ONE & ONLY

CANTON, BOOK 1

VIV DANIELS

WORD FOR WORD

One & Only

Cover design: Sarah Hansen

Photo credit: @Couperfield

For all the fans of
Secret Society Girl

ONE

I WAS six years old when I found out my father had another family. I knew he didn't live with my mom and me, but that wasn't so unusual in my neighborhood. He came by a few times a week and always got me presents on my birthday and Christmas. Whenever he visited, he gave me money for ice cream at the corner store. I was too young to understand he just wanted me out of the apartment. That time, though, I was taking a nap when he arrived. I woke up and heard him in the bedroom with my mom, so I thought I'd fetch the ice cream money from the wallet myself. His wallet had pictures in it. Pictures of him and a blonde woman and a little blonde girl about my age. There weren't any pictures of Mom and me.

There were rules I knew I had to follow. Like how I wasn't supposed to say "that's my daddy" if I ever saw him outside of the apartment or if his picture appeared in the newspaper. When I had my appendix out at eight, he didn't come to visit, though the wing of the hospital I stayed in had his name on it. But he paid for my braces and my clothes and the babysitter he'd hired to watch me that time he took my mom to the Caribbean.

When I was fourteen, I saw my sister again. I was on the track team that year, and we had a meet at her school, across town. I was walking back to the bus to grab my backpack while I waited for my next event, and came across a tennis meet going on, too. I wouldn't have been able to pick her out of the group of slim, tan, blonde girls on the court, except I saw my father in the stands. He was shouting her name—Hannah—and cheering. Every time she scored a point, she'd preen in his direction. I folded my fingers through the diamond links of the fence separating the path from the court and watched her play. She was way better at tennis than I'd ever be at sprints or hurdles or whatever other event the coach assigned me to. But Dad hadn't been there when I won the county science fair in the fall, either.

If Dad saw me near the court that day, I never guessed. But it wasn't long after that that my mother reminded me of the truth. "You need to be more careful."

"Huh?" I said, mouth full of spaghetti, head full of my Algebra II problem set.

"It's only natural to be curious about...her. You think I haven't wanted to see myself?"

Her? "You mean Dad's other daughter?" Or his wife?

"But we can't. This apartment doesn't pay for itself. Neither does the food you eat or the clothes you wear." Mom's art didn't pay for it either. Sometimes, when she was in between commissions, she worked at clothing stores or as a secretary. Never for long, though. Whenever it got in the way of her latest project, the whole grind of a 9-to-5 gig killed her creativity, and Dad always stepped in. "Steven has been really good to us. He doesn't have to be."

"Actually, he does," I replied with all the surety a fourteen-year-old girl could muster. "It's the law."

"The law wouldn't give us half of what he does on his own, Tess," my mother scoffed. "He helps us because he loves us. He loves you. You're his daughter."

I thought about the way Dad had cheered Hannah on at the tennis match. Dad was my father in this apartment. Nowhere else. I hardly even looked like him. I looked like Mom, with her dark hair and pointy chin and figure like a Hollywood star out of an old black-and-white movie. Only my eyes were Swift— large and bright, with that indeterminate color that wasn't blue or gray or green or brown. When we'd studied genetics in Biology, my lab partner had been stumped until our teacher told him to put down "hazel."

"We owe him a lot, Tess. And if we hurt him, we'll lose everything else."

———

I DIDN'T UNDERSTAND what that meant until three years later, when I got accepted to Canton University. Dad's alma mater. All the Swifts' actually, for nearly a hundred years. Like the hospital where I got my appendix out, it had buildings bearing his name. It also had one of the best bioengineering departments in the country—thanks to a generous endowment by Canton Chemicals, one of the few businesses in the town that my dad didn't have his fingers in—and they wanted *me*.

I figured Dad would be proud. Even if we had to keep it secret, I was following in his footsteps.

"Canton?" he'd said when he came to the apartment the week after I got my letter of acceptance. "I don't understand. Did you get a scholarship?"

"No." Something very cold starting winding its way through my belly. "I figured with loans and—"

"I don't like the idea of you going into debt for your schooling, Tess," he said. My mother beamed and squeezed his arm. "Tell you what I'll do. If you go to State and take that 'bright futures scholarship' they give kids with your SAT scores, I'll pay for everything else. Room, board, books—whatever."

"Oh, Steven!" my mother gasped and laid her hand on his arm.

I looked at the Canton acceptance packet in my hand. The glossy cover was filled with pictures of smiling, happy students on the grassy quad, the soaring archways of the Swift Library, a kid practicing violin and another with safety goggles shielding her eyes as she filled a beaker with a glowing compound. The bioengineering department at Canton boasted a Cole Award winner, two recipients of a Sloan Fellowship, and a state-of-the-art lab. Graduates of the rigorous programs went on to top-tier medical schools and PhD programs. I'd researched the program at State, of course, since it was my back-up school. It was solid and respectable but not nearly so well-regarded, and I'd have to fight hordes of other students for the higher-level classes and access to the labs.

But Canton meant private school tuition. Even with loans, would I be able to swing something so pricey?

"What do you say, kid?"

"What if," I began slowly, "we set aside that money to help with Canton tuition, instead? If I went to Canton, I could live here. That would save some money…"

Dad's lips became a tight, sharp line, and his eyes looked like hard chips of granite. "That wasn't what I said. I *said*, if you went to State, which is basically free, I'd pay for your living expenses. Provided you keep your grades up, of course."

That wasn't a question. My grades were always up.

When I didn't say anything, he sighed and shook his head at me. "You always seemed like a really practical girl to me, Tess. I'm going to let you think it over for a bit. You sleep on it, okay? I know you'll choose the right thing. State is the place you belong."

I slept on it, as Dad asked, and more than that, I made up a detailed spreadsheet of the costs associated with each option. I was good at spreadsheets. Like he said, I'd always been a practical girl. But when I presented it to my mom the next morning, she barely glanced at the tallies I'd so painstakingly budgeted.

"Tess," she said, shaking her head at me over her coffee cup. Over the years, her lipstick had left an indelible stain on the rim. "You don't understand. This isn't money your father is giving you for college. It's money he's giving you to go to State."

I pointed at a few figures. "But if you look here, you can see—"

Then my mom sighed, exactly as my father had. "Sweetie, it's time you started to face some facts. You're going to be eighteen next month, and your dad won't be required to give you a cent, legally or otherwise."

If Mom had hauled off and slapped me across the face, it wouldn't have stung any more. And it must have shown on my face, too, since she softened things with her next words.

"I know you think the program at Canton is something special, but I also know that you're an excellent student, and you can make your time at State work well, too. If you go to State, it'll make your dad happy, and if you do really well there, it'll make him proud. And maybe he'll help with grad school or med school or whatever you want to do next."

I looked down at my spreadsheets, aligned so neatly on top of the Canton acceptance package.

"Do you understand what I'm saying?"

I did. I'd understood when I was in the hospital at eight and had my braces off at twelve and stood outside that tennis court at fourteen. Steven Swift made the rules, and we played by them.

I chose State, and Dad wrote a check, but I didn't think any of us were fooled. When I was the runner-up in the state science fair that year, my mom was there to cheer me on, but Dad didn't even send flowers. When I was named a regional Siemens competition finalist, my name—Teresa McMann—appeared in a national newspaper, and though my mom had the page framed and hung in our hallway, I secretly hoped Dad wouldn't notice— lest he say anything about the $3,000 scholarship that came with it.

He might not owe us anything anymore, but we still owed him everything.

TWO

THE SUMMER after high school graduation, I traveled away from home for the first time. Along with several hundred other teens, I'd received an invitation to spend three weeks studying at a science camp at Cornell. Three survey classes taught by real professors, space in the dorms, food in the dining hall—and all of it paid for by a grant for gifted and talented high school students who planned a career in the science and technology fields. Mom and I only had to cover spending money and airfare, and I had the Siemens money for that.

When I boarded the plane, I felt freer than I ever had in my life. We hadn't had to ask my father for a single cent to pay for this trip, and that meant I didn't need his permission to take it. I wasn't sure what to expect from Cornell. High school had been neither the best nor the most traumatic experience teen movies had made it out to be. I had friends—a group of us had even gotten together and rented our own limo for a girls' group to prom. I'd participated in the occasional slumber party my friend Sylvia would organize at her sister's cramped apartment. But aside from Sylvia, I knew the girls I hung out with in high school weren't lifelong friends. It was hard to make close friends when your whole life was a secret. And I'd never had a boyfriend or anything. I was "that science girl" to most of the kids in my class. But here, we were all the science ones. That was the point.

My roommate, Cristina, was a Puerto Rican biology major from Brooklyn. She had curly hair and eyelids painted to look like peacock tail feathers. "Dermatology or plastic surgery," she said to me as soon as we exchanged names. "You?"

"Bioengineering?" I asked rather than said.

Her peacock eyes widened in appreciation. "Hardcore."

I shrugged, as self-conscious as I'd ever been at those science fair presentations. "Well, I think there's a lot science has done to wreck life. Maybe we can score some points for the good guys, too."

"Look at you, all noble," she said, smiling. "And here I'm just out to make people pretty."

Cristina, I learned, was a lot more than eyeliner. She'd been a New York City Science Scholar, and her field of study was skin grafts for burn victims. But the makeup was no joke either. She'd worked for two years at a MAC counter in some department store in Manhattan she was shocked I hadn't heard of. She was also staying at Cornell come fall. "In-state tuition, baby."

"Yeah, I'm going to a state school, too." It just wasn't *also* an Ivy.

This was how most of the introductory conversations with the other campers went throughout orientation. We all had to report on what we were studying, what project had brought us here, what we were going to do with our futures, and where we were going to college. It seemed like everyone was headed off to Harvard or MIT or CalTech. I even heard a few Cantons in the mix. My practical, sensible side kept me from concocting an elaborate lie that I was going to Oxford, which turned out for the best, since I met a budding physicist who actually was. I retreated to the buffet.

"Good choice," said a voice as I was picking through the cheese plate.

"I'm sorry?" I turned around.

His eyes were blue and framed by glasses rimmed in

gunmetal gray. His hair was black and flopped down over his brow just a shade too far. "The cheese. It's an artisanal kind from the School of Agriculture here."

"Oh," I said, looking down at the white cubes on my plate. "Well, eat local, right?"

"Absolutely. Smaller footprint, et cetera." He held out his hand. "I'm Dylan Kingsley."

"Tess McMann." I waited for the inevitable *what are you studying where are you going to school why should I care who you are,* but it didn't come. I put a piece of cheese on a cracker.

"Wait," he said and spooned up a dollop of the black stuff sitting in a ramekin on the cheese tray and, without even asking, smeared it on top of my cheese. "Try it with this."

I did. The sharp, tangy bite of the cheese exploded in my mouth, soothed by the sweetness of the dark, creamy paste. Dylan watched, the corner of his mouth quirked up in an approving smile.

"Yum," I said once I swallowed, though yum didn't quite cover it. "What is it?"

"Organic date-blueberry compote. The blueberries are from Cornell, too."

"I'm guessing the dates aren't, though."

"No. It's pretty hard to get dates around here." A flush stole over his cheeks as he realized what he'd said. "I mean—" The flush grew deeper. "Can we, uh, pretend I never said that?"

"Sure thing."

He chuckled to himself. "Thanks. I was hoping to sort of leave the whole Dylan the Dork thing behind in high school. I was going to make a new start being all handsome and mysterious."

"And pick up chicks with your sexy cheese factoids?"

"Of course," he said, mock-affronted. "Any girl worth having is impressed by sexy cheese factoids."

"That's been your experience?" I asked wryly.

"Not as such, no." The flush was gone, but the smile remained. It did nice things to his cheekbones. I had a hard time imagining him having problems getting dates if he wanted.

"Tess!" I craned my neck to see Cristina waving to me from across the room. She was standing with a host of other headed-to-Cornell campers. "Come here and explain your whole algae thing to these people."

"Algae?" Dylan asked.

"*Way* more nutritional than cheese," I quipped as I headed over to my roommate and her new BFFs.

Cristina was still staring behind me when I arrived. "Who is that?"

"Another Cornell guy," I guessed. After all, he knew everything about their cheese.

"Cute," she said. "Teach him how long pants should be and you've got a hottie, too."

I cast a glance over my shoulder. Dylan waved, a piece of cheese in his hand. In truth, I hadn't even noticed the length of his pants, which were, as Cristina had said, just a touch too short. I'd been too busy thinking I'd never seen gunmetal-gray glasses before.

I dragged my gaze away. "Well, have at him, then," I said as if I hadn't a care in the world.

She cocked her head at me. "Boyfriend, or not into guys?"

"The latter," I replied.

"Cool," she said. "I'd actually been wondering, what with the no-makeup—"

"What?" I said, realizing what she'd meant. "No. I'm not—"

"It's totally cool, girl. I don't judge."

How could I explain? My mom had been into boys and love and the whole sweep-you-off-your-feet romance thing. And look where she'd ended up—a mistress to a married man, raising a secret daughter, able neither to live the life she'd forged nor escape it. Sometimes I heard her with her friends, talking about how happy her arrangement was, how everyone got what they needed, but I knew better. I'd also heard her on the phone with him, begging when he hadn't come over for days or weeks. I knew the promises he'd made her when I was younger and they didn't think I was listening. There'd been times over the years when she'd thought Dad would leave his family for us, times she'd even put me in the car and driven past "our new house" on the nice side of town. But they'd never panned out.

I didn't want to be dependent on anyone, the way Mom and I had always been. I knew I was weak like her, willing to give up the things I wanted—like Canton—to make the people I loved happy. I knew I was weak like her and wouldn't be able to be with a guy without falling for him.

I hadn't flown all the way to Ithaca to date some boy. I was here to work—to prove to myself that I could do something extraordinary all on my own.

———

NOT ONLY WAS Dylan in my lab, but because we were assigned seats alphabetically, we shared a burner.

"Cheesemonger," I said as I dropped my bag on the floor next to my stool.

"Algae girl," he replied.

"So you're a biologist?" I asked him. He was wearing an open button-down blue shirt over a gray tee. It made his eyes darker, almost the same color as the frames of his glasses.

He shrugged, and his shoulder brushed mine. "Closest fit." He watched me pull out my notebook and freshly sharpened pencils. "I read up on you, you know."

"Stalker." I wrote the date on the top of the page, tapping my eraser against the edge of the paper to cover my nerves. Why hadn't I looked him up? I'd spent a good half hour last night thinking about gunmetal gray glasses. One little visit to Facebook, and I might have gotten this all out of my system.

"That was some project."

My science project—the one that had finaled in all those competitions—had been on algae. Specifically, on the potential for growing algae as a food source for livestock. But I could freely admit that no cute guy had ever seemed interested in it before. "Thank you."

"You should have won."

"You should have been on the jury."

At the front of the class, our professor cleared her throat to begin the lecture. The room hushed.

Dylan chuckled again, soft and low, and leaned over to whisper in my ear. "You're kind of prickly for someone obsessed with the mushiest plant matter alive."

"Good to know," I said without looking up. "My next project will be about cactuses."

The professor began speaking, and we both settled down to take notes. At least, I tried to, but my penmanship was jittery, and my heart pounded in my chest. I felt my cheeks flush and leaned my head over my paper, glad I had my hair to act as a screen.

That, Tess McMann, is what is known as flirting.

When the professor handed the syllabus around, I passed the stack to Dylan. Our hands touched, and all my nerve endings thrilled. This was insane. I glanced down toward the bases of our stools, where he'd hooked his sneakered feet around his footrest. His pants were still too short. That was good. Good to remember. He shifted in his seat, and my gaze snapped up. He was staring at me, his hair falling over the rims of his glasses, skimming his cheekbones.

Oh God, since when was I someone who noticed cheekbones?

"Drop something?" he asked me.

I shook my head and returned my focus to the lecture. The professor was outlining the entire syllabus. It was designed much like a college course, with most of our coursework being done either outside of class or during the lab session. We'd have a midterm and a final project, all in a three-week session.

"For your project," Professor White said, "you may either work alone or on two-person teams."

There was a rumbling in the class. I kept copying notes down from the board, unconcerned. I'd never been much of a team project kind of girl. In my experience, I'd always ended up doing the work while my slacker partners ended up with the benefit of my blood, sweat, tears, and grades.

When class ended, I managed to pack up my papers and notebook without looking at Dylan. Much.

"So...," he said. "Tess." My name in his mouth sounded longer than four letters. He savored the syllable like it was a bite of cheese and organic blueberry-date compote.

My mouth watered. I pretended to be very busy arranging my pencils into the little canvas pencil holders on the inside of my bag.

"You headed to lunch?"

"I was going to grab a sandwich or something," I said. I had a lot of planning to do if I wanted to complete a worthwhile project by the end of the term.

"Great," he said. "I'll grab one with you. We can chat more about"—he grinned—"algae."

I slung my bag over my shoulder and took a deep breath. "Look, Dylan, you're"—*Cute. Funny. Disconcerting.*—"fun and all, but I should probably tell you something. I'm not here to flirt and I'm not here to date and I'm not here to hook up. I'm here to work. Since you read up on me, you already know that I didn't win my science fair or the Siemens regional, and so the fact that I have an opportunity like this...well, it's really important to me. I aim to have the best project in the class. And that means I don't have time for any kind of nonsense."

He blinked, taken aback. "Oh...kay. So, no sandwiches, then?"

I rolled my eyes and turned away and, thankfully, he didn't follow.

Back in my room, I booted up the computer, my mind already scrolling through concepts for a kick-ass three-week project. I tapped my fingers idly against the keyboard, groaned, then clicked over to Facebook. There were seventeen Dylan Kingsleys, but it was easy enough to spot mine—I mean, to spot the correct one. His profile pic showed him outdoors, grinning broadly—was that a dimple?—with his glasses glinting black in the sun. I read the stats. He lived in Pennsylvania, listed himself as single. Schools: Sacred Heart, *Canton University.* I caught my breath. Canton. He never had told me where he was planning to go to school, unlike everyone else I'd met at the party. I felt a stab of jealousy. Private school, private college, designer glasses. Must be nice. No wonder he thought his time here could be used eating cheese and chasing girls. The rest of the profile was nothing special, the usual wall messages from friends and family. Lots and lots of family. Dylan had an older sister, a little sister, a very tiny baby brother, and a mess of cousins and aunts and uncles and grandparents. I clicked through to the photo albums—not as many as I would have thought. I wondered if he'd scrubbed his account and why.

One photo album featured a lot of guys in suits on a stage. I opened it up. There was a short, chubby kid on stage, shaking an older man's hand as he accepted a plaque. Short and chubby, huh? Suddenly, the ill-fitting pants and the lack of photos made a lot more sense. The Dylan I knew was tall and on the slim side, with a physique more like a runner. Must be what they called a late bloomer. Better late than never, I supposed. The picture linked to a news article. I clicked through and started reading.

Five minutes later, I picked my jaw up off the floor.

Dylan, it seemed, was something of an environmental science wunderkind. While doing a run-of-the-mill science fair project in ninth grade studying frog populations in a local pond, he'd noticed some chemical readings that were off. Hypothesizing that there was degradation from an old coal mine nearby, he'd tried to bring it to the attention of the company responsible for maintaining the site. They'd blown him off. Undaunted, Dylan had taken water samples from all over the area and actually pinpointed the exact location of the leak. He'd reported his findings to an environmental watchdog group, who'd nailed the mining company on their environmental violations. Dylan, meanwhile, got himself a grant from said environmental watchdog group, a commendation from the EPA—that was the ceremony in the pictures—and kept working.

While the rest of us were dicking around with school science fairs, Dylan had been out doing *real* science. I dropped my head into my hands and groaned.

Then I noticed the new message in my inbox. I saw his name and my heart raced. Was there some way Facebook could tell you when people were looking at your profile?

Tess,

After consideration, I've decided to accept your strongly worded proposal to be my biology project partner.

In all seriousness, I think we'd make the perfect team. Ask around. I'm good with water stuff, but I have a desperate need for more algae in my life.

However, on one point I want to be absolutely clear. If we are to work together, you should know that I require very high standards from my coworkers. And that means that from now on, it's not cactuses. It's cacti.

Dylan

THREE

FOR THREE WEEKS, I never heard the name Swift. For three weeks, no one once told me to be careful or I'd risk ruining my future. Cornell was a respite from all the expectations—or lack of same—that had marked my high school experience. I don't think I was alone there, either. Everyone around me seemed to be breaking free of the stereotypes that had followed them through their teens, whether it was class dork or freak or "good girl" or what. I even saw Cristina heading to class a few times with no makeup on at all, and she taught me how to do a smoky eye and the proper use of a lip pencil.

And for three weeks, there was Dylan. When he explained his idea to me, I jumped at the chance to be his partner. Piggybacking on my algae experiments, he wanted to study the relative potential of types of feedstock algae as a sink for marine pollution. "Double duty," he called it. "We could even do some biofuel stuff."

Okay, I'll be honest: I might have jumped anyway.

But the work was fun and challenging and engaging. Dylan was a meticulous partner—maybe even more dedicated to the research than I was. I'd often get emails detailing new avenues of research that were time-stamped 3:00 a.m.

Your roommate must hate you, I wrote back when I read my email at 7:00 a.m.

His replies always came lightning-fast.

My roommate dropped out midterm. Computer science guy. Too much gaming, not enough coding. What did you think of that paper I sent?

Me: *Haven't read it. Some of us need sleep.*

Him: *Amateur.*

This was par for the course for Dylan. Lots of hard work, seasoned with liberal joking. The behavior I'd taken for strong flirtation when we'd first met seemed to be my partner's standard setting. Every statement was tinged with sarcasm; every conversation ended in a quip. If he'd ever been interested in me as more than a project partner, he gave no indication. He was friendly, kind, generous, and professional. We spent most of our time talking about algae blooms and phytochemical reactions. Sometimes we talked about food—Dylan was very disappointed in the college dining options ("For a hotel training school, I'd expected more")—and occasionally he'd start in with a story about his family. He came from a huge family, full of busybody cousins and cheerleader sisters and a student-teacher aunt who'd apparently campaigned to get him a prom date.

"Most embarrassing experience of my life."

"Well," I prodded, "did she get you one?"

"Yeah." He smiled mysteriously. "She was way hot."

I spent the rest of the evening alternately glaring through my microscope and wondering exactly how hot the prom date—and the prom night—had been.

But if our research remained platonic, I was certain other project pairs didn't fare quite so well. Cristina, who was always up on the campus gossip, filled me in. She had a boyfriend back home in Brooklyn, so she was living vicariously through all the hormones running amok across campus. Hook-ups, cheating, broken hearts, people who'd been caught with their pants down —literally—despite the campus's rather firm open-door policy.

"And what about you and Dylan?" she asked, sculpted eyebrows waggling. "Are you *doing* it?"

"No!"

She smirked. "Are you *not* doing it?"

"We're project partners," I insisted. "That's all."

And that *was* all, even if his words made my heart beat faster, the accidental brush of our skin set my nerve endings on fire, and I spent hours every night after our work ended turning over in my head every look and smile and conversation. One night, he leaned over my shoulder to point at some numbers on my computer screen, and I felt the weight of his chest against my back, his breath in my ear. Another night, he caught a strand of my dark hair with the tip of his pinky and swiped it off my face. Yet a third night, I could have sworn I felt his eyes on me every time I looked away. Day after day, night after night, study session after study session, we exchanged emails, we talked about our project, we read and worked and researched together, and there were times that I wanted him so much, I worried if he so much as touched my hand, I'd split right open and spill my soul all over the floor.

I might have denied it to Cristina, but there was no point in pretending to myself. And as long as it was *only* to myself, I figured there was little harm. I'd told the truth to Dylan after our first class: I was here to work and to do well. He respected that, and with his help, I was doing exactly what I'd intended. Anything else was my own personal problem to deal with. And I wasn't like my parents, who did what they wanted with no regard for the effect it may have on their lives or the lives of others. I had the project, my position at the camp, Dylan's own undeniable scientific fervor…and honestly, it was enough.

It was amazing.

In high school, it had been hard to find anyone as interested in research as I was. I'd never been bullied or ridiculed for the amount of time I spent in the bio lab or my commitment to the science fair and other competitions, but I hadn't exactly had friends who shared my interests, either. Sylvia, my closest friend in school, never even took science past the minimum requirements, and though she'd always politely asked how my projects were going, her eyes would glaze over after the second mention of cellular structure.

Not so with Dylan or the other people I met at Cornell. Dylan and I could debate for literally hours over various methodologies or ramifications or avenues of research. Behind the rims of his glasses, his eyes were blue flames, lit up with intensity as he argued about the dangers of frakking or listed case histories of water contamination or declared that he didn't care if it took us an extra two hours every night, we just had to include some linear regression graphs in our final presentation.

And then he would back off, and his cheeks would darken, and he would apologize like I used to with my high school friends. But he never needed to, because I was right there with him, late night after late night, pleading with the lab managers for just fifteen more minutes, wrestling with graphics programs I'd never heard of and which were certainly way more complicated than the simple Excel spreadsheets I'd used on all my high school projects.

One night, after hours spent crunching numbers and hunching over petri dishes, I collapsed in one of the lab chairs with a moan and grabbed my shoulders, kneading my aching muscles in vain.

"You can't massage your own shoulders," Dylan's voice floated over. "It's an anatomical impossibility."

"Better than nothing." But he was right. In order to rub, I had to contract the very muscles I was trying to relax. I gave up, rolled my neck, and yawned.

Seconds later, I felt his fingers brush my hair to the side. His thumbs caressed the base of my neck and his hands curved over the tops of my clavicles. "Let me," he said softly as my skin started tingling and warming beneath his touch.

I caught my breath. I couldn't. *I couldn't.* His thumbs pushed against the knot of muscles in my back and I bit my lip to keep from groaning.

"Does that feel good?"

I turned around in the seat and faced him, kneeling on the chair. His hands dropped to his sides in surprise. "Yes," I said, staring at him staring at me, inches away. His glasses were off. There were tiny red marks on the bridge of his nose. He looked older with them off, more refined, cuter than ever. He didn't step back, he didn't look away, he didn't say a thing.

And I knew. If I reached for him, he'd let me. If I kissed him, he'd drag me off the chair and into his arms. He wanted me to. He wanted me, too. My heart pounded blood so hard through my body that I was surprised the windows of the room weren't rattling. Dylan had no interest at all in stopping what was about to happen.

So I did it. "I have to go," I said and grabbed my bag. He didn't say anything, and I didn't dare turn in his direction before I ran from the lab.

———

THE NEXT DAY, we both acted like nothing had happened. Fortunately, it was our final day of work. We put the last touches on our presentation and turned it in to Professor White for her review.

The morning after, she asked us both to stay after class.

"I took a look at your project last night," she said when everyone else had gone, "and I have to say that I'm very impressed. There's a level of meticulous detail here that is uncommon for early undergrads, even in a program of this caliber. If it's all right, I'd like to share your work with some of the other faculty members here."

"We're scientists," said Dylan. "We always want our work shared."

"Miss McMann," the professor said, turning toward me, "I

took a look in your file last night. I understand you're interested in bioengineering?"

I nodded. "They have a really limited program at my college, but I'm going to do my best to get in—"

"I doubt you'll have much trouble," Professor White said. "In fact, I know a professor there you should meet. If you like, I'd be happy to contact Dr. Stewart and put you two in touch."

I brightened. Maybe things wouldn't be so gloomy at State after all. "Thank you!"

"I think he only teaches upper-level classes, but I'll let him know that if he's in the market for a research assistant, he couldn't do better than you."

I was speechless. I probably managed to stumble out a thank-you. And here I was thinking I'd be making ends meet by slinging coffee.

It wasn't until we were dismissed that I noticed she'd made no explicit promises to Dylan. Perhaps, though, she figured he wouldn't need any extra help at a school like Canton, whereas I was going to have to scramble to make sure I could take all the classes I needed for my major in the overpopulated crush of State.

Dylan was beaming as we waited for the elevator together. "Well played, algae girl. Who knew you might get a job out of this?" The doors dinged open and we stepped inside.

I still felt a little breathless. I turned to Dylan, who was pressing the button for the lobby, and threw my arms around his neck. "Thank you," I whispered, hugging him tight. Yes, the project was mine, but I hadn't done it alone. It was Dylan's idea, Dylan who'd helped push everything to the next level.

His arms slid around my waist as he returned the hug. "Tess..."

To this day, I don't know who started it, who moved first. But suddenly, his mouth was on mine and my hands were weaving into his hair and he'd grabbed the back of my shirt in his fists and crushed me against him. By the time the elevator door dinged open, we were both breathing hard. We flew apart, staring at each other. Forever. *Forever.*

"Are you going to run away again?" he said at last, with a kind of anguish in his voice I'd never heard before.

"No," I replied and came at him again. "No."

We kissed until the doors shut on us and the elevator started lifting, and then we stopped and retreated, faces flushed, hair mussed. On some upper floor, the doors parted again, and some students got in. No one I knew, thankfully, though I might not have recognized my own mother in that instant.

On the ground floor, we left with everyone else and walked back to the dorms, first side by side, then hand in hand, then running until we reached his room.

"I wasn't sure...," he managed to get out as we wrapped ourselves around each other and fell back on his narrow dorm room bed. "You said you were here to work..."

"Shhh," I admonished. "Project's done. Didn't you hear Professor White?"

The sound Dylan made then was half laugh, half groan, and it did strange things to my insides. His body was heavy against mine, and for a long time, all we did was kiss, our limbs tangled, softly moving against each other, until that friction wasn't enough.

"Tess," he breathed into my ear. "I..." He held his breath for a moment, his forehead pressed hard against mine as if he was trying to read my thoughts. "What do you want?"

I looked at him. His pupils were dilated, his mouth parted and swollen from my kisses. I reached up and removed his glasses, folding the frames and laying them on the table near his bed. I shifted my legs and he settled between my thighs and I saw him bite his lip, then squeeze his eyes shut as I softly bucked my hips.

"I want you," I said, though those words sounded so ridiculous. So canned. So vague. "I want us to take our clothes off."

His laugh this time was a painful sound. "Okay. But I feel like

I should tell you that, um…" He sighed and opened his eyes. "I haven't exactly done that before."

So the prom hadn't been *that* hot of a night. Or maybe Dylan just wasn't that kind of guy. I reached up and cupped his cheek. "Neither have I. But I want to now."

Of course, it wasn't as easy as all that. He had to go dig out the condoms he'd brought with him "just in case" and I did my fair share of giggling and it wasn't all soft-focus candlelit perfection like in a movie. To start with, it was lunchtime, and the sun streamed in bright and glorious from the dorm room windows, striping our skin in light and shadow from the blinds. Dylan kissed each stripe as it dappled my torso.

"You look like a tiger," he said.

I clawed at his back. "Rowr."

But we stopped joking around soon enough. Dylan touched me everywhere, and I returned the favor. His hands encircled my wrists and his fingers traced the line of my throat and my sternum and my hips on their way to their destination. And as they moved inside me at last, his mouth explored the undersides of my breasts until my animal sounds got a lot more realistic.

"Tess," he rumbled against my skin. "God. Don't do that. I'm going crazy."

"Go crazy," I urged him. "Please."

But even then, he took his time, asking all the while if I was okay and kissing the tip of my nose when I promised I'd tell him if I wasn't. I'd heard it would hurt, but it didn't. I'd heard it would be bad—but how could it be? It was Dylan.

Afterward, we lay around, sheets haphazardly covering body parts as the sun slanted farther and farther away from the windows.

"You are so beautiful," he said, running his finger across my jaw.

"Oh, is that why you wanted to be my project partner?" I asked wryly.

"No, I wanted to be your project partner because I thought you'd be good at it," he said. "I flirted with you because I thought you were beautiful." He rolled on top of me and smiled down. "But it's really the combination of those two things that made me spend the last few weeks taking only cold showers." There was no self-consciousness in his tone as he said this. There never had been with Dylan. He wanted what he wanted, and he was never ashamed. I'd never known anything like that. "I liked you so much, Tess, but you made it clear you only wanted to work. I didn't think I had a chance."

My breath caught. "If we'd done this, we wouldn't have finished the project." Because this was all I wanted to do. This should be all anyone wanted to do, ever.

"Your self-control is astounding." He had no idea. But as he leaned in to kiss me, I let him. I let him do a whole lot more, too, until I came, trembling, in his arms, and he had to go get another condom.

It started getting dark outside, but neither of us were interested in dinner. So it began.

I thought of the man lying next to me. His huge, loving family waiting for him at home. His future attendance at Canton, where no doubt he'd make a splash, doing his studies and maybe even living in a building named after my father.

"When are you leaving for school?" Dylan asked, as if he could read my thoughts. "The Canton dorms open early. I can be there by the end of August. I can see you before you leave."

I shrugged. "I don't know if that's a good idea." I pictured myself coming home on weekends so I could be sure of meeting up with Dylan. Trying to balance research opportunities with my need to see a boyfriend who lived three hours away. I imagined all the things I'd end up being, all the things I wouldn't be able to be, if I tied myself to a man in Canton.

Just like my mother had.

"Why? Are your folks really strict? Because I can be so charming. Parents love me." He cleared his throat. "'Mr. McMann, I'm here to take your daughter to a scientific lecture.'"

My smile faded. "My dad's not...Mr. McMann. He doesn't live with us." I took a deep breath. "I'm not exactly...legitimate."

A burst of laughter escaped his lips. *"Legitimate?* No one says that anymore, Tess." He tilted my chin in his direction. "I think you're totally legitimate."

I didn't argue with him. Why ruin what time we had left? Before I flew home, he told me when he'd be at Canton. He promised to call. I kissed him in response, because I couldn't bear to say that I couldn't promise him anything like that.

———

DYLAN DID CALL. He called six times, texted twelve, and emailed once, concerned that something might have happened to me. I never replied to any of them. I did see when he unfriended me on Facebook, and I convinced myself it was better this way.

I went to school three hours away, became that botany professor's research assistant, and only came home for major holidays and my mother's birthday.

I didn't see Dylan again for two years.

FOUR

Two years later

"OF COURSE I'm happy for you, honey," my mother said when I told her the news of my scholarship. "You always wanted to go to Canton. I just don't know what your father is going to say."

"There's not much he can say about it," I replied airily.

Twenty-year-old me knew a lot of things seventeen-year-old me—and my mother—never had. Like how to get scholarships and interest-free student loans and line up research assistant positions that would defray the cost of textbooks. For two years, I'd given State my best shot, but their program didn't have what I wanted. Canton's did. Landing the transfer and the academic scholarship required to pay for it had meant everything. Even my old boss, Professor Stewart, had approved of my move.

"Everything is going to be paid for, so we don't have to ask Dad for anything. And I'm going to pick up a few shifts at Verde downtown—you know, that restaurant where Sylvia works? So I can even help you with the rent and food—"

"You don't have to help me," my mom began. "I got a new commission last month."

Well, I would if Dad decided to take my transfer to Canton

out on Mom because she couldn't keep their most dangerous secret three hours outside of town. If it were possible to hide my transfer from Dad, I would, but I knew that wasn't Mom's style. I just hoped that he wouldn't punish her for my choice.

Like I said, two years—especially two years away—had given me all kinds of insights. But there was no point in stressing my mother out about that. And that was why I presented the whole thing as a *fait accompli*. I was already registered at Canton for the fall semester. I'd given up my apartment at State, sold my crummy thrift-store furniture, and packed every single one of my belongings in the back of my junky old car to move home, Canton course schedule clutched in my hand like some sort of talisman. Whatever arbitrary reasoning my father had convinced Mom of several years ago, she wouldn't risk my academic career. My attending Canton wouldn't pose the slightest danger to the maintenance of our little family secret. They would soon see that I was right.

I couldn't have been more wrong.

———

ON THE LAST night before classes started, there was a reception at the bioengineering department. Though I wasn't really much for receptions, I figured it was a good idea to go and try to meet as many faculty and fellow students as possible before the year started. The only professors I'd had a chance to talk with so far had been the head of the department who'd interviewed me during my transfer application and two others he'd had sit in at the time. As I knew after my experiences with Professors White and Stewart, a lot of opportunities came from connections. I was a transfer student, which meant I was that much more of an unknown, even if I did come with stellar recommendations from my old teachers and a scholarship specifically due to my academic achievements. I wanted to make sure everyone in the department knew they'd made the right choice.

I dressed with more care than usual for the reception,

eschewing the usual jeans and T-shirt look for one of my mother's sheath dresses. My mom was only just forty, and she and I wore the same size. I had her curvy bombshell figure, though I was a few inches taller. The dress was pretty but conservative—a tailored, dove-gray sheath with a boat neck and pin tucks, and it fell to my knees. I paired it with stockings and a set of low, black slingbacks. As I stood before the bathroom mirror, pulling my hair up into a twist, my mother peeked in and smiled.

"That color's nice on you," she said. "Makes your eyes look almost like slate."

"Thanks," I mumbled. I knew what was coming.

"You have your father's eyes."

Yes, I did. My father's mercurial, impossible-to-pin-down eyes. Every time I looked in a mirror, there he was, staring back at me, reminding me who I was and the rules guiding my life. My ex-boyfriend Jason had once written a rather awful poem about all the colors of my eyes. And he wondered why we didn't last.

I applied some eyeliner and a touch of mascara. Cristina had taught me the technique—Cristina, who was still kicking ass at Cornell and had responded to my announcement about my transfer to Canton with the following text:

OMG HAVE YOU TOLD DYLAN?!?!?

Which, of course, I had not. I was not in touch with Dylan Kingsley, I had steadfastly resisted looking him up on Facebook, and I wasn't about to indulge in my friend's love of drama.

That being said, I'd definitely made sure to map out routes around campus that would bypass the environmental science department completely. I didn't fear seeing Dylan—after all, it had been two years—but I wasn't going to seek him out, either.

After all, it had been two years.

A touch of pink lip gloss, and I was done. The last time I'd dressed up this much was at my interview. Maybe I was giving the wrong impression after all. Most days, I had on a lab coat and a ponytail. At the same time, this was Canton. I hated to admit it, but I really wanted to impress them.

I climbed into my beat-up old hatchback and drove over to the campus. I'd brought my shiny new student parking pass and hung it from my dented rearview mirror as I entered the lot behind the bioengineering lab. Where State had been large and impersonal, its original central campus overspilling into masses of utilitarian outbuildings that would never show up in a college catalog, Canton University was filled with gorgeous architecture. From the picturesque brick quad where all the old buildings were located—including the one with my dad's name on it—to the soaring glass walls and atrium that marked the famous bioengineering building, every location on campus dripped with the power and prestige of the Canton name. Coming here had always been my dream. I could only strive to live up to it.

When I entered the reception, which was being held in the central lobby atrium, I felt an unexpected wave of panic. I didn't know a soul in the room. Some of the attendees had dressed up, others seemed to have come rolling in from the quad or even just sneaked away for a minute from their labs, as a few still wore their lab coats and were clearly grabbing dinner as they filled their plates with towering piles of shrimp from the buffet. I took a deep breath and decided I needed to find something to do with my hands.

In line at the bar, I found Dr. Cavel, who'd been at my transfer interview.

"Tess!" she said brightly. "I'm glad you came." She tapped the shoulder of the elderly man in front of her. "John, this is Teresa McMann, who just transferred from State. She'll probably be taking your Biophotonics course next term."

"I hope to," I said out of habit. It had been nearly impossible to find space in the courses I'd needed at State. "You must be Professor Chen."

We chatted for a bit about my move and my past research.

"Algae, huh?" Dr. Chen said when Dr. Cavel, who'd apparently memorized my CV, brought up my old Siemens project. "What is it with the kids and algae these days?"

"I'm sorry?"

"Don't mind him," Dr. Cavel said with a shrug. "He's biomed. We need more non-health folks around here or people will start to think we're just a feeding program for Canton Chem." She cast her eyes about the room. "There's another student here who is interested in biofuel applications. I'll remember to introduce you if he shows up."

Armed with a sparkling water, I let Dr. Cavel introduce me to a few more faculty members and fellow students. I got asked the same questions and listened to their stories of summer projects and travels. They seemed nice enough, but naturally, they all knew each other better than I knew anyone. After a while, names and faces started to blur and I excused myself to find the buffet.

Perhaps it was fate that I was once more picking through a cheese tray when I heard his voice.

"Tess? Tess McMann?"

I looked up to find Dylan Kingsley standing across the table from me. The glasses were gone, the hair was tamed, and whatever baby fat might have lingered on his eighteen-year-old features had disappeared entirely, leaving behind perfectly planed cheekbones and a sharp jawline. The slim teenage body I'd never quite managed to forget had matured too, and he nicely filled out the expensive-looking gray sportscoat he wore over a close-cut Oxford open at his neck. Though I couldn't see, I was pretty sure his pants were just the right length.

I found my tongue. "Dylan. Hi."

He blinked at me. "Did you transfer to Canton?"

I nodded. Algae. Biofuel. I should have guessed that the other student those two professors had been talking about was the one I'd once slept with. This wasn't State, with its tens of thousands of science majors. "Are you a bioengineering major now?"

"With a focus on sustainable resources," he said. He stared at me for a second, but his expression was neutral. "It's good to see you."

"It's good to see you, too." I sounded like a parrot.

After a moment, he said, "You know, you never called me." There was no malice in his voice and only the tiniest hint of scolding. He might have been talking about a string hanging off my sleeve.

I swallowed. I had no excuse, or at least, none that I was willing to share with a guy I hadn't seen since my teens. "I know. I'm sorry, I—"

"That hurt." He certainly hadn't lost any of his frankness. "For a week or two."

A week or two? I narrowly resisted my impulse to gape. "Well," I said, doing my best to smile. "I'm glad you got over it quickly." I had kept his messages on my voicemail for months. Just because I hadn't called him back didn't mean I hadn't *wanted* to. Even without seeing him, Dylan had taken up too much space in my head. A relationship with him would have been too dangerous. "How did you manage?" I asked lightly and popped a cube of cheese in my mouth.

"I slept with a lot of girls," he replied.

I choked. I could not believe we were having this conversation over cheese.

He handed me a napkin. "Okay there?"

I snatched the napkin and glared at him as I attempted to get my coughing fit under control. Okay, I deserved that. I could admit it. Dylan was smirking at me, but his eyes held amusement, not anger.

Two could play that game. "Oh, I did the same. *Lots* of girls." In truth, there had been zero girls and only two guys.

He raised his eyebrows and his grin grew wide. No blush though. The teenage blush was gone, completely masked by a nice summer tan. "Really? *That* I'd like to hear about."

I laughed. I couldn't help it. "Sure you would."

Dylan was who he'd always been: friendly and funny, gentle and genuine. I had little doubt he had been mad at me, but doubted even less that he'd held on to that anger. Long before we'd been lovers, we'd been friends.

"It's good to see you, Tess," he said after a moment, his tone more serious. "Welcome to Canton."

And just like that, I knew we would be friends again.

———

IT WOULD BE LYING to say that I had anything else on my mind but Dylan that night. In between reading for my first classes, I scrolled back two years on my email to our old exchanges. I read them all, from his first email inviting me to work with him, through every note and message and quick reminder that came in between, to his final email—the only one out of all of them I'd never replied to:

Tess,

I'm worried something has happened to you. I don't know why you won't answer me or call me back. I wish you would, if only to say goodbye.

Love,

Dylan

Love, he'd written. *Love.* At the time, I'd told myself that was silly. It had only been one day. But it hadn't. All these emails, read in a row. It hadn't been a day. It had been weeks of seeing him every day, working with him night after night, studying and researching and laughing and joking. That one afternoon in his bed had led from the runway of our entire acquaintance. He'd told me so at the time.

Not that it made the slightest bit of difference. I didn't regret any of the choices I'd made except one—that I hadn't been clear to him that we didn't have a relationship. I might have saved him the hurt evident in his last email. But as he'd said at the reception, the pain didn't last long. He'd slept with other girls.

Lots of girls, he'd said. Lots.

I was glad I'd gotten him on a roll, then. And if I didn't quite have the same scoresheet, well, I'd had other things on my mind. School, work, transferring to Canton and figuring out how to afford it. There'd been Jason, who I supposed was my first real boyfriend. I liked him because he hadn't complained about seeing me only once or twice a week. After about three months of that, though, he'd said he didn't "see where this was going," and I really couldn't blame him. There had also been Sean, whom I'd met at a friend's party one night and taken home. It was…uneventful, to say the least. I wasn't sure how to tell the guy that the virgin I'd lost my own virginity to had made me come more.

After that, the whole enterprise seemed to be more trouble than it was worth. I'd even wondered if that thing with Dylan was sort of a fluke—exciting because it was new and naughty and forbidden by the rules of the summer camp. Maybe it was genetic that I only liked sex if it was somehow wrong. After all, that was how I'd been conceived.

I highlighted all the emails from Dylan, and my finger hovered over the delete button. I really should've gotten rid of them. Emails about a two-year-old project cluttering up my account, emails about a two-year-old fling that the other party had just this evening told me he'd gotten over in a week? What purpose did they serve?

But I didn't. *Curse you, unlimited storage space. You indulge me in all my worst habits.*

————

AFTER MY FIRST day of classes, I was coming down the wide steps in the bioengineering building's center atrium when I caught sight of Dylan passing by at the bottom of the staircase. My steps faltered as he looked up, those blue eyes shining out of his tanned face like beacons.

"There she is." His smile hadn't changed as much as the rest of him. Last night, reading his old emails, I'd almost convinced myself he was still eighteen, with floppy hair and too-short pants. They were gone now, like his glasses. I missed those glasses—without them, there was nothing protecting me from the power of those baby blues. But as for the rest...I couldn't complain. The cuteness evident in the teenager had morphed into full-blown hot. No, *handsome*. Handsome was safe. Objective. Hot meant I cared.

"Hi," I said as casually as I could, coming down the last few steps to meet him on the tiled atrium floor.

He shifted his laptop from hand to hand. "How have your classes been?"

"Good," I said. "Nothing too early, which I appreciate."

"Lucky you." He fell into step beside me as I headed for the door. "I have one at eight fifteen this term. Do you have your schedule on you?"

I pulled it up on my phone and handed it to him. He perused the list.

"Ah, Haverford. You'll like him. Really no-nonsense. Try not to get the redheaded TA for your section, though. He doesn't like chicks."

"'Chicks'?" I pursed my lips.

"That's what he calls you, and believe me, it's just the tip of the iceberg," Dylan said, still looking over my schedule. "We have Transport Process Design together. People are going to be jealous you got in. Didn't you lose a semester transferring?"

How did he know that? "I got a few strings pulled."

He cast me a glance over the top of my phone. "More than a few, I'd say." He pushed the door open for me, which only gave me a second's pause. "Org 3, Stats...too bad you didn't get into Tissue Comp with me."

"I need a few more prereqs." We hit the sunny part of the pavement. "Part of the reason I transferred is because I could never get a full course-load at State."

Dylan handed back my phone. "Then it sounds like you made the right choice, coming here."

There was something odd in his tone, and the silence that fell in between us was even weirder. "Any other tips?" I forced myself to say.

"Um, don't bother with the red book in Stats, make sure you sign up for the early lab in Org 3, and if you make friends with Dr. Chen, he'll let you into the Photonics lab after hours."

"Great," I said with false cheerfulness. "Thanks."

"No problem." He shrugged. A shiny silver BMW pulled up to the curb. "Ah, my ride."

As he opened the passenger door, I caught a glimpse of blonde hair and heard a female voice say, "Hey, honey."

"Hey—oh, this is Tess McMann. She's new to Canton."

The girl leaned across the seat to smile up at me. Our identical eyes met and I reeled back, my entire body going cold despite the late summer sunlight.

From somewhere very far away, I heard the rest of Dylan's introduction. Not that I needed to. I knew who she was.

"Tess, this is my girlfriend, Hannah Swift."

My sister.

FIVE

"HONESTLY, Tess, I always thought your little plan of never running into him was kind of naïve," Sylvia said, tying the black apron with the embroidered green leaf on it around her waist. "Canton's not that big of a school."

"We weren't even supposed to be in the same department," I argued. It was my first day of training at Verde, and Sylvia was running me through the basics before the lunch shift started.

She rolled her big brown eyes at me as she swept her hair off her neck and secured it with some carved leather clasp that looked like it came right from the prop department of *Game of Thrones*. Which, considering Sylvia, it probably had. "It's not like he was an art history major or anything. You both study life sciences. You both study *algae*, for Pete's sake."

I shook my head and looked away. "Whatever. It's fine. He's not even mad. He told me all about how he got over me…"

Annabel Warren, Sylvia's sister, paused as she passed us and set down her carafes of coffee on the stainless steel counter. "I'm sorry. Back that up a minute. He *told* you how he got over you?"

"Yeah," I said. "He said he was upset for a week and then he slept with lots of girls and then he was fine."

Annabel threw back her head and gave a big, throaty laugh.

"Oh yeah, he's not mad at *all*. He just felt he had to point out his significant sexual prowess five seconds into seeing you for the first time in two years."

That gave me pause. I pursed my lips, which made Annabel start laughing all over again. The sisters were a few years apart, and they both had the same peaches-and-cream skin and dark-red hair, but that was where the resemblance ended. Sylvia was tall and willowy, and when she wasn't working at Verde, she was singing in a variety of local nightclubs, coffee shops, and Renaissance fairs. Annabel, several inches shorter to start with, had never lost the weight she'd gained after getting pregnant at sixteen. Her son, Milo, was seven now, and Annabel was juggling his care, two jobs, and the occasional night school class to try to get a degree in nursing.

"Tell her what happened the next time you saw him," Sylvia singsonged as she filled ramekins with chopped chives.

"He gave me some pointers on my class schedule," I said. She had me slicing lemons. I hated slicing anything. There was a reason I'd gotten into algae, not higher life forms.

"*After* that," she prompted, blowing a tendril of hair out of her eyes.

I sighed. "We walked to the parking lot, and his girlfriend was there to pick him up."

"His rich, blonde, beautiful girlfriend," Sylvia added. She looked at her sister. "I mean, if I were friends with this Dylan guy instead of you, I'd be congratulating him on how well his revenge scenario was working out. The only thing that could possibly have made it at all better for him is if instead of you being a gorgeous, brilliant transfer student with a fat academic scholarship, you'd become some dirty old bag lady."

"Thanks for the gorgeous and brilliant part, at least," I said.

"No problem, honey." She went back to filling ramekins, and Annabel trotted off with her coffee jugs.

What neither of the Warren girls knew was that Hannah Swift wasn't just a hot blonde girlfriend for Dylan to show off to me. She was my secret sister as well. It was funny. I'd often thought of Hannah—or at least, of the existence of Hannah, since I'd never met her before—when I was hanging out with Sylvia and Annabel. They lived together, with Milo, in a little two-bedroom apartment in a building not far from my mom's. They'd both had some awful crap to wade through, especially after their parents kicked Annabel out of the house for getting pregnant and her creepy babydaddy left her in the lurch...but they'd had each other.

I also had a sister, but she was a stranger.

"Well, even if you're right," I said at last, "and he *was* trying to rub it in my face a little, it's done. And actually, I'm happy for him. I was the one who walked away, remember? He didn't do anything to hurt me. He deserves to, you know..."

"Sleep with lots of girls and have rich, blonde girlfriends with BMWs?" Sylvia asked.

I winced. Did we have to keep repeating it? "Exactly."

Annabel swung by again. "Look lively, girls. The Ladies Who Lunch are back."

"Who?" I asked.

Sylvia groaned. "Bunch of bitchy Canton sorority girls. They like to stop here after they've maxed out their daddies' credit cards shopping."

Annabel nodded. "They come in, only make special orders, and then complain about everything." She shrugged. "On the plus side, they usually tip well."

"Of course they do," said Sylvia. "They aren't paying the bills." She considered me for a moment. "I think this will be your first assignment. Go fill their water glasses and give them their menus." She handed me a pitcher. "Not that they'll use them."

I snagged a bunch of menus from the hostess stand on my way to the table. It was still early, so there weren't many people in the restaurant, and the table of the Ladies Who Lunch was obvious to spot, given the shopping bags clustered around their chairs and the chattering of the occupants. Verde was located in what had once been an alley between two buildings, so the restaurant featured soaring glass ceilings like a greenhouse, brick walls, and industrial details like metal rivets and exposed pipe. Real trees lining every aisle softened the picture and lent an explanation to the restaurant's name.

"Good afternoon, ladies," I said as I started to pass out the menus. There were five of them, all blondes, all with giant designer sunglasses shielding their eyes from the light filtering down from the glass ceiling. Three took the menus and actually paged through them. Two more had their noses buried deep in their phones. I started filling glasses with water.

"Oh my God, Hannah, look. He's texting me again." One squealed and pointed her cellphone at the blonde beside her.

My grip tightened on the pitcher. It *was* Hannah. Dylan's Hannah. My Hannah.

"Oooh," Hannah teased her friend. "He wants you *bad*."

I retreated to the kitchen at the fastest pace appropriate for a waitress.

"How'd it go?" Sylvia asked. "Did they ask you to pledge?"

"Syl," I choked out. "It's her. Dylan's girlfriend. She's a Lady Who Lunches."

Sylvia and Annabel piled over to the pass-through and peeked out at the table. I kept my distance.

"Which one?" Annabel whispered.

"The blonde."

Sylvia turned around and glared at me. "Honey, they're all blonde."

"Who is it?" Annabel asked. "I'm going to go out there and tell them about the specials."

"The one in the coral jacket," I said begrudgingly. The slim, stylish one in the designer sunglasses and the two-hundred-dollar shoes. The one with the perfect fall of silky hair and the eyes that look exactly like mine.

"Awesome." Annabel straightened her apron. "Off to do some recon."

As soon as she was gone, I turned to Sylvia. "I don't want or need recon," I said. Everything there was to know about Hannah Swift I already knew. She was my father's *real* daughter. She was dating the boy I'd lost my virginity to. End of story. "I don't care who he dates."

"Did she recognize you when you went over there?" Sylvia asked, still staring out the pass-through.

No, thank God. I didn't want us being friends. "She didn't even look up from her phone," I said. And it was a good thing, too. Who knew what would happen if she started contemplating how similar our eyes were?

Sylvia snorted. "Figures. Bunch of snobby little rich girls who can't imagine their servants are actual people."

"Would you stop it?" I asked. "We don't get to hate this girl just because she's dating some guy I slept with a long time ago." And I didn't get to hate her because her father paid for every single cent of her Canton education even while arguing that I shouldn't get one.

Sylvia turned back to me, her eyes big and round. "Sorry! Geez, Tess, who made you Miss Manners?"

I wondered if that was why Dad had tried to talk me out of Canton. Because he knew Hannah was going there and he didn't want to risk having us at the same school, maybe even living in the same dorm.

Annabel returned. "The usual." She affected a high, squeaky voice and a valley girl accent. "'Can I get the breaded filet without the breading and do you have any pomegranate today and can you roast the cauliflower without the truffle oil?'" She tossed the menus back in the holder and began entering the complicated orders into the computer. "Dylan's girlfriend went easy on us though. Seared salmon salad, hold the nuts."

Sylvia laughed. "Let's *not* hold the nuts."

"Sylvia!" I exclaimed. "What if she's allergic?" Was she? Dad had never mentioned if Hannah had a nut allergy. Of course, he hardly ever mentioned her at all.

My friend nodded. "Good point. Can we put salt in her iced tea?"

"Sylvia!" Annabel and I cried in unison.

"You're making me sorry I told you who she was," I added.

"Honestly, I'm sure she's a perfectly nice girl." Dylan wouldn't be dating her otherwise, right?

"I'm sure she's *not*," Sylvia insisted. "What twenty-year-old owns a BMW? Spoiled brats who get everything they want all the time are never nice girls."

"If I could, I'd give Milo everything he ever wanted," Annabel pointed out. "You think that would ruin him?"

"Yes!" said Sylvia. "That's why they call it 'spoiled.'"

I didn't say anything. I was sure Dad had given Hannah everything. He'd even gone so far as to make certain that her college experience wasn't marred by the presence of her bastard half-sister. Lucky Hannah.

Somehow, we managed to change the subject to Milo's collection of matchbox cars, and then a few more tables came in and Sylvia started showing me the ropes. I was to train at her side for today, then help expedite and assistant serve for two more shifts. After that, I'd get my own tables and my own tips. Sylvia was working the row of tables on the other side of the Ladies Who Lunch, and I made sure to keep my back to Hannah whenever we were out there. She'd only seen me for a moment at the car the other day, but I didn't need her to ever see me again.

Sylvia was explaining the menu to a couple who clearly didn't understand the meaning of the word "confit" when I heard Dylan's name come floating up from Hannah's table. I couldn't help it—I diverted my attention away from Sylvia. After all, I knew what confit was.

"Seriously, girlfriend, in six months, you have re*made* that boy." It was one of the Blondes, talking to Hannah.

"I take some credit for his newfound sense of fashion, yes," Hannah was saying. "But I had *great* starting material."

There was a chorus of snickering around the table. My fingers started tingling with a two-year-old memory of what Dylan's body felt like beneath my hands. I straightened and squeezed my eyes shut before other parts started remembering too.

"That's true," said a second blonde. "He has kind of an Adam Scott thing going on. Geeky but adorable."

I practically nodded in agreement before catching myself.

"If you say so," said Blonde #1. "But Inever would have noticed the raw material under all that nerdy covering."

"Oh, he's still a nerd," said Blonde #2. "We were out at dinner the other day, and I swear the only thing he wanted to talk about was seaweed-powered cars." More laughter.

"Laugh it up," said Hannah. "I'll keep my nerd boy, thank you very much. When he's the billionaire owner of that seaweed-powered car company, you'll change your tune."

"All hail Seaweed Zuckerberg and our very smelly future cars," said Blonde #3 and I heard glasses clinking.

I breathed in very long and slow through my nose, then opened my eyes. Sylvia finished going over the menu with her table and gave them a few minutes to think it over. I trailed back to the kitchen with her in silence, my heart pounding, my cheeks inflamed.

"Oh. My. God," Sylvia said when we got back to the kitchen.

I kept breathing.

"She might as well have just come out and said she was only dating him for his future earning potential!"

I swallowed thickly. "And they don't get it at all!" I blurted. "'Smelly cars?' Come on! The whole point is to convert the seaweed to ethanol. It's not going to smell like low tide or anything."

Sylvia blinked at me, then chuckled. "Leave it to you, Tess, to get all worked up about precisely the wrong thing. If Dylan's as big a nerd as they seem to think he is, then you two are perfect for each other."

I wiped my clammy hands on my apron. "I'm going to go out there and tell them about the potential for kelp forests as a marine pollution sink and—" I stopped. No, I wasn't. Because out there was Hannah Swift. If some waitress came up and served them a lecture on algae instead of their lunch, Hannah would be certain to remember. And if she mentioned it to Dylan or her dad...

Sylvia was shaking her head at me sadly. "Kelp forests? Tess, come on. Let's focus on the issue here. Your ex is dating some total bimbo who's only after him for his money. There's no point in being noble about that. If you want him back, you have the moral authority to strike."

"But I don't want him back." It sounded very convincing. "Dylan is a really nice guy, and I like him a lot, and once, a long time ago, we had one good night together. But *I* was the one who walked away. I don't want to be with him."

Sylvia's shoulders slumped as she looked at me. Inwardly, I begged her not to ask *why not?* "Okay," she said at last. "But still, if he's such a nice guy, he should know that his girlfriend is using him."

I rolled my eyes. "You figure out a way to let him know that without making me sound like some creeper stalker ex who *does* want him back, and I'll consider it."

Sylvia, of course, could not, so she dropped the subject and went back to training me. Later, Annabel called me over to the computer so she could show me how to split checks. She handed me a stack of black pleather bill cases. "Ladies Who Lunch want a five-way split."

I opened the top bill case. The platinum American Express card inside read *Hannah K Swift.*

Sylvia wanted me to resent Hannah because she was dating Dylan. She wanted me to be jealous of her because Hannah had the affection and attention of the only guy I'd ever really liked.

Sylvia had no freaking clue. I couldn't allow myself to begin hating Hannah Swift. If I started down that path, I'd never, ever stop.

SIX

THE TOTAL on the bookstore register read *$1,534.71*. At first, I was sure it was a mistake. An extra number typed in. A decimal in the wrong place. I asked to look at the breakdown.

It was right. I almost fainted, right there on the floor of the Canton Campus Bookstore.

"I said I was looking for *used* books," I told the clerk, trying not to choke.

She shrugged and pointed at two textbooks in the pile before me with little red "USED" stickers on their spines. "Those are the only ones I could find used. Not as many people take the upper-level courses, and most of them keep their books."

I bit my lip as I studied the pile before me. I'd always gotten by with used texts. This was twice what I'd budgeted for text-books this term, and I hadn't even gotten my online course packets yet. But I wouldn't despair. They'd surely have a few of these at the campus science library. I'd just do some of my reading there.

No such luck. At the library, I couldn't find several of the most expensive. "Excuse me," I said to the student behind the desk. "I'm having a hard time locating this book, *Tissue Engineering*, in the stacks. But your computer says it's here."

The guy didn't even look up from his screen. "Maybe someone's using it."

I checked out the nearly empty reading room. "I don't see anyone using it. I'm wondering if maybe it's been mis-shelved..." I gestured at the overflowing book cart behind him.

"Maybe," he mumbled. "Or maybe someone hid it so they could always be sure to get their hands on it for class readings. Or maybe they stole it..."

"Well, maybe you should buy more than one copy!" I argued.

He rolled his eyes. "Maybe you should write a letter to the acquisitions department about that."

"Thanks for your help," I replied through gritted teeth as I turned and headed out the door. My next class started in less than ten minutes, so I didn't have time to argue with the grumpy librarian anyway.

I'd figure this out. It would just take a little scrambling. I had about three hundred dollars available on my credit card, but I might be able to get them to increase my limit. Mom had a new art client. Maybe that meant she had a little extra cash to lend me. Dr. Cavel had all the research assistants she needed this term, but she said she'd keep a lookout for me and would even ask around a few other departments. Now that my training was done at Verde, I could pick up a few more shifts...

"Lost in thought?" Dylan fell into step beside me. "Or just trying to work out some of the stickier issues in our reading for Biotransport?"

"I...uh, haven't done that reading yet," I admitted, sparing him a glance. Maybe if I looked at him more often I'd stop having to catch my breath every time he showed up. I could vaccinate myself against him. That was totally possible, right? "I can't seem to get my hands on the textbook."

"This textbook?" he asked and held up a shiny new copy of *Tissue Engineering*. "You should have called me. I'd be happy to share until you find one."

Called him? For the first time in years? My eyes burned as I took the book from him. "Thanks. I can get this back to you...

whenever. I can—" What? Email him daily to schedule time with his textbook? Drop by his dorm room to say hi to him and his girlfriend? No, that wasn't going to fly at all.

He gave me a kind smile, and it seriously stung. "We can work something out."

"Thanks," I repeated. "I owe you."

He didn't say anything.

In class, it seemed almost natural that Dylan would sit next to me. After all, we'd walked in together. There were about twenty other students in the class, but only three other girls, all of whom gave me a once-over as I came in the door at Dylan's side. He opened his laptop and slid it into the space between us so I could see his reading notes.

"Come prepared next time," he whispered, and every hair on my neck stood on end.

Class started, and I tried to put my concerns about textbook pricing and Dylan Kingsley out of my mind and concentrate. But it was pretty difficult to do the latter, with him sitting right next to me, tapping his blunt fingertips against the table and answering the professor's questions in his usual no-nonsense style.

Near the end of class, the professor, Dr. Yue, said, "I wanted to leave a few minutes at the end to go over the syllabus and see if you had any questions. I also wanted to talk a bit about the Design Symposium at the end of the term. Given that this is a 400-level class, any of your term projects will be eligible for entry into the symposium, which, as you know, comes with a five-thousand-dollar grand prize. So if anyone here is interested in that, my office door is always open."

A chorus of chuckles went around the room. My mouth had gone dry. Five thousand dollars would go a long way toward defraying the unexpected costs of attending Canton.

After class, I packed up my bag, my mind already whirling with possibilities. I certainly wasn't going to approach Dr. Yue before I'd caught up on his course materials, but if Dylan would let me keep the book for the next couple of hours...

"Earth to Tess," came his voice.

I looked up at him. Vaccination.

"At the risk of getting attacked, are you up for a sandwich? A nice, friendly, utterly innocent sandwich?"

"I can't believe you remember that." But of course he did. Well, I wasn't the silly teenaged girl I'd once been, who read all kinds of invitations into a simple request to share lunch. Besides, the man had just lent me his textbook. How could I say no? "A quick one," I agreed. "I want to make sure I do this reading and tomorrow's, too, so I can get the book back to you ASAP."

"I trust you're good for it," he said.

On the way to lunch, Dylan was greeted and waved at by a good dozen fellow students. That had never happened to me, even after two years at State. The campus was just too large, too populous. I'd made a few friends there, but no one I expected to keep in touch with for long. I wondered if things would be the same here at Canton, especially since I wasn't living on campus.

"So how are you liking it here so far?" Dylan asked.

"Other than the textbook trauma, it's been nice. I'm loving the class sizes."

"It's weird they sold out at the bookstore," Dylan said. "Dr. Yue is usually really good about making sure they're ordering the right amount. Any idea when the new shipment might come in? Or you could try online."

Inwardly, I cringed. He thought they'd just sold out. What would it be like to live in Dylan's world? In Hannah's? In a place where the only reason you couldn't buy something was because the store had an inventory problem? "I'm working on it."

"Well, you're free to use mine until you can get your hands on a copy. And you can just drop it by my apartment this evening. I'm over in Swift." He pointed at the brown sandstone complex at the other end of the quad. "Apartment 202."

Pretty sure I could remember that. Something perverse inside me made me speak again. "Swift. That's your girlfriend's name, isn't it?"

"Yeah." He shrugged. "Big legacy family. She's actually a townie, like you."

I don't think you call them "townies" if they own half of the town.

We entered the sandwich shop and placed our orders. "So," I said when we sat down with our food. "How did you and Hannah meet?"

He paused, his turkey club halfway to his mouth. "Asking questions about my girlfriend?"

I shrugged. "Making conversation."

The glint in Dylan's eye said he didn't buy that for a second. "Nothing too interesting. We were at a frat party and neither of us wanted to be there, so we wound up talking."

"Not into frat parties? Isn't she in a sorority?" I asked.

"No." He furrowed his brow. "What made you think that?"

Sylvia. Common sense. Girls like Hannah were in sororities. They wore pearls and drove their daddy's cars and had bright, shiny futures where they married soon-to-be scientific billionaires like Dylan. I took a bite of my sandwich, and when I swallowed, spoke up again. "What's she studying?"

"Communications," he replied. "This week, at least. She's had about six majors since we started dating last spring. I think she'd rather take a gap year or something to figure herself out, but her parents won't have it. Her dad, really. He's kind of an asshole."

I very nearly spewed my soda across the table at him. "You've met her parents?" I choked out.

"Sure," he said. "Plenty of times. They live right here in town. Anyway, enough about Hannah. You don't have to pretend you're oh-so-interested in my girlfriend. We're all grown-ups here. Let's talk about Bio-E."

So we did. I told him all about the work I'd done at State, and he gave me a rundown of the department at Canton and what he'd been up to for the last two years.

"Actually, I owe it all to you," he said, his blue eyes alight with what I'd decided to call scientific passion. "I'd probably still be in environmental science if it wasn't for our Cornell project. It made me think that I didn't want to just study these things, I wanted to be more proactive in trying to stop it."

"That's great," I was able to say honestly.

"I think about that summer a lot," he said, then stopped himself. "You know what I mean. About the work."

"Of course." I chased a few stray bits of shredded lettuce around my sandwich wrapper as an awkward silence fell over the table.

We could say whatever we wanted about how we were grown-ups and how it didn't matter anymore, and we could act the part, too. But that didn't mean we didn't remember. You don't forget your first time like that. Not when it was like it had been for Dylan and me.

I decided to just press through to the other side. "I think about it too. I mean, I could have easily given up on algae after high school, but you kind of made sure I remained a fan for life. My new thing is biofuels and ethanol production. I was actually thinking about it in class today when—"

An alarm buzzed on his phone. "Crap, I have a one thirty," he said. "I can't believe it got so late."

Of course Dylan set alarms for his class times. Otherwise he'd get so involved in his research he'd probably forget to breathe. He'd been just like that even back at Cornell.

He stood up, crumpling his lunch wrappers into a ball. "Can we put a pin in this for later? I want to hear all about your ideas. I just have to get to lab."

I waved my hand at him. "Yeah, sure. Go on. I'll get your book back to you by six."

"Great!" He sprinted off, and I worked on getting my heartbeat back to normal.

———

MY LAST CLASS was at three, so I spent all the time in between trying to get the reading finished for Biotransport. After my stats class, I finished up the last few pages of the assignment in *Tissue*

Engineering, then headed over to the Swift building to give Dylan his book. I wasn't exactly sure what to expect from his place, but I prepared myself, just in case it included Hannah.

The door marked 202 opened a few seconds after my knock, and a wave of heavenly smells emerged. Something spicy and tomatoey. My mouth watered, and that was before my eyes even landed on Dylan, casual in a pair of low-slung gray sweatpants and a dark-red Canton U T-shirt. His dark hair was mussed and almost as floppy as it had been when we were teens. He must have taken his contacts out because the gunmetal-gray glasses were back—oh, boy, were they back.

"Hi," I said, trying not to drool. Instead of vaccination, staring at him felt more like feeding an addiction. "Here's your book, as promised."

"Thanks." He reached to take it and our fingers brushed. Sparks shot up my arm and the book clattered on the threshold.

As Dylan leaned over to pick it up, I got a glimpse at the apartment behind him. It was a studio-type setup, with wide windows, a modern, granite-topped kitchenette, lots of book-shelves, and a rumpled futon opened up into a platform bed.

"Oops." He dusted off the cover, then caught me checking out his place. "Want to come in? I'm actually in the middle of cooking. It's just pasta, but there's plenty if you're hungry."

Yeah? And where would we sit? On that big old bed in the center of the room? "No thanks," I trilled. "I have to go home to my mom, so…"

"Right, of course." He shifted the book from hand-to-hand. "Listen, Tess, about what you were saying earlier…" He trailed off as if thinking better of his words. "Never mind. See you in class tomorrow."

I waved and departed, though I wondered the whole way home what it was he'd wanted to say.

———

WHEN MY FATHER came to visit, he always parked behind our

apartment complex so no one spotted his car. It wasn't a flashy car or anything, just a beige Lexus SUV, but he still didn't want anyone to recognize it. He was there when I got home that evening.

I bore no illusions that Dad would be happy to see me. We dispensed with the usual pleasantries even more quickly than usual.

"I can't believe you didn't consult with me before making such a huge change," Dad said, his voice filled with fatherly concern but his eyes doing that hard, flinty thing they always did when he was angrier than he was letting on. "Your mother tells me you've lost a whole semester in this transfer of yours. Is that true?"

"Yes, sir." I was sitting across from him on the couch, my hands folded in my lap. Mom was in her usual armchair, perched on the edge and listening. She wore the same concerned expression as my father. Tattletale.

"And that doesn't bother you?" he asked. "I thought you were a serious student, Tess. To give up a whole semester..." He clucked his tongue.

I resisted the temptation to roll my eyes. "I wasn't going to graduate in eight terms at State, either," I said. "I couldn't get into half the prereq courses I needed. I hardly lost any credits in the transfer, but I have to catch up on prereqs. I was going to need another semester, at Canton or at State. This way, my final degree will say Canton on it, and that's worth an extra term."

"This scholarship of yours is going to cover it?" he asked skeptically.

"Yes." Well, as much as it was covering anything. I wasn't even going to be able to afford books pretty soon if I didn't figure out an extra source of income. Like that symposium...

"What I'm most baffled by, Tess, is that you didn't even think to ask me if this was all right. After all the money I invested in your schooling at State...you just threw it all away."

My eyes shot up to meet his. I hadn't asked him because I knew he'd say no. "I didn't throw anything away. I made the best decision I could for my future." What did he want me to do? Pay him back for eight credits' worth of lost room and board at State?

He was shaking his head at me, his face a mask of disappointment. "And I can't imagine what your professors think. That nice botanist who gave you a job in his lab—what was his name?"

"Dr. Stewart," Mom supplied.

"Stewart. I can't imagine he's happy that you transferred. You might as well have said to his face that you don't think he or his program is good enough for you."

"As a matter of fact, Dr. Stewart wrote my recommendation." I could have added a lot more, but I didn't. Dr. Stewart was the one who'd told me about the Canton scholarship going vacant. He'd known it was where I wanted to be but that financial constraints kept me from attending, and there wasn't much he could do for me in Bio-E from the botany department. We'd both agreed it was the opportunity of a lifetime.

"The whole thing just strikes me as so…ungrateful," Dad said. "And all for what? A few extra lab hours? A microscope or two? You don't know anyone at Canton—"

Au contraire, *Dad. I know your daughter's boyfriend* quite *well.*

"And you aren't likely to find another research assistant position, either. I'm guessing all those slots have already gone to their own students."

"I am 'their own student'," I pointed out, irritated. "Transfers aren't second-class citizens, Dad."

"Sweetie," my mother pleaded. "Give your father a break. He's just trying to show you some cons that you may not have thought through entirely."

My mother could take her peacekeeping efforts and shove them. I was an expert at examining my options, after years of trying to fit every choice in my life into my father's rules. I'd made a pro and con list back when I'd gotten my scholarship acceptance. The only thing tripping me up at the moment was textbook prices, but I'd have that resolved soon enough. And I resented my father's insistence that he be involved in the decision when I knew the only thing he'd want was for me to stay far, far away.

I wasn't asking him for money—in fact, I was asking for *no* money—so he could just stay out of it. "It's a little late for that," I said instead. "I'm here at Canton. Bought and paid for, credits transferred, semester started. It's too late."

"Yes," my father said. "You worked that out very neatly, young lady. You didn't even tell me. Didn't even ask for my advice about what was best for your future or what I, who've spent so much money on your education, might think about all this." He stared at me for a moment more, then sighed. "I just can't believe that after everything I've done for you, you'd act this devious. This selfish. And I honestly don't see why you don't think State was good enough for you."

"I don't know," I snapped. "Why wasn't it good enough for Hannah?"

It was as if all the air got sucked out of the room. My mother's mouth dropped open.

"What did you just say to me?" His voice was nearly a whisper.

"She's at Canton," I said as tears began to burn my eyes. "I saw her there. So it's fine for her to go, but not me?"

He stood up, tall, broad, big, like the Canton U football player he'd once been. His tone was still low, still dangerous. "Did you talk to her?"

"Of course not!" My voice caught on a sob as the tears began to roll down my cheeks. "I know the *rules*." And I did. I'd always known them. But staying away from the Swifts shouldn't mean staying away from everything else I wanted in my life.

I needed Canton. Hannah didn't need anything.

He said nothing, but I felt his eyes on me. Abruptly, he turned. "We'll finish this conversation later." He headed for the door, and my mom followed after him, down the narrow halls of our apartment.

I just sat there and gulped down big breaths, wiping the tears off my face. Saying her name had been a mistake. If he was unhappy about me going to Canton before, letting him know that I hadn't been there a week before I'd run into his real daughter was not going to help the situation.

My mom only came back down the hall as I was getting up to go into my room. "Oh, Tess," she said, shaking her head sadly. "Why do you insist on making everything so hard on yourself?"

I paused at the door. "Trust me, Mom. It was pretty hard already."

In my room, I booted up my computer, still fuming. How dare he tell me where I could go to school if he wasn't paying for it? How dare he call me selfish for wanting the best out of my education, for wanting to get out from under his control for good?

There was a new email, sent to my shiny new Canton address, from Dylan.

Tess,

I kind of lost my nerve back there at my door, but apparently I'm better over email.

All other unfortunate history aside, you and I both know we did awesome work on that project at Cornell. You're new here, but I can tell you right now that there's no one else in our Bio-E class that you want to do a term project with. And I know the only person I'd partner with again is you. I think you mentioned you have a few ideas. I do too, and together, I think we can rock the symposium.

What do you say? For science?

Dylan

I pressed reply.

Absolutely. For science.

-Tess

SEVEN

I WAS REVIEWING my notes before Biotransport when a shadow fell across my desk. I looked up to see a female student I recognized from our first class staring down at me. "Tess McMann, right? I'm Elaine Sun."

"Nice to meet you." I shook the girl's hand, and she slid into the seat beside me. *Dylan's seat*, I thought to myself for a split second before I banished the notion from my brain for all time. Nothing here was Dylan's.

"It's good to see the proportion of women in this department increasing," Elaine said. Her dark hair was twisted into a messy bun, and strands of magenta reached back from each temple. "Even one makes a huge difference around here."

"Well," I said with a sheepish shrug, "I'm glad to help in any way I can."

"What are your plans for the symposium?" she asked abruptly.

I blinked. "I'm—not quite sure. I think Dylan Kingsley—"

"Dylan Kingsley?" she sneered. "Figures. You've been here for a day, and he's already got his claws in the fresh meat."

"Pardon me?" I asked.

"There aren't enough girls here as is," she said. "We should really stick together."

I wanted to hear more of what she was saying about Dylan. He'd sounded genuine enough in his email. But I hadn't seen the guy in two years, while Elaine had presumably been in several classes with him. Who knew what he was like these days better than she? And what did she mean by "fresh meat"?

"Nothing's set in stone yet," I tried. "I just told him I'd be happy to talk about potential—"

"And I'll tell you one thing," she said. "You won't win unless you do biomed. Not at Canton."

"I'm not doing biomed," I said. "With or without Dylan. I've got an environmental concentration."

She snorted now, so hard I was surprised snot didn't spatter my textbook. "Well then, aren't you two a perfect match."

"A perfect match for what?" Dylan's voice hovered above us. He was standing there, his stance casual, his smile not quite reaching his eyes. "Poaching my partner, Elaine?"

She rolled her eyes, swiped her things off the table, and stalked away. Dylan slid smoothly into the spot she'd vacated.

Nothing here is Dylan's, I repeated to myself.

"What was that all about?" I asked him.

He shrugged. "Elaine's a sore loser. I beat her in the freshman year final project, and she's never forgiven me."

I pressed my lips together. Maybe I'd rushed into things last night, letting my anger at my dad fuel my response to Dylan. I shouldn't commit to partnering with him. Not until I heard more about his ideas or got to know some of the other people in the class.

Not until I could be sure I was capable of working alongside him.

"She said you always preyed on fresh meat." I eyed him carefully. "What does she mean by that?"

He looked amused. "She did? I have no idea what she means by 'always,' but she's smart. She probably figures that if I snatched you up this quickly, I have secret info about how good you are." He leaned in and dropped his voice to a whisper. "And of course, she's right. I *do* have secret info about how good you are."

I swallowed. Why did he have to say it like that?

"Because we worked together before, Tess. Geez, what did you think I meant?" He grinned, and I prayed my face wasn't as flushed as it felt. He nudged me with his elbow. "Come on, lighten up. Either we're going to joke about this or we're going to be awkward and horrible."

My body told me awkward and horrible would rule the day, no matter how many jokes might come out of my mouth. But I wanted to get over it, the way Dylan so obviously had. I wanted to work with him, because he was right, we had worked so well. I wanted to be all grown-up and professional.

"Besides," Dylan coaxed. "You don't want to work with Elaine. She's biomed all the way. She won't touch algae with a ten-foot pole."

"I told her I was enviro."

"See?" Dylan said with a flourish of his hands. "Elaine was right about one thing. We are a perfect match."

Stop saying it like that. Just stop.

"Like I told you last night," he went on, "you can ask around if you want. I'm certainly not going to pressure you into anything. But I think with the two of us working together, we can really wow them, knock them on their biomedical asses."

I chuckled. He beamed. Somewhere across the room, Elaine Sun was scowling.

And I could do this. I knew I could. Two years ago, I'd had enough willpower to keep my hands off Dylan the entire time we were working together. Two years ago, I'd had enough willpower to walk away from a relationship with him because I knew it would be bad for my future. I certainly had just as much willpower now. Besides, all that was back when Dylan had actually wanted me.

This time, he had a girlfriend, and even if he didn't—well, I'd screwed him over. Broken his heart. Dumped him. And though he didn't seem bitter about it at all, he also didn't seem *interested*. I was ancient history, water under the bridge, whatever other thing meant he could laugh and tease and introduce me to his girlfriend like he'd never once told her the name of the first person he'd ever slept with.

Wait—he *hadn't*, right? I thought about my ex-boyfriend Jason, who'd definitely told me about both of his prior girlfriends. Just as I'd told Jason about Dylan. Didn't everyone do that? But if Dylan had told Hannah, then wouldn't she have been a little more interested in me when he'd introduced us the other day?

Just like that, my mind was filled with images of Dylan in bed with my sister, having pillow talk with her about the time he lost his virginity…to me. Oh, God.

"Ms. McMann?" Dr. Yue's voice broke into my waking nightmare. "Care to give us your thoughts on cell surface plasmon resonance?"

"Yes!" I said, relieved to be flipping through notes tangled with chemical equations rather than my even more tangled thoughts. "When you're dealing with a dissociation constant higher than the expected value of K-delta…"

Even when I was done answering the professor, I kept all my focus on the rest of the lecture. I might have written down every word spoken in that classroom for the next fifty minutes.

It was nice for my brain to have something to do other than worry about what Dylan may have told Hannah, or wonder if I could be the disinterested scientist I longed to, or process the aggravatingly delicious scent of the guy sitting way too close.

———

THAT AFTERNOON, I did something that I'd somehow managed to avoid doing for my entire life. I looked up Hannah Swift on Facebook.

There wasn't much there. Her profile pic was one of those candid shots that had clearly had other people in it originally. I saw the corner of someone else's arm near her shoulder—maybe even Dad's. It listed her schools: the high school that served the nice part of town, Canton U. She was "in a relationship" with Dylan, and there were a bunch of pictures of him there, too. Her wall was filled with posts from friends, pretty girls with pouting selfie profile pics, sending her exclamations points and Xs and Os and clippings of news items about her favorite TV shows and movies.

Hannah liked horror films. That was unexpected. She read a lot of books—or at least, she wanted everyone on Facebook to think she had. I tried to imagine Hannah in my father's house, nose stuck in a book. It didn't jibe with the image I had of her. Or maybe the image I wanted to have. Hannah, the beautiful rich girl, living in my dad's house, spending his money, smiling out from a silver frame on his desk at work. I wanted to know who this girl was who had attracted Dylan. He wasn't into Ladies Who Lunch, that much I knew. So what did he see in her? Maybe he liked the girl who listed *One Hundred Years of Solitude* as her favorite novel. I'd never read it, but I'd heard of it. Maybe he liked the girl who didn't squeal when the murderer ripped the co-ed's guts out in the slasher flick. Maybe he liked her tennis serve.

I didn't know anything about that girl. She was my sister, and I didn't know. I glanced at her friends list—other Canton kids, other kids from high school. Did she have exes in this list? Her senior prom date, her first kiss, the guy she'd lost her virginity to? God, I hoped it wasn't Dylan. It wouldn't be though, would it? Not if they'd only been together for six months.

No way, Tess. She's twenty years old. Probably hadn't even waited as long as Dylan and I had to start having sex. Hannah was too outgoing, too pretty, too popular, too *Swift.*

But that wasn't the info anyone ever put on Facebook.

————

THAT EVENING AT VERDE, I helped Sylvia with prep work and gave her the latest scoop. She chopped lemons, threaded olives and pearl onions onto toothpicks, and listened patiently until I was through.

"You know, Tess," she said at last, "for someone who isn't interested in dating Dylan, you sure care an awful lot about what he told his new girlfriend about you."

I chose not to dignify that with a response. Besides, I didn't care because of Dylan. I cared because of Hannah. "But if he did tell her that we'd slept together, don't you think she'd have been a bit more interested when she met me? I mean, wouldn't you be?"

"Yeah," Sylvia agreed. "So then he probably didn't tell her."

I shook my head. He would have told her. Dylan—frank, honest, open Dylan—would have given her the names of the girls he'd slept with. Then again, that was teenaged Dylan. And since then, he said he'd slept with lots of people. Maybe that list was just a tad too long to trot it out these days.

But number one—I mean, that was worth a mention, right? *I* was worth a mention. What we'd done had meant a lot to me, even if I hadn't called him again. I'd always thought that since Dylan had wanted to keep the relationship going, it had meant a lot to him, too.

Oh God, was I bad in bed? Maybe it hadn't been those other guys' fault.

"And anyway, who cares?" Sylvia asked, breaking me out of my spiral of neuroses. "Are you worried that if she knows, she'll freak about about you two working together?"

"Yes." This, at least, was most of the truth. Added scrutiny from Hannah Swift was bad on any level, and there'd be enough chances of us running into each other if I worked with Dylan. If she was suspicious of me because Dylan had told her our past history…well, that was definitely against Dad's rules.

"You know what you can do, of course."

I waited, hopeful.

Sylvia blew a strand of hair out of her eyes and started in on the trays of nuts. "You can *ask him*."

"Excuse me?"

"'Hey, Dylan,'" she quoted in a falsely casual tone, "'before we commit to this science fair thing, can you tell me how much your girlfriend knows about the nature of our former relationship, and, if she does know, if she's cool about us working together now? Because I don't want a beaker of acid in my face.'" She shrugged. "Like that."

"A beaker of acid?" I asked dryly. "Seriously?"

"You're right," she replied. "A Lady Who Lunches wouldn't be smart enough to blind you with science. She'd just key your car or something."

"That's okay then," I said. "The paint job's so bad, I wouldn't know if my car had been keyed."

Syliva laughed at that, and we finished our prep work. Tonight, Sylvia had me on bar training, and soon my head was filled with formulas for various cocktails, the difference between sweet and dry vermouth, how many seconds of pouring equaled one or two or one-half of a jigger, according to the recipe booklet behind the bar. Sylvia, the more experienced bartender, would be making most of the drinks tonight, but I had been assigned the role of barback, pouring beers and wines and helping her out when things started getting rushed.

"This should be easy for you," Sylvia said as people started showing up. "Just pretend you're in a lab."

"Labs are quieter," I said. "And not full of guys looking to flirt with you."

"Really? Isn't that how you met Dylan?"

"Good point." And that was pretty much the end of all conversation that wasn't "two draft beers and a pinot grigio" or "pass the lime juice" for the rest of my evening.

After my shift had ended, I drove home, yawning and wondering how much coffee I'd need to consume to be able to finish my homework that night. What I didn't expect was to find my mom waiting up for me. She was seated at our kitchen table, reading a magazine and having a cup of tea.

"I know, I know," she said, giving me a dismissive wave. "You're all grown up. But somehow, now that you're living here, it's harder to keep up this fantasy that you've been home in bed at 8:00 p.m. every night for the last two years."

I smiled. "Is there any coffee?"

"At midnight?" She clucked her tongue. "Tess, you can't keep this up. You're going to burn out."

"It's my only option if I want to stay at Canton. Dad won't help."

She pursed her lips and looked down at her magazine. I knew that look. It was the one where she cast Dad's latest edict in the most positive light possible. "He'll come around eventually. I think the other night he was mostly just mad you went behind his back. You're his daughter, Tess. He wants to talk over big decisions like that with you."

More like he wanted to *make* big decisions like that for me.

"It's hard to feel like his daughter when just mentioning my sister's existence gets him angry."

She gave me a long, thoughtful look. "It's hard for him too, Tess. He's so proud of you—of all your accomplishments. He'd love to boast about you to everyone."

Hard. *For him*.

"You don't know. There were lots of times, when you were younger, where he'd wonder what he could do to get...her...to act more responsibly, be a little more focused on her schoolwork and her goals."

Well, at least Hannah was lucky enough to be spared the stereotypical parent "why can't you be more like your sister" lectures.

"And what did you say, Mom? That it was due to your superior parenting skills and maybe he'd married the wrong woman?"

She smiled. "Should have said that, you're right." She cocked her head to the side. "Do you really think that? I always thought

I just got lucky. You certainly didn't get your ambition from my genes. I was never the scholar you are, and I couldn't have cared less about science in school."

"But you never dissuaded me from trying to achieve the most I could," I replied. Unlike my father.

"Oh, sweetie, I don't think I could have. You always go after what you want."

I bit my lip. "Not always, Mom." I'd walked away from Dylan once, and I was trying my hardest to do it again.

─────

AT THE FIRST planning session with Dylan, in the Photonics lab after class the following week, I decided that Sylvia had the right idea. Before I spent the next few months fretting about secrets when I should be formulating equations, I should just find out from Dylan what he'd said to Hannah about me.

"Before we get too far into this," I said, tapping my pencil a bit too hard against the page, "I have to ask you something."

"Oh...kay," Dylan said slowly, looking a bit worried.

It came out in a blurt. "Did you tell Hannah about us?"

"About how I was doing this project with you?"

"No," I said. "About...us."

"Oh."

"Because it usually comes up," I rambled on. "With girlfriends. And...histories."

"It does?"

I looked up, not even realizing until that moment that I'd somehow become fascinated with my notebook. "Doesn't it?"

"I don't know, Tess," he teased. "You're the one who made that claim. I assumed you had data to back up your hypothesis."

"Well, you're the one with all the experience!" I shot back. "'Lots of girls,' remember?"

He laughed. "Right. I did say that."

My mouth dropped open. "It's not true?"

"Well..." He rolled his shoulders. "'Lots' isn't an exact

number, Madam Scientist. What is the precise definition of 'lots'?"

I straightened and looked him in the eye. "Ten."

He blinked. It was a guilty blink.

I threw my pencil at him. "I knew it!"

He ducked. "What did you want me to say, Tess? I'm standing there, minding my own business, and a girl I hadn't spoken to in two years suddenly appears across the cheese tray like some sort of hallucination in a gray miniskirt."

"It was a dress."

"It was a *shock*, is what it was." He folded his arms. "Okay, fine. Three. Not including Hannah."

I didn't say anything, partially because *three* changed my perception of the situation a lot, and partially because the "not including Hannah" part made me cringe a bit on the inside.

He was staring at me, and when he spoke again, his voice was much softer. "And now you know a lot more about my sexual history than my girlfriend does. Does that answer your question?"

I nodded wordlessly, because I couldn't trust my voice not to say all the things whirling around in my brain, especially the biggest—*why*? Why hadn't he told Hannah about me, if we were so firmly and forever in the past?

"Now you tell me if what you said over the cheese tray about dating girls was true. Because I think it would help my ego a lot to learn that your real issue was that you had decided guys weren't your thing."

Okay. So I hadn't exactly told him the truth, either. I took a deep breath. "No. No girls."

"Well, there goes that fantasy. And my whole prepared speech about how, as a friend, I think you can do way better than Elaine Sun."

I forced a smile. "Not into girls, Dylan."

He said nothing, but I heard the question anyway. I saw it in his deep, blue eyes. And I knew I owed him an answer, after all these years.

"I...wasn't ready for a relationship," I admitted. "Truthfully? I was kind of scared of where we were going. I was only eighteen, and... I just wasn't ready."

He seemed to mull this over for a bit. "Yeah. I get it," he said at last. "Well...it all worked out for the best."

"Yes!" I agreed, relieved. "Now we'll be partners and friends, and it's perfect."

"Yeah."

We were such liars.

EIGHT

IT STARTED SIMPLY ENOUGH. Since my shifts at Verde ran Thursday and Friday nights, and all day Saturday and Sunday, Dylan and I planned Monday through Wednesday evenings to work on our project.

On Monday, we worked from five until nine, when he said he had to go meet Hannah.

On Tuesday, we worked from five until ten. He'd been saying he had to go meet Hannah for a full hour before he finally left the lab.

On Wednesday, we looked up from our work to discover it was eleven-thirty. Dylan pulled out his phone. "Three missed calls."

"Hannah?"

He nodded. "I should have told her I couldn't meet tonight."

Now it was my turn to nod. That was the rule. I'd learned it from years of living with my mother. When your married lover starts complaining to you about some issue with his wife or real family, you simply nod and don't make eye contact.

Except Dylan wasn't married. And he wasn't my lover—not anymore. But that didn't stop me from mimicking my mother so perfectly I shocked myself.

"I should go," he said now.

I nodded again, not even looking up from my laptop this time.

"Tess?"

I raised my head. He was looking at me, an unreadable expression on his face. "Yeah?"

"Do you want me to go?"

His words scooped something out of my chest, leaving behind a hollow, sucking place. "Sure," I said lightly as the ache spread from my heart to my stomach. "I'm ready to crash myself. I'll have those notes to you tomorrow morning."

He stared at me, saying nothing, and for a moment I could almost imagine that he knew exactly what it cost me to act as if I didn't care. That I didn't even give a second thought to the fact that he was going to leave me here and go back to his apartment and be with her.

And just like that, the images were back. The ones where Dylan was with *her*. Hannah. My sister. *He'd walk into his apartment. She'd wait for him on the tangled blue sheets of his futon bed. He'd pull off his shirt, revealing muscles that had only been hinted at back when I knew him, back when he'd been mine, but were now fully formed...and fantastic. She'd run her hand across his chest, through his hair. Her perfect, manicured hand, glinting with rings, especially the big, fat diamond one on her left hand.*

I squeezed my eyes shut. What the hell was wrong with me? I was not my mother. I'd had two years in which I could have gone after Dylan if I'd wanted to. I was not going to pine over what was lost to me now that he'd found someone else, as if the only reason I could possibly be attracted to him was that he was unavailable...

His hand covered mine, then swept up my sleeve, softly stroking my arm. "Tess? Are you all right?"

I opened my eyes, feeling stupid. "Sorry. My head hurts a bit."

"You're overtired. I shouldn't have kept you out this late.

And you have your shift at the restaurant tomorrow..." He frowned. "You okay to drive home?"

"Fine." I snapped down the lid of my laptop, annoyed he was calling my bluff.

"I don't like the idea of you driving."

"I don't like the idea of sleeping under the lab table."

The corner of his mouth quirked up. "You can stay at my place."

I gaped at him. Was he serious? Was he stupid? Was he just so clueless as to what was going on here that he could invite me back to his campus studio apartment to sleep?

Or was he inviting me to something entirely different?

"I can stay with Hannah," he finished.

Oh. *Oh.* The visions started up again, only this time, he was taking his shirt off in what I imagined would be Hannah's immaculately maintained and lavishly furnished condo. No simple dorm room or townie commute from her parents' mansion for the precious Hannah Swift. I was quite sure of that.

"No," I said quickly. "Don't do that."

"What?"

"Don't stay with Hannah." The words were out of my mouth before I could stop them. His eyes widened. "I mean...don't bother her. At this hour." His stare was molten. "I'm fine. I can drive myself home."

I was already stuffing my things in my bag, already looking away. I threw a rushed goodbye back at him and fairly ran from the lab. This was wrong, I thought as I took the stairs two at a time. This was not part of the rules, I thought as I hurried across the parking lot to my beat-up old car. Girls like me didn't give orders to boys about whether or not they should go home to their girlfriends.

And the second I thought it, I wanted to throw up.

Instead, I got in my car, jammed the key in the ignition and drove home, trying the whole time to ignore the drumbeat in my head.

Girls like me.

Girls like me.

Girls like me.

———

I'D NEVER SKIPPED a class in my life, but I was deeply tempted to skip Biotransport on Thursday. As soon as I walked into the class, I realized the challenges existed beyond just facing Dylan again after my cowardly dash from the lab the previous evening. From what Dylan had told me, competition for the symposium prize was pretty cutthroat. If I chose to sit somewhere other than the desk we'd staked out as ours for every class thus far, what would it look like to everyone else?

I sat down in the usual seat.

I felt rather than saw Dylan sit beside me, since I kept my nose buried in my notebook. He said nothing. I slid his textbook over to him. He took it without a word. I died a little inside.

Class began, and I found I missed his nudges, his whispered asides. How was I going to get through a whole semester like this? No, forget about that. How was I going to get through a weekend of not seeing him, wondering what he was thinking? I couldn't even bear to wonder what he was thinking now. I stole a glance.

His focus was completely on our professor as his fingers moved across his laptop keyboard.

Across the room, Elaine Sun was sitting with another female student, sharing notes and pointing out things in the open text-book on the table in front of them. I tapped my pen against the edge of my notebook, thinking. It flew out of my hand and rolled off the desk, and I reached down to get it at the same time as Dylan.

Our hands met under the table, each of us with our own end of my pen. I raised my gaze to his face and saw, for the first time, that he was wearing his glasses today.

"Hi," he whispered.

"Hi."

Time stopped. It was two years ago at Cornell, glasses and all. I could have happily lived under that table, half-bent over, with Dylan's face an inch away. But the professor probably would have noticed. The other teams definitely would have. He straightened, and after a second, I did too, back up into the harsh, fluorescent light of the classroom, where there was schoolwork and students and Dylan had a girlfriend and I wasn't interested anyway.

He angled his laptop screen at me and tapped my notebook. I looked over and there, between the equations and lecture notes, was a single line of text, all on its own.

Don't run away from me.

I caught my breath. Then, I bent my head over my paper, my dark hair falling forward as I scribbled my own secret note.

I'm right here.

I looked over at his screen.

If there's something wrong, I want you to tell me. We're not 18 anymore. If you can't do this, tell me now. It's better to quit now than get into it and risk our chances at the end.

Well, that stung. Humiliated, I felt a flush stealing up from my collar toward my cheeks. So now Dylan thought I was the girl who couldn't keep her hormones under wraps long enough to do a project with him. I bent my head over my notebook once more, the strokes of my pen strong and black.

I can do it. And YOU can stop inviting me to spend the night in your bed.

I sat back and tapped the paper, and then when I was sure he'd read it, I drew a thick black line across the words, scribbling them out. I didn't need that kind of note in my records. I looked up at him. He was staring at me, his expression impossible to divine underneath the glint of his glasses. I gave him a smug little smirk and returned my attention to the professor. Round to Tess McMann. I might have acted like a scorned ex last night, but he'd started it. "Friends" was one thing, but we weren't so buddy-buddy that I could just sleep at his place.

When class ended, I started gathering up my things without looking at him.

"Are you working all weekend?" Dylan asked, his tone as casual as if nothing at all had transpired.

"Pretty much," I said. "But if you want to find a time to meet and do work, I can probably arrange something."

"No need," he said. "I was actually just making conversation. Wondered if you had any big plans."

I tossed my hair out of my face and turned to him. "Nope. Working. You?"

"I was going to go to the football game with some friends this weekend."

Oh right. Canton Football, where you didn't have to fight for your tickets months in advance the way you did at State. "Sounds fun."

"We may tailgate." He let the words hang there a minute. "Hannah's not coming."

I nodded. "Well, have fun. Think of me when you're out there and I'm stuck chopping lemons."

"Don't worry," he said. "I'll think of you."

———

"HANNAH'S NOT COMING"? Sylvia repeated, incredulous. "He actually said that to you?"

"Yep," I said, blowing a strand of brown hair out of my face. We were doing prep work behind the bar at Verde before things got busy. Because so many students didn't have class on Fridays,

Thursday nights in a college town could get just as wild as the weekend. "It's sketchy, right?"

She raised an eyebrow at me. A single eyebrow. I didn't know anyone who could do that except Sylvia, and she'd practiced for ages to get it right. She'd even put it on her audition sheets under "talents," along with crying on cue.

And I was glad she agreed with me that it was suspicious. First Dylan had invited me to stay at his place and now he was inviting me to social events when he knew his girlfriend wouldn't be there? I knew this game. I was *born* because of this game.

I just never suspected Dylan would be anything like my father.

"It's definitely sketchy," she said. "Especially after him exaggerating his sexual history and what that other girl in your class said about him going after fresh meat..."

Annabel, on waitress duty, swung by the bar with a drink order. "What's up, ladies?"

While Sylvia got started on Annabel's martinis, I filled her in on the latest with Dylan.

"I don't know," she said when I finished. "I wouldn't be so quick to condemn him."

"You're a softie," said Sylvia, stringing olives on toothpicks.

"Let's just analyze what's going on here before we jump to any conclusions," Annabel said. "You know this guy, and he's never been a jerk before, right?"

"She *knew* him," Sylvia corrected, popping the lid on her shaker. "Two years ago. And now he's all Hottie McHotHot. That changes a guy."

Well, I'd always kind of thought he was Hottie McHotHot. Or at least Cutie McCuteCute.

Annabel ignored her sister and starting ticking off her arguments on her fingers. "He thought you were tired and he offered to give up his room, not share it with you. There's a difference. Maybe he was just sincerely worried about you driving home by yourself.

Also, he knows that you're new at Canton and might not have made a lot of friends yet. So he invited you to a group tailgate. *Group*." She glared at Sylvia. "I think he's just trying to be nice."

"Then why would he stress that his girlfriend wouldn't be present?" Sylvia pointed out.

"Well, he already knows that Tess feels uncomfortable around her because of that whole 'they once slept together' thing. Maybe it was just his way of saying, 'Come hang out with my friends. You won't even have to deal with the girlfriend weirdness.'"

Sylvia poured the martinis into Annabel's waiting glasses. "Maybe it was his way of saying, 'Come give me a little somethin' somethin' on the side.'"

Annabel rolled her eyes and went off to deliver the drinks. But she'd given me a lot to think about. The Warren sisters didn't know it, but I was all too familiar with the ways and habits of wandering men. My dad never invited my mother out with his usual social circle. They did have "friends" they saw when they went on trips together, other men and their mistresses who all had as much to lose if they weren't discreet about their secret lives. She never went to dinner with him in this town. Too much chance of being discovered.

"I honestly don't know how she does it," Sylvia grumbled beside me as I poured glasses of pinot grigio for a group of girls at the end of the bar. "I don't know anyone who's been screwed over as thoroughly by men as Annabel, and yet she always wants to think the best of them."

"Maybe because of Milo," I suggested. "He's going to be a man someday and she wants to make sure he's one of the good ones."

"He'd better be, or I'll wring his neck."

I smiled at my friend. "Well, at least you're admitting there *is* such a thing as a good man."

"Milo isn't a man yet," she said. "We'll see in ten years."

Annabel had indeed been screwed over. Her first boyfriend, Marcus, had been a thief and a thug and probably some other things I wasn't entirely sure about yet. He was in jail now, thank goodness, but back in the day he'd managed to hurt Annabel quite a bit, both before and after getting her pregnant. When she'd refused to abort the pregnancy, her parents had kicked her out of the house. When she'd asked Marcus's dad for help, he'd called her a lying whore and insisted she take a paternity test before she "ruined" his son's life. That was rich. When Milo was about six months old, Marcus had gotten arrested after breaking into his neighbor's house and, after he'd gone to jail, the whole question of him paying child support had become moot, anyway. I thought Milo was better off without his father in his life. If there was one man I'd prefer not to influence any future generations, it was Marcus.

At yet Annabel had never lost her faith in humanity. Milo was her shining light. It was her sister Sylvia who had grown cynical. If I thought I'd made men a low priority on my life list, it was nothing compared to the "stay off my lawn" attitude of my best friend.

Then again, Sylvia's motto was "guilty until proven innocent." She hated everyone until she knew they were on her side, and those who'd made the cut were few and far between.

As the night continued, I found I didn't have much time to talk further with my friends about the situation, though since pouring beers wasn't exactly taxing my mental capacity, there was plenty of time to think about it. And of course, the stuff I was thinking about wasn't exactly the kind of thing I could share with the Warrens. Sylvia believed there was a type of guy who cheated and a type of guy who didn't, and maybe she was right. But maybe it was more than that. Maybe there was a type of woman that you cheated with, too. Women like my mother, who let out some kind of special pheromone only cheating guys could sense that said, "Yeah, I'll put up with this bullshit. Let's have at it."

And maybe I was that type of woman too.

Either way, I was not skipping out on work Saturday to attend the football game with Dylan and his buddies—and *not*

Hannah. Instead I tried very hard to figure out the exact proportions of the amaretto sours that the sorority girls at table thirty-five were throwing back like Kool-Aid. Maybe it was the biochemist in me, but I preferred tending bar to being a waitress. Or at least, the part of tending bar that didn't require me talking to the patrons.

"Hey, sweetheart," a voice drifted above the din. "You there. Miss?"

Slowly it dawned on me that I was being called. I turned to see a young guy waving some cash over the bar. "Yes?"

"Three drafts for me and my friends."

I got the beers and brought them over. There were three men and two women, some with Canton T-shirts on, crowding the barstools in that corner.

"Finally, some service!" one of the girls said. "Do you do amaretto sours?"

"It's a specialty," I said, smiling as I grabbed the amaretto and sour mix from the rail and started mixing.

The guy who'd first called to me watched me shaking the girls' drinks. Well, to be frank, he watched my breasts bouncing.

"Would you like to start a tab?" I asked him.

"As long as it means you're the bartender on call, sweetheart."

I forced a smile and took his credit card. The name on the card read *Todd J. Hamilton Jr.* Todd here had a dad who loved him so much that he gave him the same exact name. Must be nice. I didn't even have my dad's last name.

The next time I made it around to that side of the bar, Todd and friends had been joined by a third woman, who'd clearly found the Verde barstool unacceptable, since she'd taken up a position on Todd's lap. As she ordered her amaretto sour, Todd didn't look at me. Not even at my breasts.

Girlfriend. Figured.

The night continued, and so did the steady orders of draft beers, G&Ts, and amaretto sours from the group in the corner of the bar. At some point, the ladies departed, leaving the gentlemen drinking on their own. As I fulfilled the latest round of orders, Todd grinned at me.

"What's your name, sweetheart?"

"Tess," I said and handed him his beer.

"Tess," he said, and it sounded like a hiss. "What are you doing after your shift?"

"Going home to study." I kept my expression open and cheerful, the pro bartender standard of, "I want a tip, but we're not really friends."

Confusion crossed his face. "You're not at Canton." It was a statement.

"Yes, actually. Just transferred in." I kept the same lightness in my tone, but there was no point in lying, right?

"Oh." He still sounded baffled. "Congratulations."

"Thanks." I left and found Sylvia across the bar. "Guy was shocked I went to Canton."

"Of course he was," she replied. "We're the help, don't you know. Not equals. Not *human*."

Todd caught my attention again. "You know," he slurred as I came near. "Since you're a Canton student, maybe you'd like to come back to our frat house after this. We're throwing a little party. Just very close friends."

"I'm not your very close friend," I said lightly, pouring him another beer.

He grabbed my hand as I passed the beer to him. "Not *yet*, sweetheart."

I jerked away. "Didn't your girlfriend leave, like, five seconds ago?"

"Eh," he said with a shrug. "She's not my girlfriend."

"Oh?" I crossed my arms. "What would she say about that if I asked her?"

His expression turned hard. "Jeez, you're uptight. I clearly had you pegged wrong. You look like the kind of girl who likes to have fun."

If he'd slapped me across the face, it couldn't have hurt more. And five minutes later, when they closed out their tab through

Sylvia and she brought me the little black pleather bill folder, I wasn't surprised to see *Bitch!* written on the tip line.

"Assholes," Sylvia said. "Their loss, though. They can't act like this and expect us not to spit in their drinks next time."

I nodded and closed out the tab.

"Fuck 'em," she went on. "Jackass guys think any waitress is fair game. And if you don't drop to your knees and blow them right there, they act as if you're the one out of line. It's a professional hazard. You have to ignore them."

"They don't bother me," I said. And it was pretty much the truth. Being hit on and screwed over for tips was annoying, but part of the landscape. It wasn't that.

You look like the kind of girl...

To Todd and his friends, I looked like the kind of girl who'd go home with a guy after watching him spend the evening with his girlfriend. The kind of girl who didn't care that he'd made a commitment to someone else, someone who trusted him not to pick up waitresses after their shifts at bars. The kind of girl my mother was.

Were they right?

NINE

I WAS STILL PONDERING the question the next morning as I got ready for my 9:00 a.m. lab, still weighing it in my mind as I drove to school and entered the building. I had a hard time picturing anyone treating Hannah the way Todd J. Hamilton Jr. had treated me last night. Was there some tattoo on my forehead, visible only to assholes, that said, "This one's fair game"?

Had it always been that way? I wasn't much of an English student, but I'd read Jane Austen in high school, just like everyone else. In *Pride and Prejudice*, all my classmates had swooned over the love story of Mr. Darcy and Lizzie Bennet, but I'd been fascinated by the response to Mr. Wickham, who'd tried to seduce several of the characters. It wasn't a part my teachers had ever stressed in class, but I'd never been able to get it out of my mind. With the rich Georgiana Darcy—Mr. Darcy's sister— and later with the heiress Mary King of Meryton, he'd sought to marry them. But with Lizzie's flirty younger sister Lydia, who had no money, he'd just run off, content to get the sex and leave her and her entire family ruined. Later, Lizzie's uncle had reported that Wickham had still hoped to marry a rich girl, despite the fact that he'd been "living in sin" with Lydia. I'd always wondered what would have happened if Mr. Darcy hadn't stepped in and forced the marriage. Would Lydia have spent the rest of her life in secret, raising Wickham's bastard children while he married some fine lady?

If there was an invisible tattoo for girls like us, Lydia Bennet had it, too.

I was able to put the thoughts aside as I finished my lab work for the week, but my mood was charcoal gray. It must have shown on my face, too, because I exited the lab, hardly seeing where I was going, and ran smack into Dylan.

"Whoa, there," he said, steadying me. "Everything okay?"

"Fine," I grumbled. "I'm just in a rush. My shift starts at ten-thirty…"

"Oh, right. How's the restaurant biz?"

I rolled my eyes. "Eh. Had some jerks in my section last night."

"Rough. Bad tippers?"

"Zero tippers," I replied. "Apparently some guys don't believe in tipping the waitress unless she agrees to go home with them."

A cloud seemed to pass over Dylan's eyes. "Does that kind of thing happen to you a lot?"

"I'll tell you when I've done this for a little longer. But according to my friend Sylvia, the answer is yes."

"I'm sorry." He shook his head. "We've got to get you out of there. I'm going to keep my eyes open for any research assistant jobs."

"Thanks." I shrugged. "It's a learning experience. I should have realized anyone with a name as pretentious as Todd J. Hamilton Jr. would be a jackass. Note to self—always check out the credit card when they open a tab. If they've got a jerk name, expect jerk treatment."

Dylan said nothing for a moment. "I'm so sorry, Tess."

I didn't need his pity. I just needed to get to work.

———

FRIDAY NIGHT at Verde passed without incident, and the Saturday lunch crowd was especially genteel, seeing how it was made up of all the locals who hadn't gone out to the football game. As the afternoon waned, however, the patrons grew rowdier and the restaurant filled with football fans eager to celebrate Canton's win. Half the booths held diners wearing Canton T-shirts and hats and jackets.

"You've got table twenty-eight," Annabel said as she swung by me at the prep table. "Six top. They asked for you specifically."

"Requests, already?" said another waitress. "Gee, someone's popular."

I was baffled. I hadn't been at Verde long enough to get regulars. I approached the table with no small amount of curiosity, and my stomach clenched as I recognized Todd J. Hamilton Jr., surrounded by some older people. But then the guy in the corner looked up and smiled at me. Blue eyes, dark hair. Dylan.

I'd been complaining to him about his friend?

"Hi, Tess!" Dylan said brightly. "Guys, this is my friend from Bio-E, Tess McMann. She just transferred to Canton this semester and unfortunately, she had to work during the game."

"Awww..." everyone echoed sympathetically.

"Tess, these are some Canton Chem folks I met at the last career day. You want to be friends with them in case you ever *do* get to come to the tailgates. They always have the best tent." He winked at one of the older women, and she smiled.

"Nice drinks, not the usual frat boy rotgut," she said. "I'm Kathleen Hamilton, VP of Human Resources at Canton Chem."

"Nice to meet you," I said.

"And of course," Dylan continued, "you know her son, Todd."

Todd wasn't looking up from his menu.

"Yes, Todd and I met the other night," I said, passing out the menus.

"I was a waitress when I was in college, too," Kathleen went on. "Tough gig. Always jerks drooling all over you."

"You don't say," said Dylan, looking at Todd. "Sounds terrible. What kind of person would be so disrespectful to a woman who's just trying to do her job?"

"Exactly," said Kathleen. "Well, Tess, if you ever want to apply to an internship at Canton Chem, here's my card." She handed me a glossy rectangle. "Dylan's been singing your praises the whole game."

"Oh. Has he?" I got their drink orders and managed to keep our interactions to a minimum through the rest of the meal. As I was ringing up their bill, Dylan found me at the computer.

"What was that all about?" I asked him, punching the buttons on the screen with a bit more force than strictly necessary. "Waltzing in here with him and his *mother*!"

He held up his hands in a feigned display of innocence. "What? You told me he'd been hassling you. I had an opportunity to fix it. And get a free meal in the process."

"I don't need you to fight my battles, Dylan."

"I know that," he said softly. "But I hate guys who pull shit like that. Who act like bullies toward people—toward women— they think are beneath them. I just thought I'd give him a little lesson in perspective."

I printed out the receipt, jammed it in the billfold, and slammed it shut. "And I think all you taught him is to be careful about who he pulls his shit around. He might be kinder to me because he knows I'm Bio-E and so Canton Chem will suck up to me, but what's to keep him from being a jerk to other waitresses —say, my friend Sylvia?"

Dylan stared at me for a second. "Maybe. But it's a start. He shouldn't have hit on you."

"Hmph."

"He has a girlfriend."

I looked away. "That doesn't stop some guys." And look who was talking. Had I pegged Dylan wrong? Had Annabel been right, that he was really just trying to be kind to me when he'd offered to let me stay at his place? When he'd invited me out to the game? Had he been planning nothing more insidious than trying to hook me up with an internship at Canton Chem?

"Plus, he has no idea what a heartbreaker you are."

Still safely facing the register, I laughed.

"Plus…he doesn't deserve you."

I turned back to him. The look in his eyes was raw, unrestrained, and brimming over with longing. I drew back in shock.

"Tess…" He reached for me, then stopped himself. "I'll—take the bill back. You can see to your other tables." He grabbed the case out of my hands and vanished.

I pressed my hand to my chest. Under my palm, my heart pounded like I'd run a mile. What was that? What *was* that? One second he was telling me it was inappropriate for guys with girlfriends to hit on other women, and the next second he looked like he wanted to tear my clothes off right there by the cash register.

At least he'd gone away. If he hadn't, I might have let him tear my clothes off.

The next time I passed table twenty-eight, it was empty. Along with the tip Kathleen Hamilton, VP of Human Resources at Canton Chem, had written in with the credit card slip, I found a twenty. On the top was scrawled, *Sorry -TJH.*

Okay, I didn't *need* Dylan to fight my battles. But I couldn't argue with the results.

———

ON SUNDAY, Dylan showed up at Verde again, around two, right as the brunch crowd was dispersing. I was working the bar again, mixing Bloody Marys and mimosas all morning. I finally thought I'd get a break, and then I saw the hostess setting a place at the bar. Moments later, Dylan sat down.

I folded my arms. "Are you my first regular?"

"Looks like it." He grinned and opened the menu. He was in Sunday casuals—jeans, a Canton T-shirt, and those damn glasses. If I didn't know better, I'd think he was wearing them just for me. "What's good here?"

"Well, you just missed the brunch prix-fixe, so I'm afraid it's going to be a lot of sandwiches and salads."

He eyed me over the top of the menu. "What do you like?"

"The BFG." I pointed. "It's bacon, fig, and goat cheese. Perfect for you."

He snapped the menu shut. "Aww. You remembered."

I remember everything, I very nearly said but stopped myself just in time. I wasn't going to add to the collection of vague and confusing statements he'd thrown at me in the last few days. "So, the BFG?"

"And a Coke."

I put in his order and busied myself chopping lemons the bar didn't need until I delivered his meal. But as I was about to turn away, he stopped me.

"Are you so very busy?"

"Did you come in here just to hang out with me?"

He unfolded his napkin. "Truth?"

"Truth."

"Maybe."

I smiled. "What, five hours a day Monday through Wednesday isn't enough?"

He looked at me. "No."

I caught my breath. This wasn't fair. The bartender reaction would be to keep things light and flirty—friendly enough for a tip but not so friendly that the customer thought there was something really going on between you two. The lab partner reaction was to tell him we'd have plenty of time to work when we were actually in our lab. And the ex-lover-trying-to-be-friends reaction was to tell him to go home and call Hannah.

I did none of it. "I was about to take my lunch break as well. It's cooling down here and I get a free salad with every shift."

"Eat with me?"

So I did. For the next forty-five minutes we sat across from each other at the bar, talking about our project, about our classes, about our favorite foods and movies and what we thought of current environmental regulations regarding GM foods. Dylan joked about how hard it was to be simultaneously a foodie and a budding bioengineer.

"I can appreciate an heirloom tomato without trying to ban all other types," he said with a laugh.

"I think you might be wasted in biofuel." I pointed my fork at him. "Obviously your calling is food."

He shrugged. "Still that fat kid on the inside, I guess."

I let my gaze travel over the part of his chest and arms I could see over the bar. Trim, lightly muscled, like a runner. "Don't worry. It doesn't show."

He said nothing, and I dragged my eyes back up to his face. He'd stopped eating and was staring at me, watching me look at him, an expression I didn't dare to identify in his deep blue eyes.

"I mean—"

"I know what you meant." He popped the last bit of his sandwich in his mouth and wiped his hands on his napkin. "I should probably head out. Hannah will be back in town this evening."

Inwardly, I flinched. "Okay. Have a nice day."

"And I have some work to do before then," he finished awkwardly as the ramifications of his words sank in. "Tess, I didn't mean 'my girlfriend's back, so, later…'"

"I know what you meant," I echoed, clearing away his plate. And boy, did I ever. How many weekends had my father spent in our apartment when his wife was away on a spa trip with her rich friends, or off on a shopping weekend in Manhattan with Hannah? How many Sunday afternoons ended with him saying those exact words to us?

"Thanks for lunch," he said.

"Don't thank me," I said. "You're paying for it."

"I meant for you having lunch with me."

"Oh." I actually *hadn't* known what he meant that time. "Well, like I said, I was taking a break anyway."

"You didn't have to take it with me."

"You didn't have to come to Verde."

"I did," he said, and from the tone of his voice, he sounded like he wanted to say so much more. "If I wanted to see you."

After Dylan had gone, I opened the leather folder. His bill had come to twelve dollars. Inside was a twenty-dollar bill. I swallowed. Had it been anyone other than Dylan, I wouldn't have thought twice about that tip. Sure it was big, but it wasn't outlandish, and it wasn't that unusual from a single diner who'd gotten some extra conversation from the wait staff. Yet from Dylan it felt like he'd paid me to have lunch with him, like he was saying, "Poor Tess, not rich enough to attend Canton without filling your days with menial labor, not nearly as rich as the girlfriend I *should* be spending my time with."

Sometimes, when Mom was between jobs or feeling blue, Dad would write her checks. Big ones. Dad would pay for her to get a new wardrobe or have a Botox treatment or some other lavish indulgence that felt really good until you thought about it and realized that it was nothing compared to what he gave his wife.

Eight dollars from Dylan. Twenty from Todd, which Dylan had also arranged. One hundred and fifty from the rest of the weekend. At this rate, I'd have that *Tissue Engineering* textbook paid for in no time.

———

THE NEXT THREE weeks passed in much the same manner. Monday through Wednesday, as soon as class was done, Dylan and I would meet in the bioengineering labs to work on our project. We'd decided to resurrect our work from Cornell and do an advanced version, using the skills we'd gained after two years of college and, of course, Transport Process Design. On Thursday and Friday, as soon as I was done with class, I hurried to Verde for my shifts. Either way, I never came home before 11:00 p.m. On lab days, I smelled like the nose-tickling chemicals they used to keep things clean. On waitress days, I smelled like garlic and frat boy sweat. Mom had stopped waiting up for me. I never saw my father, which I think suited both of us pretty well. After that, it was at least two hours of homework before I set my alarm for six and got up to start all over again.

Dylan's crazy email schedule didn't let up, and it was soon clear that every hour I spent at the restaurant, he was spending working on the project. I hated the idea that he was doing so much more work than me, but what option did I have? There was literally zero time for anything else. I'd been at Canton for a month and so far, I didn't even know the names of most of the other students in my classes. I'd often see them leaving together for lunch or playing Frisbee on the quad while I rushed from class to library to class to work to lab. My fellow students would head off to eat in the cafeteria or any of the little shops dotting campus, and I'd bring a bag lunch to save cash.

I tried to tell myself that it was okay. I wasn't at Canton to make friends. I was here to get my name on a Canton diploma. Besides, it wasn't as if I'd had so many friends at State, either. I'd had acquaintances in class and people I called friends who I went out with on weekends, but no one I was really close to. And hadn't it always been that way, anyway? Maybe I just wasn't the type of person who had close friends. Even Sylvia, whom I'd always thought of as my best friend, didn't know the truth about me.

It was safer that way. The more people who knew about my father, the more chances there were that the story would become public. These were the rules. I knew the rules.

On the weekends, I worked all Saturday at Verde, then Sunday afternoons, too. Dylan always came in on Sundays, once the brunch crowd had departed. He always seated himself in my section. He always cajoled me into having lunch with him.

On Sunday morning of the third week, after what seemed like an endless weekend of Halloween revelry by the entire Canton student body, I met my mom, bleary-eyed, over the coffee pot.

"You look like hell," she offered and poured me a cup.

"Thanks, Mom," I grumbled. I had, in fact, worn a sparkly

devil horn headband most of the weekend, to play off Sylvia's angel wings and silver glitter halo. Quite a pair we'd made behind the bar, but the tips had been worth it.

"You can't keep this up," she continued. "Look at you. Something's got to give, Tess, and the way you're going, with work and school and this Symposium project, I'm afraid it might be you."

"What, old before my time?" I snapped. "Guess I'll never find a man, then."

She sighed. "I don't care about you finding a man, sweetie. I do care about you getting sick and flunking out of college, though. How are you ever going to prove your father wrong if that's what happens?"

I looked at her. A hint of a smile ghosted across her face.

"Mom!" I said, impressed. "What did you put in your coffee this morning?" Prove Dad wrong? I'd never heard her so much as disagree with him over the weather.

"Oh, come on," she replied. "You never were rebellious as a teenager. It's nice to see that you do have it in you. Which is why I don't want you turning into a drudge over this school thing. College is supposed to be fun. You need to be able to go out, make friends, and yes, meet boys...and I do mean *boys*, Tess."

"Not married men?" I couldn't help but ask.

"Not married men." My mother had been even younger than me when she'd met Dad, a college intern the fifteen-years-older-than-her Steven Swift had found irresistible. When she'd gotten pregnant, she'd dropped out, he'd agreed to support her, and the rest was history. "I don't regret any of the choices I've made, the life I've had with you and your father, but I know that's not for you. So...no married men, Tess."

What about boys with girlfriends? I almost asked her. I wondered what my mother would do in my situation. Damn the torpedoes, probably. She'd had no compunction muscling in on a marriage, she'd have no trouble trying to break up a simple dating arrangement.

When I was younger, I'd wonder why, if my father loved my

mother so much, she hadn't been able to get him to leave his wife for her. Later I understood. It was Hannah. She was only a few months my junior, and my mother had once let slip that Dad and his wife had struggled for years with infertility. The powerful Steven Swift getting divorced and marrying a younger woman was not an earthshaking revelation. Abandoning his pregnant-at-last wife for the intern he'd knocked up—well, that was a career-ending scandal.

When I was a teenager myself, I'd wondered why my mom had submitted to this arrangement. Why she hadn't told Dad where to shove it, taken me, and started our lives free and clear. But I saw how hard it was on Annabel. She was twenty-four now and still working on her nursing degree, taking the odd class here and there while working two jobs. Sometimes, she said, it was like she worked just to pay the babysitters.

And it wasn't just the money, either. Mom loved Dad. Even if she'd been as ambitious as me, she might not have left. She loved him then, she loved him still. You couldn't help your feelings, no matter what obstacles stood in the way. She'd always believed that, and I had to admit she was right. Though I was making different decisions than my mother, I knew that it didn't change how I felt. I'd spent two years wishing away my connection to Dylan Kingsley. But even though I had more reason than ever to deny my attraction to him now, I couldn't make myself stop wanting him. It was a part of me, and wishing it away would be like trying to banish my left foot by power of will alone.

Mom always claimed I got my brains from my father, but it wasn't that. She wasn't stupid, my mother. She was just more willing to let her life be guided by her emotions than Dad was, than I was. I believed he loved my mom, just not enough for him to ruin his life over. I'd cared for Dylan, too, two years ago, but I'd chosen to walk away, to not let my life be guided by my relationship to a man.

And I wouldn't let it happen now, either. There was far too much to lose.

That afternoon, Dylan came to Verde again and asked to be seated in my section. I hadn't seen him since class on Thursday. He'd probably spent the weekend partying, in costume, with Hannah. I bet she'd made a beautiful kitty cat, or princess, or nurse.

For the sake of my weariness, my libido, and my sanity, I decided to go on break. Let someone else handle his table for today. I didn't have any fight left.

TEN

I WASN'T EVEN to campus on Monday morning when I got a text from Dylan.

We need to talk. Meet me in the atrium ASAP.

Fear bubbled in the pit of my belly. Was he breaking off our partnership after I'd blown him off at Verde on Sunday? Or because he realized that working together was just too weird? Or maybe it was because I wasn't good enough? He couldn't do that! I needed this project. I needed the money. I needed…Dylan. I took a deep breath.

What's wrong?

There was no reply. I sped to campus, parked, and tried to look calm as I approached the glass doors to the bioengineering lab. Dylan was standing by the stairs, and his face was grim. Today, the glasses were absent and his frown left me cold. I'd honestly never seen him so serious.

He saw me, and there was no brightening in his expression. I'd never before realized it, but there was always a hint of a smile when he first caught sight of me. The fear boiled over. Maybe this didn't have anything to do with our work at all. Maybe he somehow found out about me and Hannah. About my dad.

That was silly, though. It wasn't possible. Even if he'd noticed our eyes, most people would write that off as a coincidence. Lots of people had similar eyes. I smoothed my hands over my jean skirt, tugging down the folds that always formed over my hips when I sat. What I wouldn't give sometimes to have tiny little hips like Hannah.

What I wouldn't give to have a lot of Hannah's things.

I took a breath, pulled my shoulders back, and walked over.

"Good, you're here," he said, his tone flat. "You have to see this."

He led me over to the lab sign-up sheet posted on the board outside the admin offices. Elaine Sun was signed up for Monday through Wednesday evenings every week for the rest of the semester in the lab we'd been using for our sessions.

"She's trying to sabotage us," he growled. "I know it. She's studied our schedule and she must know you can't make it at any other time."

"So this thing really is cutthroat." And to think one of the things I was looking forward to at Canton was not competing for lab space.

"When it comes to Elaine?" His tone was grim. "Yes."

I laid a hand on his arm. "We'll find another lab space."

"Not with all the equipment we need, and not for as much time as we'll need it. She arranged this very neatly. And, lest you think I'm being paranoid, look at this." He pointed at erasure marks on some of the pages, and I could see the ghost of Elaine's name. "She erased every Thursday or Friday slot she had and every slot she had where we had classes. Now she's only reserved *our* lab for the times *we* need."

"Maybe her schedule changed?" I suggested. "I can't imagine someone going through all this trouble just to mess with us."

"Well, you're a better person than Elaine."

No, I was just a busier one. I could barely get my own shit together, let alone figure out how to fuck up someone else's.

He slammed a fist against the board. "I'm so angry at myself right now. I don't know why I didn't sign up for the whole semester right off the bat." Up until now, Dylan had just been signing us up for the labs when he came in for his early Monday morning class. "But in two years, I've never had a hard time reserving a space. I've ruined everything."

"Hey," I said. "This is going to be okay. I'll go talk to her—"

"Yeah, you do that," he said ruefully. "You go talk to Elaine and see what she does. My money's on gloat."

"I never gloat," said a voice behind us. Dylan and I turned to see Elaine standing there, her computer bag slung over her shoulder. "It's so petty."

"No, you know what's petty?" he asked. "You know you can't compete with us on real terms, so you're just trying to make sure we can't do our project as planned."

She rolled her eyes. "It's not my fault you didn't plan ahead, Kingsley. Might be good for you to realize you aren't the center of the universe for once."

I stepped between them. There was no need to go nuclear. I'd learned well from my mother how to arrange things so everyone got what they needed. "Elaine, the problem here is that I have shifts at my job on Thursdays and Fridays, so really our only time in the lab is Monday through Wednesday evenings. I'm sure we can work out some sort of schedule so we can all finish our projects on time—"

"Oh, please. You made your bed with this guy, so now you can lie in it. I told you he was bad news. Anyone with half a brain knows that if you need Lab A and all its equipment to finish your project, you'd better reserve your time well in advance. But Kingsley here thinks he's above all that."

How did she know what kind of equipment we needed? Dylan's paranoia was sounding a lot more plausible.

"Elaine, seriously," Dylan said. "Get over it."

"Screw you," she replied sweetly, turned on her heel, and left.

Dylan looked like he wanted to punch the wall again.

"Okay, that girl has issues," I said to him. "What precisely did you do to her again?"

"I told you. I beat her in the freshman end-of-year competition."

"She *hates* you," I said, skeptical. "It's not just rivalry. She honestly hates you."

"Yeah." He shrugged. "Like you said, issues."

I shook my head. Something didn't add up. "Are you sure all you did was beat her that one time? You didn't, like, strangle her kitten or spill wine on her silk dress or sleep with her and never call her again?"

"No!" He was quiet for a second. "I did sleep with her room-mate freshman year."

I gaped at him. "You *what?*"

"I slept with her roommate. Two years ago. Fall." He looked contrite. "She was the first of the three."

I smacked his arm. "Dylan!"

He flinched away. "What! I was eighteen. I was new at school. And I'd just had my heart broken by…" He gestured. "Well, you know all that." He hung his head. "I made a mistake, Tess. Haven't you ever made a mistake?"

"Yes." I made a mistake not calling him back all those years ago. I made a mistake breaking his heart, letting him go.

But Elaine's roommate having an ill-advised hook-up with Dylan two years ago was no excuse for Elaine to sabotage our project now. Even if she was mad at Dylan, that was bullshit. And I'd never done a thing to her.

"Yeah," he grumbled. "Partnering with me, that was your mistake. I can't believe I've screwed this up for you."

Partnering with Dylan might still end up being a mistake, but not because of any of Elaine's ham-handed machinations. Clearly, she had no idea who she was dealing with. I had a whole lifetime's worth of experience working around people who didn't want me to have nice things. If Tess McMann screwed something up, she screwed it up on her own damn terms. If I wasn't going to let Dad get the better of me, there was no way I was going to let some Canton co-ed do it.

"We're not going down without a fight, Dylan. Elaine doesn't own the lab. I'll switch my shifts at Verde to early in the week. We'll reserve every Thursday and Friday instead. We'll come in at 6:00 a.m. if we have to."

"You need your Friday-night shifts at the restaurant. That's when you make the most in tips."

He'd been paying attention. "I'll be fine. As long as we win, I'll be fine."

He shook his head. "And if we don't win?"

I shrugged. "I'll figure it out then."

Dylan looked at me, his blue eyes keen and penetrating. "You're a marvel, Tess. You know that?"

"Give me your pen," I said brusquely, trying not to let his words sink in. "I'll sign us up for every space left on the chart."

"I mean it. I know why you've really been borrowing my textbook. I'm actually a pretty smart guy."

"Yeah," I said, concentrating on filling in the slots. "Is that why you've been tipping me out the wazoo lately?"

"So you'll quit borrowing my textbook? Yes," he joked. "I don't like your sticky notes."

I looked at him, my expression dead serious. "I don't want you giving me money, Dylan. And I don't want you bullying jerks into giving it to me, either." I returned to writing our names down.

Tess McMann and Dylan Kingsley. Tess McMann and Dylan Kingsley. Dylan Kinsley and Tess McMann, just to switch it up. *Kingsley/McMann. Tess + Dylan.*

No, I wasn't going to write that last one again.

"Jerks don't deserve their money as much as you do for putting up with them," he said softly. He'd moved in so he stood right behind me. His voice was nearly a whisper.

My pen stilled on the page. "Stop," I whispered.

"Why?" He was so close. Heat poured off his body in waves. His breath stirred the hairs on my neck.

"You know why." I closed my eyes for a long moment, waiting for the feelings to pass. If I just concentrated on breathing, if I thought about anything else—my classes, the weather, that strange knocking noise I heard in the engine of my car from time to time—it would pass. I wouldn't want to jump all over him. I could be better than my parents. I could overcome this.

"Yeah. I do." He stepped back and I breathed a sigh of relief. When I turned around to look at him, he'd pulled out his phone and was entering the new schedule into his calendar. "I should get to class," he said without glancing up. "I'll email the new hours to you so we both have them."

"Okay."

"If you want, we can meet later to figure out our plan of attack." He looked up. "After all, it's not like we have other plans tonight."

"Okay."

"My place? Five thirty? I'll make dinner."

"Okay," I said again, automatically. I don't know why. I should have been smart enough to realize what would happen.

We both should have.

———

WHEN I ARRIVED at Swift 202 that night, I could smell Dylan's cooking from the other side of the door. By the time he answered my knock, I was already drooling.

The way he looked didn't help. The contacts were gone, the glasses were back, and the hair was damp and mussed and downright floppy. He was wearing a pair of jeans and a T-shirt and his feet were bare and his collar was worn and *I could have had him. I could have had him two years ago and I walked away.*

"Come in," he said. "I just got out of the shower. Went to the gym this afternoon."

Tell me more about this shower, I thought, stepping across the threshold. The gym part was obvious. His T-shirt was thin, and the definition in his arms and chest were there to remind me that despite those glasses and the untamed hair, I was no longer dealing with the eighteen-year-old boy I'd once known.

"What are you cooking?"

He grinned, then practically bounded into the kitchenette. "I hope you like it. It's this Greek shrimp thing, with feta and tomatoes."

"I love feta and tomatoes. And shrimp. And Greeks."

"Me too," he said. "My family went to Greece last summer and I have been on a Greek cuisine kick ever since." He picked up a bottle of wine from the counter and presented it with a flourish. "Ever have retsina?"

"No," I said. "I'm not much of a drinker."

"Oh." He lowered the bottle. "I didn't know—"

"No," I clarified. "I'll drink alcohol. I just mean, I'm not a wine aficionado. Before I started working at Verde, all I knew was that white went with fish."

"Well, retsina can be an acquired taste. It's resinated—tastes a bit like pine needles." He looked at my face and laughed. "I told you. Acquired. But I definitely acquired it this summer. Brought some back. This is my last bottle."

And he was using it on me? Sweet. "They let you have alcohol in the dorms?"

He started taking the cork out. "Well, they haven't shut down my speakeasy yet. Besides, I turned twenty-one before the school year started. You?"

"Next week."

He turned to me. "Really?"

I nodded.

He yanked out the cork with an audible pop and poured me a glass. "Then happy early birthday."

I took a sip, painfully aware that Dylan was watching me, just like he had the night we'd met at the Cornell party. Watching me as if my reaction to what I was putting in my mouth was the only thing in the world that mattered. On second thought, I didn't need wine. That thought alone was enough to knock me sideways.

Dry white wine with just a hint of pine hit my tongue and brought me back to the moment. "Not bad," I said.

"You'll love it with the food." He turned back to the pans on the stove, and I tried a large gulp of wine this time, just to fortify myself.

Maybe it would be better if I put some space between us. His kitchenette was just too crowded. I circled around the bar, into the main living space. His futon was in sofa-shape tonight, all evidence of its use as a bed tucked away somewhere. Textbooks and pens lay scattered across his coffee table, and his shelves were lined with cookbooks, DVDs, and video games.

"I don't know how you have any time for these," I said, pointing at the games and movies. What with all his labs and trips to the gym and cooking experiments...and Hannah.

"I'm an excellent multi-tasker," he called from the kitchenette. I turned to see him poking his head out over the bar. "Plus, you know me. I never sleep." He winked and went back to cooking.

Don't wink at me, Dylan Kingsley. I'm trying my hardest here. I continued my self-guided tour around his studio. There were pictures of his family hanging on the wall above the bed—I mean, above the futon. There were no pictures of Hannah out. I knew because I checked as I circled the place, studying everything and, as it turned out, finishing my wine. By the time I made it back to the kitchenette, my glass was empty.

"More?" he asked, holding out the bottle.

I stared at the glass in my hand, my heart pounding. How had I consumed an entire glass of wine already? I hadn't eaten since lunch. This was a bad idea. Coming here had been a bad idea. Drinking while alone with Dylan Kingsley in his apartment was quite possibly the worst idea I'd ever had.

"Sure," I said before I could stop myself. I watched the green-gold wine splash into my cup and I raised my eyes to his and he smiled and I smiled. Then, my eyes never leaving his, I had another sip. He watched me drink, the movement of my jaw and tongue and throat, blatant and unmistakably an invitation. "Mmmm."

Here's the truth, unvarnished and inalienable: I wanted him. I'd *always* wanted him. I could pretend otherwise, I could walk away, I could avoid him for two years, but it didn't change a thing.

Dylan was mine. First, last, and always. I stood there in his apartment and I looked into his eyes, allowing the full force of my desire to shine out, raw and intense. I didn't care that he was dating someone. I didn't care that she was Hannah Swift. For perhaps the first time in my life, I understood what my parents thought about when they did the things they did.

"Tess..." Dylan's voice was pained.

I blinked at him, slow and languid. "Hmmm...?" I was the daughter of seduction; I was the product of lies. I was born for this.

"Stop."

I stopped. I looked down. His hands were fisted against his sides. "You poured the wine," I mumbled.

For a long time, we just stood there. I didn't know if he was looking at me or not. Blood rushed in my head. I shouldn't have come here. I shouldn't have done that. I shouldn't, I shouldn't, I shouldn't.

I was so sick of all the things I shouldn't do.

"I...can't...I can't take this anymore," he whispered at last. "I think about you all the time. Where you are, what you're doing, why I'm not with you. I go to Verde on Sundays because two days without seeing you is two days too long."

I turned away and put my hands on the counter, pressing down as if I could somehow leave marks on the granite. As if I could somehow imprison my hands here and keep them from grabbing him. "I'm sorry."

"Don't be *sorry*," he said from behind me. "Be *honest*. You feel it too, don't you?"

"Dylan..." I hung my head, in agony as every nerve tingled,

and I forced myself not to turn around. If I saw his face, I was a goner. "I don't know what you want."

"Isn't it obvious?" He came up close behind me, his chest against my back, his hips against my butt, his voice in my ear. "I want *you*."

Oh God, it *was* obvious and I wanted to melt against him. I shouldn't. I shouldn't.

His left hand gripped my waist, his fingers curling into the hollow of my hip. "Tell me," he pleaded. "Tell me you want me too."

I gasped. I shouldn't. I wasn't that kind of girl.

"Tell me." His fingers felt like a brand against my flesh, holding me hard, forcing me to acknowledge the truth.

I swallowed, and when I spoke, my voice was a breath. "I want you too."

I felt his forehead rest, ever so gently, against the nape of my neck. His sigh of relief sent cool air rushing across my fevered skin. He brushed my hair to the side with his free hand, stroked my neck.

"Tess," he said now, cupping my chin in his hand, running his finger over my bottom lip. "Tell me to stop."

I turned in his arms. "No."

ELEVEN

WHEN PARTICLES COLLIDE, they explode, strewing pieces of themselves in waves across the universe and combining to make something entirely new.

And when I kissed Dylan in his dorm room kitchen, the universe expanded. It had to, because this—*this*—was not something that had belonged to our reality before.

It was two years ago and it wasn't, all at once. It was right, it fit, as it had always fit, from the first moment in the elevator at Cornell. And at the same time, it was so much better. We knew what we were doing. *He* knew what he was doing. Oh, God, did he ever. His fingers stroked my jawline, lifting my mouth to his, his lips and tongue moving against mine until I surrendered to the simple realization that my mouth had been made for Dylan to kiss. How could I ever have doubted it?

He tasted like white wine and pine needles. He tasted like two years of waiting. I wanted to breathe for him, I wanted to swallow him whole. I ached with a sudden, pulsing need, an overwhelming desire I'd never felt before.

His hands slipped to my waist, holding me firmly against him as I wrapped my arms around his neck. I needed him closer, closer. He pushed me against the counter, arching me backward until the edge of the granite cut against my spine, but I didn't care. Nothing mattered but never moving my mouth off his. I wrapped my legs around the back of his calves for leverage.

Dylan's fingers dug into my hips and lifted me until I was sitting on the counter. Instantly, we were even closer. My thighs circled his waist, my skirt riding up around my hips. I felt his hands under my shirt, moving across the skin of my stomach, grazing upward to cup my breasts through the satin of my bra. I rocked against him, teasing us both, the edge of his belt pressed against the center of my panties, so close, so close.

There were wordless moans coming from my mouth and I could tell they were driving Dylan crazy. His fingers dug into my thighs as if to mark me as his, first, last, and always. I rocked faster, feeling him, hard and ready and trapped beneath layers of clothes. It wasn't enough. I wanted this. I needed this. I didn't care about anything else.

I was just like my parents.

"Stop," I choked out. "Stop!"

Dylan pulled away from me, breathing hard and staring at me, hurt and confusion overtaking the raw lust in his deep blue eyes.

I yanked my skirt down and ran my hands across my heated cheeks, smoothing my hair. "I can't be the girl you cheat on Hannah with," I blurted out. It may have been the most honest thing I've ever said in my life.

His eyes widened. For a single horrible second, I thought the truth was written on my face. I slid off the counter. There wasn't enough room in this kitchenette. There might have not been enough room in the country, but I'd do what I could. I escaped to the living room, then turned around and took a deep breath.

He'd followed me, standing a respectable few feet away, his arms slightly out as if to catch me if I ran. As if to reach for me again.

"I don't want to be the other woman," I admitted. I couldn't be. Not with Hannah. Not with anyone. I wasn't that kind of girl.

"I don't want you to be, either," he said at once. "I want to be with you, Tess. Just you. That's all I've ever wanted." Dylan came forward and brushed his fingers gently across my cheek. There was reverence in that simple touch of skin on skin.

"But...Hannah..." I gestured futilely at some imaginary Hannah, somewhere beyond these walls. If he wanted me, why was he dating her?

"I like Hannah very much," he said now. "She's a sweet girl. But she's not...you. Tess, I love you." His voice broke on the words.

I broke, too. *Don't love me. You have no idea what an awful person I am. You have no idea I'm standing here, stealing my sister's boyfriend.*

"For two years, I've loved you. I'm not afraid to tell you that."

No, he wouldn't be. Dylan was always forthright. He'd never had to keep secrets, never had some innate part of him be too dangerous to speak aloud. And he loved *me*. My heart was pounding again, but it wasn't lust this time. Fear, hope, wonder that this could remotely be true. That a man would stand here and choose me.

"Now you're here, and I want to be with you. I love you. Nothing has changed, except I'm not going to let you get away again."

Each declaration rang like a wrecking ball against my resolve. I wanted to throw myself at him again.

"Tell me you want to be with me, too. I'm breaking up with Hannah the next time I see her. I don't want to hurt her, but I can't be with her anymore. Not when I feel the way I do about you."

His eyes were clear, pleading. This wasn't lust talking. This wasn't a single glass of wine. Dylan was being as frank as he always was. Hannah was nice, but she wasn't forever. They weren't married, no one was pregnant, and this wasn't the end of the world. He wanted to be with me; I wanted to be with him. It was as simple as that. We were lucky, in a way, that we'd caught it so early, when it *could* be simple, when we could make this decision and get it over with and no one had betrayed anyone else. It was unfortunate, but sometimes things happened this way.

I stepped backward. "You'll break up with her tomorrow?" I asked, hardly trusting my voice. How does one say something like that without sounding like a total bitch?

He gestured between us. "I'm pretty sure I have to."

"Okay." I gave a curt nod, then wrapped my arms round my torso, squeezing tight because Dylan couldn't be there. I would not start our relationship with a betrayal. "Tomorrow."

He understood immediately. I gathered my things and went to the door. I couldn't stay here. I couldn't eat his shrimp and feta and drink his wine. I couldn't trust myself with Dylan tonight. As I went to turn the knob, he put his hand on the door jamb. Not on me. He couldn't touch me, either, or we'd both fall apart. I turned to him and his blue eyes burned with questions.

I smiled. It was all so very clear. "I love you, too," I said.

"Good." He breathed out. Relieved. Satisfied. Happy. "Tomorrow."

It was the only word in my head as I left.

———

SO HERE'S A FUNNY STORY: Dylan skipped class Tuesday morning.

My first thought was that he'd slipped in his shower and was lying on the floor of his apartment with a broken neck. Because that was the only possible reason Dylan Kingsley wouldn't show up at Transport. He was a guy who went to class, barring a life-threatening emergency. A significant part of me wondered if I should call 911, but instead I texted him the second that class ended, before I'd even packed up my books.

Where are you?

The answer came flying back:

Something came up. Talk later?

Okay, so at least his texting hand was operative. But I was baffled. Something came up? Something. Came. Up. Things that might make Dylan skip class did not just "come up."

Unless it was me and our very-near miss last night. Unless it was the words we'd said to each other, the promises we'd made. Maybe retsina was some kind of crazy hallucinogenic Greek wine. Maybe it was the Mediterranean equivalent of eating a mezcal worm. Maybe he regretted every single instant of last night and was avoiding me...

"No little boyfriend today, Tess?" I looked up to see Elaine standing over me. "Drop/add's going on for one more week. Maybe he realized he's in over his head here."

"You really need to let it go," I said. "This isn't high school anymore. I never did anything to you." I thought about the way Dylan had dealt with the Todd situation. "And you might not want to be on Dylan's bad side either. You're biochem, right? Well, Dylan's got some really good friends over at Canton Chem HR."

"Oh, yeah, real charmer, isn't he?" She rolled her eyes. "He doesn't even want to work there and he hogs all the attention, makes all the friends. He knows full well he's never going to take a job at Chem."

"He *lets* a bunch of rich alumni give him beers at a tailgate?" I pressed my hand against my chest in mock shock. "Call the cops. What an outrage."

"You don't know him," she repeated. "He takes everything and he doesn't care who else might want it. He made sure you were off the market the second you arrived here, but don't get too cozy. When he has what he wants, he'll ditch you, too."

Boy, did this chick have her wires crossed. It was really the exact opposite.

"He used me freshman year to get to my roommate."

"That's not the story I heard."

"Oh, and you believe Dylan!" she scoffed. "Figures. Are you

in love with him or something? Because you can talk to my roommate about how well that works out."

My jaw tightened. I didn't want to listen to this anymore. I didn't give a shit about Elaine's bitter, petty view of Dylan, the situation freshman year, the entire world that was apparently arrayed against her. Her poison couldn't touch us.

And yes, Elaine, you snide bitch, I do believe Dylan. And so what if I'm in love with him? He loves me, too. And he wasn't in class because of...something. Something, just as he'd said.

Maybe he was in the middle of breaking up with Hannah even now. You never knew.

———

BY TWO O'CLOCK, I still hadn't heard back from Dylan, and I had finished all my homework and course reading in the bioengineering library. Since I had no lab access today and no shift at work, I found myself at loose ends. I didn't want to go home. I didn't have any friends on campus.

God, it was November and I didn't have any friends on campus.

Before I let myself spiral into some sort of pity party, I packed up my things and drove out to Sylvia and Annabel's apartment. Who needed friends on campus when you had friends off it?

The Warrens lived in a one-bedroom apartment smaller and dingier than ours. Annabel had done what she could to brighten the place up, and the walls were covered with photographs of Milo as well as his childhood artwork in cheery, cheap frames. When I arrived it was "reading time"—Milo was in the big armchair with a chapter book, and Annabel had stuck a book-mark into one of her nursing school textbooks to mark her place.

"Kitchen?" she said when she saw my face.

I nodded. "Coffee."

Crowded around the little card table in the kitchen, I gave Annabel the short, PG-rated rundown of the events that had transpired over the last few days.

She still fanned herself. "Holy shit, Tess. You're a femme fatale."

"No, I'm not."

She gave me an incredulous look over the rim of her coffee cup. "You made out with him on his countertop, then insisted you weren't going a step further until he dumped his princess girlfriend? And he agreed? The CIA should hire you."

I looked down into my mug. It hadn't been like that.

"And to think," my friend continued. "Last time we spoke about this you were still claiming you didn't want him back. I *so* knew you were lying. I always know when you or Sylvia are pulling a fast one. Sylvia may think she's the actress in the family, but I had her beat—sneaking around with boys and no one the wiser…well, until I got knocked up."

I rolled my eyes. It was the end of the story that troubled me. Why hadn't he called?

"I don't know," Annabel said when I asked her. "Maybe he's had a harder time getting in touch with Hannah than he'd planned. If he's the guy you say he is, he'll want to break up with her in person, right?"

"True."

"Don't let this Elaine chick plant fear in your head. She's the one acting devious, not Dylan."

"Except for cheating on his girlfriend," I pointed out.

"He didn't cheat. Not really."

I wondered if that would be Hannah's take on the situation. Too bad Annabel was home tonight and not cynical Sylvia. I felt like I needed both the angel and the devil on my shoulders right now.

It wasn't that a few hours were making me doubt Dylan. It wasn't that Elaine's words were haunting me. It wasn't anything I could put my finger on. But somehow, the security, the certainty I'd felt last night when I left Dylan's apartment had faded. Then, I'd trusted that it would all work out as we'd planned. He loved me and I loved him, and he was going to break up with Hannah and we'd be together. We'd be happy. But every hour that passed made me wonder more and more if that was a bigger fantasy than the ones lining Sylvia's bookshelves.

I'd told myself all night and all day that everything was going to be fine, but why did I expect that? Why did I think I even deserved it? It *shouldn't* be easy to steal my secret sister's boyfriend.

I wondered what Dylan was telling Hannah about why they were breaking up. Dylan was always so honest and open. I hoped he wasn't telling her he'd met someone else. I hoped he was giving her the "it's not you, it's me" speech. Because it wasn't like that was a lie. It *was* Dylan—Dylan, who didn't love Hannah the way he loved me.

I was an expert on lies of omission. Maybe I should have given him some tips.

Another check of my phone, just in case it had buzzed since I'd gotten to Annabel's apartment. Nothing.

"Tess, honey." Annabel put her hand on my arm. "You're going to drive yourself nuts. Go do some homework or something."

"Done."

"Go to the movies."

I made a face. "Alone?"

"Go get your nails done!" Annabel threw up her hands in frustration. "Whatever it takes to put your phone away for a few hours. A watched pot never boils."

I slipped my phone back in my purse. True. But what if I didn't even realize the stove was broken?

————

SO I GOT my nails done at the mall. It felt weird to have polish on them, since I rarely bothered with stuff like that. Spa treatments were always more Mom's thing. I'd purposefully left my phone in my car, and after the manicurist pronounced my hands dry enough to let me leave, I even spent what felt like forever wandering up and down the mall, window shopping. Nevertheless, when I got back to my car to check my messages, I'd only managed to kill an hour and a half.

Even worse, Dylan still hadn't called. There was nothing left for me to do but go home.

I spent a quiet evening with Mom and around midnight, I finally gave up and went to bed. Correction: I got into bed and stared blankly at the ceiling, going over everything with as much scientific precision as I could muster without resorting to charts and graphs.

Hypothesis 1: *All Dylan wanted was a lay, and when I didn't give it to him, despite him throwing around the L-word like it was nothing, he decided to cut his losses.*

Evidence for: *Plenty. We met at his place, he plied me with wine, he only stopped when I asked him to, then he said yes to everything I laid out there, as if I'd throw caution to the wind and sleep with him if he promised to break up with Hannah. I thought back to all those times when Dad swore he'd leave his wife for Mom. Mom gave in; the divorce never happened.*

Evidence against: *"Tess, I love you." If that was fake, he should drop out of Bio-E and join the Canton Theater department.*

Hypothesis 2: *This is all some big revenge scenario. He doesn't want to get back together with me. He wants me to want it, and he's never ever going to call me, just like I never called him two years ago.*

Evidence for: *Sylvia had suspected as much, hadn't she? The first time I saw him with Hannah. The perfect revenge. And he's not calling.*

Evidence against: *Then why bother texting me with: "Talk later?" He could have just said "Sucker!" and bolted.*

Hypothesis 3: *Elaine is right, and in the ensuing years since I first met Dylan he has turned into a ladykilling jerk.*

> *Evidence for:* He admitted he slept with Elaine's roommate
> (and two other girls) he had no real feelings for. He made
> out with a girl who was not his girlfriend.
> *Evidence against:* Elaine's got it in for him. Plus, the
> aforementioned "Tess, I love you."

Okay, I'll admit it. Those four words had been on repeat in my head all day, especially as there hadn't been any further conversations with Dylan to help supplant them in my mind.

But he hadn't called. He hadn't called. He hadn't called.

> *Hypothesis 4:* You deserve any and all of these outcomes for
> trying to steal your sister's boyfriend.

On my nightstand, the phone started buzzing. When I looked at the screen, I noticed two things: 1:30 a.m. and the name Dylan.

Swallowing, I slid the button to answer and held the phone to my ear. "Hello."

"Hi." His voice was low, nearly a whisper. "Is it too late to call?"

"Almost," I said. I went boneless beneath the covers. I'd *almost* talked myself out of the whole thing. But it was going to be all right. He said he'd call, and he did. All those hypotheses, the doubts that had plagued me all day long—they meant nothing. "Everything okay?"

There was a split second of hesitation. "Yeah. I mean, today was tough, but yeah. I hope so."

He hoped so? What did that mean? "How is Hannah?"

"Not so great," he admitted.

A stab of pain shot through my chest at those words. I wish there'd been some way to do this without hurting her. I'd never met Hannah, but she was still my little sister. "What did you tell her?"

I heard him sigh on the other end of the line. "It's so late. I'm really tired. I can't go through everything tonight. I—just wanted to hear your voice."

"I'm right here," I whispered. I knew what he meant. His voice on my pillow—it was like he was lying right beside me, in a way he never truly had. Back at Cornell, we hadn't spent the night together, fearing that we'd get caught if I wasn't back in my own bed by curfew. So many firsts to come, even if we were two years late.

"You're everything to me, Tess. I want you to believe that."

His words were warmer than any blanket. I wanted to believe it too. "Do you want me to come over?"

"No," he said, his voice harsh in my ear. "It's really late. We'll talk tomorrow."

I immediately felt like a heel. *Hey, Dylan, now that you've ditched your girlfriend, wanna bang? It's been thirty minutes, right? Plenty of time for decency's sake!*

Of course, we hadn't worried about decency last night, when we'd almost ripped each other's clothes off in his kitchen.

Not true, said a little voice inside me. If I hadn't been concerned about decency, I would have finished the job then, not insisted he break up with Hannah before we got together.

But what difference did that really make, in the scheme of things? If I were Hannah, would I really care whether or not he'd had sex with, or just made out with, the woman he was leaving me for? Wasn't that girl equally evil either way? A girl who went after guys with girlfriends? Wasn't that exactly the person I swore I'd never be?

Dylan was right. It was late. Far too late to be contemplating these sorts of questions. "I'm just glad you called," I said sleepily as a yawn threatened to knock the receiver away from my chin. "I was beginning to worry."

"I thought you might be." Dylan's tone was soft, almost like a lullaby. "I'm sorry if you waited up for me. I know how much you need your sleep."

"Mmmm," I murmured. My eyelids felt heavy, as if all the concerns of the day had wrung me out.

"Oh, Tess, I miss you so much. I can't wait to see you tomorrow."

"Me too," I murmured, half asleep already.

I mean, I *must* have been nearly asleep. I don't remember the rest of our conversation. I don't remember how it ended. And I'm sure he couldn't have said:

"—I'll explain everything."

But I swear I heard it anyway.

TWELVE

I AWOKE the next morning bleary-eyed but blissful. Everything would be okay. Dylan, the project, Canton—all of it. The weather outside was the type of brilliant day you only get in the fall—crisp air, scorching color, a sky as deeply blue as my lover's eyes.

I was in such a good mood, I even decided to splurge on one of those fancy coffee drinks from the shop on campus instead of my usual cheapskate homemade cup of joe. The shop was promoting its fall lineup of pumpkin mochas and maple lattes. I was trying to decide between a cinnamon caramel shot or a pumpkin spice foamer when I heard the girl next to me shout.

"Hannah! Over here."

As smoothly as I could, I ducked behind the pastries. Canton was entirely too small a campus. I knew I'd run into her sooner or later, but I'd hoped to put at least twenty-four hours between my breaking up her relationship and our first hello.

"Miss?" the barista said to me. "Do you know what you want?"

"Pumpkin spice," I chirped.

Behind me, the girl greeted my half-sister. Spiders started marching down my back.

"What size?"

"Large?" No, wait. Hadn't I read somewhere that larges just meant they added extra milk, not extra espresso? I didn't want to pay another dollar-fifty for steamed milk.

"Why didn't you answer your phone all weekend?" the girl was asking Hannah. "Were you off on some romantic trip I didn't know about?"

"No," Hannah said softly. I flinched. "But that sounds better than what I *was* doing. I'll have to suggest it to him for fall break."

I stiffened. Suggest it to *whom*?

"That'll be four-fifty," the girl said, and I blindly thrust a five-dollar bill at her, then started sidling away. The coffee-making process seemed to take forever. Maybe it was the pumpkin spice. Finally, they handed me the cup, and I breathed a sigh of relief and tried to back out through the crowd of people waiting for their drinks.

"Hey!" Hannah's voice called. "I know you."

I froze, head bowed. Was there any possibility of pretending I didn't hear her, even though we were standing less than five feet apart?

"Tess, right?" Oh, God, she said my name. This was against the rules. This was *so* against the rules. Then again, hadn't the rules gone right out the window when I'd let her boyfriend put his tongue in my mouth?

I looked over, into eyes that matched my own. I wondered if she noticed it. "Yeah."

She turned to her friend, a cute redhead with freckles and a frizzy pom-pom of a ponytail. "This is my boyfriend's new lab partner. Tess just transferred to Canton."

The red-haired girl shook my hand and probably introduced herself, too, but my brain was busy trying to process Hannah's words.

My boyfriend's lab partner…

"How's the project going?" Hannah asked me, her many-colored eyes clear and guileless. "All I can make out about it is Dylan's been working his ass off. I know that's his style, but I hope he's not driving you crazy." Her smile was gentle, almost patronizing. I wanted to die.

"I'm so sorry," I choked out. "I have to run. I have a class—" I made a gesture that I hoped indicated "across campus" and made for the door.

"*That's* your boyfriend's lab partner?" I heard the redhead say to Hannah. "Oh, honey, I'd watch out..."

Correction: *now* I wanted to die.

The second I was away from the doors, I started sprinting, ignoring the scalding hot pumpkin spice concoction splashing onto my hands. Why the hell had I decided to get coffee on campus when there were easily half a dozen coffee shops between school and my house? Why the hell hadn't I stepped out of line the second I heard her name? Why the hell had Hannah called Dylan her boyfriend?

Maybe she was just saving face—maybe she didn't want to get into the gory details with an acquaintance in the coffee line. After all, it had been the redhead who'd mentioned him first, and Hannah did say she hadn't exactly had the most romantic of weekends. Maybe her whole line about hoping for one in the future was just a little white lie...

But that didn't make any sense. She was the one who'd sought me out, who'd started a whole conversation about her *boyfriend* with me, as if I couldn't possibly be the party he'd just dumped her for. I could well imagine Dylan not identifying me when he'd spoken to her. But I would also suspect every girl he'd ever met, especially his brand-new lab partner. Hannah couldn't be that much of an idiot, right? She was my father's daughter. And Dylan had liked her.

So maybe he hadn't told her there was someone else. Still, he'd dumped her, and she'd immediately gone out of her way to have a chat with his lab partner? Either she was the sweetest girl in the entire world, or she was in some serious denial.

Or he never broke up with her at all.

Ugh. I hated that little doubtful voice in my head. He *had* broken up with her. He'd called last night to tell me he had.

He never actually said that, though, did he?

I looked up to find myself standing in front of the Swift building. Well, no time like the present to find out for sure, was there? I took the stairs, paused on the landing to chug the rest of the pumpkin spice and toss the cup, then strode over to apartment 202 and rapped sharply at the door.

Dylan answered, all wet, floppy hair and glasses. His eyes were bloodshot, sleepless, and his T-shirt and pajama pants were still rumpled. I wanted to climb all over him. God help me, I wanted him so badly I could taste it.

"Tess," he said, surprised. "Don't you have class?"

"Morning," I replied and pushed past him. "Why? Are you expecting company?"

"What?" He trailed after me.

"Your *girlfriend*, maybe?" I turned around.

His face fell.

Along with it went my heart. My hopes. It was true. "You said you'd break up with her."

"Tess—"

I shook my head, a short, desperate little jab. "You lied to me."

He held his arms out. "What did you…hear?" His brow crinkled, disbelieving. "Did you go talk to Hannah?"

"You *lied* to me!" The pumpkin spice churned in my stomach. That insanely expensive little coffee might have been the worst decision of my life.

"Wait, Tess, tell me what you said to her."

I was *not* going to sit here and get a lecture about the rules from *Dylan*, of all people. I knew the rules about talking to Hannah before he'd ever heard of her.

"God, let me think," I cried in mock contemplation. "I think, maybe, 'Hi'?" Had it even been that much? "I didn't seek her out or anything, Dylan. I'm not some evil bitch." Even if I would steal her boyfriend, I wouldn't rub it in her face. "She was standing in line next to me at the coffee shop. And *she's* the one who started going on and on about how I'm her *boyfriend's* lab partner, and her *boyfriend* this and her *boyfriend* that, and she and her *boyfriend* are going to go away on a romantic vacation next month."

"What?" He looked honestly baffled.

"So tell me, Dylan," I said, my voice low and dangerous, "which is it? Is Hannah Swift the most deluded person on the planet, or am I? Am I the biggest idiot in the universe for believing you when you said you were going to break up with her?"

Dylan said nothing for a long moment, just stared at me with heartbreak in his eyes. "Tess, I need you to sit down for a second. I need to tell you something and I didn't want you furious when you heard it, so…"

No way. No. Way. I had heard a variation on this speech a hundred times. I was not my mother, to be reasoned out of the kind of life I wanted for myself, the kind of person I wanted to be. I started past him toward the door. Why had I ever thought it would turn out differently? Why had I even thought I was worthy of that? A girl who would steal her own sister's boyfriend? I *was* the devil.

"Tess, please," Dylan begged. He grabbed my arm. "Please, please, I love you—"

I jerked away. "Go lie to Hannah."

"I am," he said, and there was something so desperate in his words my steps faltered. "Tess, she's sick."

What? I turned around and looked at him. "I just saw her. She doesn't look sick."

His face was as serious as a funeral. "Please, just sit down. I promised I'd tell you everything today, so let me tell you, and then you can decide."

I relented and entered the living area. His futon was still pulled out into bed form, the blankets tangled and inviting. I froze.

"Sorry. I just got up."

"Mmm." I skirted the bed and sat—or perched, rather—on the very very edge of his desk chair, poised for flight.

Dylan sat on the edge of the futon bed, leaning out over it, as if he could reach me. I rolled farther away.

"First, let me say I love you, and I'm really, really sorry I didn't get a chance to talk things over with you first—"

"Get to the point or I'm leaving," I said.

"Okay." He took a deep breath. "Yesterday, I planned to meet Hannah for lunch. I was going to break up with her then. I didn't want lies between us any longer than necessary. She's a good person, Tess."

Yeah. Better than both of us, apparently.

"But when I called her in the morning to set it up, she was totally hysterical. She'd gotten a call from her doctor's office that morning about some abnormal result on a test. The doctor wanted her to come in right away. She was really scared. Of course, I offered to go with her."

The rest of the story came together in my head before he even finished saying it, but I listened patiently as he reported on their trip to the doctor. How he'd waited alone in reception while Hannah had a long chat with the doctor about the tests she would soon undergo. How he'd held her hand during the imaging of her throat and chest, trying desperately to read the sonographer's impassive face for clues on what she might be seeing. How he'd been filled with guilt and pain as he'd thought about what he'd been planning on saying to her that day, even as he'd hugged her and told her he was there for her and that everything would be all right.

"*Is* she going to be all right?" I pressed.

He shrugged. "I don't know. I'm not able to get a straight answer out of her—she's so distraught about the whole thing, all the technical stuff is just sliding out of her head. It's like after she heard the C word, everything else sounded like it was spoken by a grown-up in a Peanuts cartoon. And they don't really tell *me* anything useful. I'm just the boyfriend."

Something cold shot through me at the word.

"But I do know there are going to be a lot more tests, and it may be be a few weeks before they know if…" He hesitated. "How serious it all is."

"Oh God," I said, as a lump formed in my throat. "Poor Hannah."

He gave me a curious look. "Thank you."

I cocked my head at him. "For what?"

"For saying that. I mean, you don't even know her."

"I don't need to know her," I said, immediately on the defensive. *She's still my sister.* I mean, she was still a young girl with some really bad news to face. I played with the sleeves of my jacket. "Has she, um, spoken to her parents?"

"Not yet," he said. "She wants to do that tonight. She wants me to go with her."

I nodded, examining my hands.

"Tess." This time it came from very near, and when I raised my head, I saw he'd ventured as close to me as he could get. "I can't believe I'm saying this—"

Oh, here it comes. The bargaining. The slippery slope to betrayal. Was this how it had started for my mother? Agreeing to keep things on the down-low for "just a little while"?

"—but I don't think we can be together right now," he finished, pain etching his brows into little frowns.

Laughter bubbled from my lips, I was so relieved. Even in this, Dylan took the high road. He didn't want to sneak around. He wanted to *wait.* "Of course we can't be together right now!" I exclaimed. "You can't dump a girl the day she finds out she may have a deadly disease. Geez, what kind of monsters would we be?"

He looked at me and I looked at him, and for a moment, I felt like we could smile. It was a bad situation all around, but we were trying the best we could to keep Hannah from being unnecessarily hurt.

"I was going to say that I understand if you can't forgive me for this." He shrugged. "I just—I can't break up with Hannah right now. I feel so guilty, like maybe if I'd been paying more attention to her this past month, I would have noticed. She's been talking about how tired she's felt, how little energy she's had and, on some level, all I thought was 'great, I don't have to feel guilty for not going over there after spending the whole evening with you.'"

"You're not to blame," I replied quickly as my cells thrilled to his admission that he hadn't been willing to go to Hannah's after being with me. I went to lay my hand on his arm, then thought better of it. The less physical contact we had now, the better. "Even if you had been around, who thinks, 'Oh, honey, I wonder if there's something wrong with your thyroid?'"

"It's just...terrible."

"It is," I agreed. I wondered what my father would do when he heard. Probably fly in a team of specialists for his Hannah. God, poor Hannah. She must be so scared. "If there's anything I can do—"

"Like what?" Dylan asked in a tone of gentle amusement. "Throw seaweed at the problem? You're a bioengineering major, not pre-med."

"I don't know. Bone marrow?"

He chuckled. "I think they go to family members first for that kind of thing."

"Right," I said. Family first.

"And hopefully we'll never get to that point. Hopefully this is all nothing."

"Hopefully," I echoed. I should ask Dylan to tell me if they got to that point. I wondered what they'd do if they did need bone marrow. I wondered if my dad would ask me.

"God, Tess, you really are incredible." He was shaking his head in wonder at me. "I've been up all night trying to figure out how to handle this, trying to figure out what you'd say, how you'd react. I've been trying to figure out how I was going to get through these next few weeks—worrying about Hannah, wanting to be there for her, and being completely and totally in love with you the whole time—"

"Please," I said. "Do not tell me how wonderful I am for almost stealing a girl's boyfriend while she's busy trying to find out if she has cancer. I'm not wonderful. I'm not even good. I'm pretty sure this is the worst thing I've ever done in my life and I'm not going to pretend otherwise."

He blinked at me, and then he grabbed my hand and wouldn't let go, even when I tugged. "You don't really think that, do you?"

"Of course I do!"

His blue eyes bored into mine. "You didn't ask for this, Tess. *I* did. I was the one who wouldn't leave you alone, who kept pursuing you, both in class and outside it. And you know what? Even if you hadn't been interested, my days with Hannah would have been numbered. Because being with you, feeling the way I do about you—I don't feel that way about Hannah. I never will. I would have left to find someone I loved. I would have wanted her to find someone who feels that way, too."

I bit my lip. *He's just not that into you.* That was the phrase, wasn't it? And it was no one's fault.

"We're barely in our twenties. We're supposed to be having fun. I'm not interested in wasting anyone's time with something that's not working." He sighed. "But I'm not going to kick someone when she's down."

I understood what Dylan was saying now. This was not about me. It was about him and Hannah. I may have been the catalyst for their breakup, but I was not the cause.

Would that make it any easier? As with everything else, only time would tell. But Dylan had one thing wrong. I was far pettier than he gave me credit for. With every fiber of my being, I hoped that Hannah was *not* sick, that these tests she was about to undergo would show that the whole thing was a false alarm and my sister would live a long and perfect life. I hoped all of these things, but at the same time, I worried. What if it turned out that there *was* something wrong with Hannah? If Dylan couldn't break up with her when she was in the middle of a health scare, what would happen if it ballooned into a real health crisis?

Was there any point in pinning my hopes on a guy who might not ever be available?

THIRTEEN

NOT LONG AFTER THAT, our conversation devolved into talk about the project, because Dylan and I were dorks like that. In truth, I was relieved to see that we could talk about other things. Whatever happened in the next few weeks, it was going to be very hard if we couldn't find any topics to discuss that weren't either Hannah or our unresolved lust.

Dylan glanced at his clock. "Um, I should probably go get ready for class." He gestured to his PJs. "Want to wait here for a few minutes and we can walk over to Bio-E together?"

"Sure." I nodded as Dylan grabbed some clothes and went to the bathroom. As soon as he was gone, I took a minute to catch my breath. I could do this. With him out of the room, I felt like I might finally get some air, like the thrumming aware-ness that simmered just below the surface of every interaction with him had abated. Even as we spoke, there was a tiny part of me that wondered if I'd be able to handle working along-side him now, after our near miss two nights ago. After all, I'd had plenty of reasons not to make out with my sister's boyfriend before our chat, and I hadn't exactly stuck to the rules then.

Nevertheless, Dylan's words put me at ease. I wasn't entirely blameless in this situation, but neither was I a boyfriend-stealing bitch.

God, I hoped Hannah was all right. I hoped Dad was okay. Maybe I should call Mom and let her know that he was about to get some scary news. It was funny; I never knew if problems in his real family made him spend more time with us or less. There had been times over the years when he'd move in for a few days or weeks at a time, when he'd take my mother on long, luxurious vacations while I stayed with a babysitter. I wondered what Hannah and her mother thought he was doing on those occasions.

But he wouldn't run away when his daughter was sick, would he? She'd need her father there with her, the same way she needed Dylan.

Good lord, did I have daddy issues.

Dylan emerged from the bathroom. Against my will, my heart skipped in my chest. He wasn't wearing anything more exciting than a T-shirt and jeans, but his hair was damp and tousled, and his glasses were on. Somehow, when the glasses were on, I felt like he was mine, not Hannah's. Kind of the opposite of Superman.

"Okay, I'm ready. Just let me grab my books." He leaned over the futon, and I saw the way his wet hair was leaving tracks of water down the collar of his shirt. Before I realized what I was doing, my hand had gone out to smooth the droplets off his neck.

Dylan froze. "Tess—"

I pulled back as if burned. "Sorry. I don't know what I was thinking." I *hadn't* been thinking. My hand wanted to touch him. My skin needed to be against his skin. It was as simple as that.

He sank to the futon beside me. It was still a bed. Still all rumpled and inviting and smelling like Dylan in the sheets. If I touched him now, we'd never leave this room. We'd miss class, we'd fall back on the sheets, and all the promises and rules we'd just made for ourselves would fall by the wayside.

"I can't lose you," he whispered. "All these years...I thought you were gone. Now that I have another chance... I can't lose you again."

His gaze burned me, blue and longing and magnetic. That's when I knew it was going to happen. All of it. It was inevitable, it was inexorable, it was impossible to resist.

Dylan's phone buzzed on the sheets. Hannah's face popped up on the screen. He dragged his attention away from me and swiped the answer button. "Hi... How are you?... No, I'm about to leave for class, so...wait, you're on your way up?"

I shot off the futon like it was made of live snakes.

He pressed the mute button. "You're my lab partner. It's not a big deal that you're here—"

"I told her I was going to class less than an hour ago."

"Oh." He turned back to the phone. "Okay, Hannah, I'll see you in a minute." He disconnected, then looked at me. "Bathroom."

I rolled my eyes but complied. It was the only choice, wasn't it? Hiding in the bathroom. This was where it began. I wondered how many bathrooms my mom had hidden in over the years.

Seconds after he closed the door behind me, I heard a knock at the outer door to his studio. Even though logically I knew she wouldn't be able to see me, I still backed up until I hit the counter. The steam hadn't yet dissipated from his shower, and the misty air smelled of Dylan's soap and shampoo.

"Good morning!" Hannah's voice floated through the door. She sounded caffeinated. Probably finished more of her coffee than I had.

"Hi," said Dylan. "How are you feeling?"

Did they kiss? Did he kiss her right on the other side of this door?

"I'm actually just on my way out," he said now. "So—"

"I'll walk with you to class," she said. "I wanted to talk to you about my folks. I'm kinda thinking of not telling them until...well, until we know what we're dealing with."

More pangs of guilt stabbed my gut.

"I don't want them to freak out," she finished. "My mom's kind of sensitive."

And your dad?

"Um...okay," Dylan said. "Let me grab my keys. I don't want to forget them, since the door locks automatically behind you when you leave."

Was it my imagination, or had he said that part just a little bit louder than necessary? *Great, got the message, Dyl.*

I heard the outer door open and close, and waited a full two minutes before I emerged from the bathroom. The steam had played havoc with my hair, and I smoothed it down some before I, too, left Dylan's room and booked it to class, trying all the time *not* to think about what it would mean for my relationship with Dylan, for Dylan's duties to Hannah, and for the rules my mother and I had always lived by had Hannah simply leaned over and opened the bathroom door.

———

FORTUNATELY, I had managed to score a shift at Verde for this Wednesday evening, which meant I could fill my head with orders and refills and split-checks-please. Unfortunately, it was dead at Verde, so I was home by nine.

Dad was there. I saw his car first and then him, sitting in the living room, scrolling through his BlackBerry like this was his home.

"Mom here?" I asked as I set my keys down on the hall table.

"Nope." He looked up from his phone. "But I'm glad you are. I feel like I've hardly seen you since you moved back to town."

That may have been by design. He patted the cushion next to him and I sat down, slowly, preparing myself for another lecture on gratitude and discretion. Deliberately, Dad put his phone back in his pocket and turned to me.

"Everything all right with you? School? Work? Have you been getting enough sleep?"

"Yeah, Dad." Had Hannah told him about her medical tests?

Was that why he was suddenly so interested in playing the part of concerned father?

"The Canton coursework isn't too overwhelming?"

I rolled my eyes. "No. I'm pretty smart, as it turns out."

"I know you are, Tess. I just—it can be hard, when you're used to one method of education, to make a big switch..."

"Well," I reasoned. "I wouldn't have had to make a switch if I'd been at Canton from the start."

The strike landed, and landed hard. Dad flinched, and I immediately felt guilty. He'd gotten some bad news tonight. I should be more understanding.

"Tess." He sighed. "I hope you know, I thought I was making the best decision, for all of us, at the time."

"I'm not sure what that's supposed to even mean, Dad."

"Encouraging you to go to State."

Forcing me, more like. "So I wouldn't get my dirty little hands all over your precious alma mater?"

He looked more hurt than ever. "That's not what I was doing. Please don't make me the bad guy here. You're old enough now to understand how complicated things are."

Actually, they seemed pretty simple to me. I was supposed to stay away from the Swifts and all they'd claimed for themselves. When I did that, things were nice and neat and uncomplicated. It was only when I switched to Canton, only when I dared to try and get Dylan away from Hannah—that was when stuff got messy. If I'd followed the rules, maybe I'd be happy right now. Maybe I wouldn't be sitting here on a couch, arguing with my father, when I'd much rather be in Dylan's bed.

Not that I'd be in Dylan's bed. But I wouldn't even be thinking about it.

"I want you to be happy, Tess. I want you to be successful and happy and brilliant and have everything you want in life. And if Canton is what makes that happen, then okay."

My lips parted in shock. "Are you serious?"

He shrugged. "Of course. I love you. I shouldn't have gotten angry at you the other day. I'm sad that you wouldn't trust me, that you thought you had to sneak around behind my back."

I bit my lip. Look who was talking. Sneaking was my illegitimate little family's specialty.

"I've done a lot of reflecting recently, and I can see that you had good reason to think I wouldn't let you come here. And whatever else we've been forced to do, I don't want you to feel that way about me."

This was the part where he opened his checkbook and gave me money for textbooks. This was the part where he started acting like a real dad, one who was proud that his daughter got a merit scholarship at his alma mater.

Except I didn't want it. I didn't want to accept another dime from him if it came with strings, with rules, with reminders that I was his daughter and Hannah was his daughter and I wanted Hannah's boyfriend and Hannah was sick, sick, sick...

I reached out and covered my father's hand with my own. His skin felt dry and I noticed, for the first time, the way the hair on the back of his hands had gotten darker and more wiry with age. His face had aged too. There were lines in the corner of his eyes and mouth, and white strands of hair mixed in with the dark blond on his head. You didn't see it unless you were up close. Was it really so rare that I got up close to him?

Whatever else we've been forced to do... As much as I hated to admit this, I understood why Dad had made the choices he did. I understood that he thought he could better provide for his families if he kept his reputation and his business intact. Divorce would have cost a bundle, and the scandal resulting from exposure of his dirty family secret might have cost him his entire career. I understood why we had the rules; I understood why I had to live my life like I didn't have a father.

But maybe my mom was right, too. I'd spent so much time thinking about how much it sucked for me, I hadn't really thought about how it sucked for him, too. For what must have been the hundredth time today, I wondered what our lives would be like if Hannah was my sister for real, out in the open, and when she'd told her family about what she was facing today, she'd told me, too. That when Dad needed some company to chase away his worries, he had a kid who would give him a hug and tell him—

"It's going to be okay, Dad. I promise."

He raised his eyes to mine, those indeterminate, every-color eyes that so mirrored my own, and for a second I thought maybe he knew exactly what I was talking about. Not our fight, not our disagreements over Canton and our secrets, but Hannah—Hannah, whom we both loved, though I barely knew her. Hannah, who was sick and scared and probably needed her father to stay home with her instead of running away here, where his other family was safe and sound, where his other daughter's biggest concern—in his mind, at least—was how long her waitressing shifts were.

"You know you're still my girl, don't you?" he said. "You're still my daughter, and I love you and I'm proud of you."

Unbidden, tears filled my eyes.

"And one day, Tess, one day this will all be behind us."

I wasn't sure what that was supposed to mean. Did Dad imagine a future where the rules no longer applied? Where after long last, he left his wife and married my mom and I could live openly, if not as his daughter, at least as his stepdaughter? Where I could know Hannah? Could that reality ever exist?

A bone-deep yearning lit up my soul. I didn't even know if I wanted that anymore. And after years of watching him dangle that possibility over my mother's head, I found it hard to imagine. It hadn't happened when Hannah had finally grown up and gone to college, which was the usual time when broken marriages officially failed. He hadn't divorced his wife, and Hannah was a junior, like me. Even Mom seemed to have relinquished the prospect of being anything other than Steven Swift's mistress years ago.

But apparently, some small part of me hadn't given up, the same part of me that yelled at Sylvia for threatening to put nuts in Hannah's salad, that wondered if she'd tell me when to hide my eyes at horror movies, that wanted to burst into tears when Dylan had told me Hannah was sick, that wanted to put my arms around my dad and tell him that whatever happened with his other daughter, we'd face it together. If Hannah needed bone marrow, we would find some way to give her mine without anyone knowing why I might be a match.

Even if I did want her boyfriend, she was still my sister.

It was funny, in a way. I had never dared ask Dad about Hannah all these years. He got too mad. And I didn't dare ask Dylan, either. He knew her better than anyone, I supposed. Knew which of those horror movies her Facebook profile said she loved were her favorite. Knew what made her laugh, her favorite color, her favorite flower, exactly what scared her most about whatever was happening to her. He knew those things, and I wanted to know them so badly right now. I wanted to know, I wanted to help.

"Dad, I know..." What? I knew Hannah told him she might be sick. How did I know that? I knew because I very nearly boinked her boyfriend the other day. I knew because I broke the rules.

I couldn't risk ruining whatever was happening here and now over telling him that.

"I know you love me," I finished lamely.

This week, two men had told me they loved me. But in the end, they both belonged to Hannah.

FOURTEEN

DYLAN SKIPPED Transport class again on Thursday morning, and I spent most of the hour with my head buried in my notebook, face flushed, trying to figure out if he couldn't face me or if he was accompanying Hannah to her biopsy. He hadn't texted to tell me what was going on, and from what I remembered of the "class participation" section of the syllabus, we only got three unexcused absences per semester.

Maybe it was because I was alone again, but Elaine approached me at the end of class.

"Hey," she said, clutching her books to her chest. "I wanted to apologize for my behavior last week."

"Okay." I flipped the cover of my notebook closed. "Apologize."

"It's not an excuse, I know that, but I was getting a little overwhelmed with midterms and stuff. My Photonics project crashed and burned, Transport is my only chance, and…I freaked out about the symposium. And Dylan and I have this competitive thing going on and he scoops up the new girl before anyone knows anything, and…well, I took my frustrations out on you. I shouldn't have. I'm just scared I can't hack Bio-E."

I stood up. "Is this your way of saying you're switching to the English department and giving us our lab times back?"

She sucked air through her teeth. "No. I mean, not the English department part, at least. But yeah, I guess we can split the lab slots if you want."

I gave her a long, hard look. How was I supposed to trust her? Dylan certainly didn't.

"I'm really sorry," Elaine went on. "I absolutely know I was in the wrong before. You're new here and I really didn't give you a nice welcome. And as much as I hate to say it, Dylan's right. I want to beat you fair and square." She looked pointedly at the empty seat next to me. "That is, if he didn't drop."

"He didn't drop. He's got some personal matters to attend to." Wait, did that sound bad? "We're still going to kick your ass."

"We'll see about that." She was silent again for a second. "Anyway, I know it's probably too late to be friends, but—could we start with lunch?"

Something inside me relaxed. Okay, so she was crazy competitive and not too fond of the man I loved. That didn't make her evil. And maybe if she saw I wasn't evil either, she could relax some. "I hope it's not too late," I said. "I've been here for two months and I don't know anyone, really."

"Dylan," Elaine pointed out.

I grinned at her. "Yeah, but you don't think I should be hanging out with him."

Elaine rolled her eyes. "Well, I say that to a lot of people. They never listen."

———

WE ENDED up having lunch at the cafe in the biology tower with her roommate, Melanie. The one Dylan had slept with freshman year. I seemed doomed to cross paths with Dylan's entire play-book. Melanie was a tiny pixie of a girl with short, spiky hair bleached nearly white in places and streaked with blue and teal. Her nose and eyebrow were pierced, and she had a tattoo covering most of her right arm.

I wasn't entirely sure what I was expecting from Dylan's first post-me conquest, but the punk rock look was certainly not it.

"Tess, Melanie. Melanie, Tess," Elaine said, setting down her tray. "Tess is Dylan's latest flavor-of-the-month."

"Oh, no," I corrected. "We're not dating. He has a girlfriend."

"I think I heard about that," Melanie said, twirling some pasta on her fork. "Don't worry, Tess, I don't share my roommate's disdain for Mr. Kingsley. She thinks I should still be mad at him for not calling me, like, two years ago. But sometimes you do crazy things freshman year. Mine was him." She smiled a secret smile. "I like to think I was his, too."

"It's not just that," said Elaine. "I don't like his attitude."

"'His attitude,'" Melanie replied, making quote marks with her fingers, "meaning that he wouldn't be your lab partner last year?"

Well, that also explained why she was so bitter. He beat her freshman year, then wouldn't help her out last year... A lot of history for those two.

Elaine pursed her lips. "I probably could have done without you telling Tess that. She's just going to go tell Dylan."

Oh, trust me, Elaine. There are plenty of things I'm perfectly fine not ever telling Dylan.

I desperately wanted to change the subject, especially considering that if everything worked out as I hoped, I *would* be dating the guy soon enough. "So, Elaine tells me you're a botany concentration? I worked at a botany lab at State. What are you studying?"

Melanie threw back her head and laughed. "Oh my God, you sound like you're still at your entrance interview. Elaine, is it, like, a requirement that you Bio-E people all have boring, one-track minds?"

"I've heard you make that claim before, yes," said Elaine.

"But I figure since you can't keep a thought in *your* head for more than five minutes, it works out well." She was smiling for what seemed like the first time ever. It was nice to see this side of her.

Melanie lobbed a pea at her. "Fair enough. Tess, don't listen to this bitch. I hear she went crazy last week and stole some poor people's lab space."

"I apologized!" Elaine cried. "What do you want me to do, commit seppuku?"

"Maybe you should just buy Tess lunch?" Melanie suggested.

I laughed. These two and their way of talking reminded me of Sylvia and Annabel. They teased and ribbed each other, but there was clearly love behind it all. And yet, unlike the Warrens, Melanie and Elaine weren't sisters. They'd only met when they'd been assigned to live together freshman year.

I wondered how Hannah was doing, and then, just as quickly, pushed the thought from my mind. Hannah and I would never be roommates, would never be sisters. We were nothing.

Perhaps I'd missed out on too much, always living alone, off-campus—first at State and now here at the apartment where I'd grown up. Being with Cristina that summer at Cornell had been fun, and we still emailed and texted a lot. She'd hated her actual freshman-year roommate, but she'd moved in with a friend off campus by sophomore year and, according to all reports, they were still having a blast.

"Have any plans for the weekend?" Melanie was asking now.

"I usually work weekends," I explained. "I'm a waitress at Verde."

"Weird, I must have totally seen you there. I go there all the time."

Well, folks never noticed their waitress.

"Are you working tonight?"

"No." I glanced meaningfully at Elaine. "I'm supposed to be in the lab tonight."

"I'm never going to live this down, am I?" she asked.

"No," said Melanie. "And you deserve it. But in this case, it all worked out. If you were waiting tables tonight, you couldn't come with us to a party."

"Oh," I said. "I can't go to a party—"

"Yes you can," said Elaine. "Nothing is really going to start until ten."

"Do you have a test on Friday?" Melanie asked.

"No."

"A hot date?"

I felt my face heat. "No."

"Some kind of religious or moral objection to people having fun?" Elaine suggested.

"No. I just..." I shrugged. "A Canton party? That kind of takes me back to high school. We used to try to crash them, you know."

"Spoken like a true townie," said Melanie with a laugh.

"You're not crashing this time," Elaine added. "And please do come. It can be part of my apology. I always say the girls in Bio-E need to stick together and I've pretty much been doing the opposite of that."

I turned to her. "You do know I think you're trying to get info about Dylan and my project off me?"

"Of course I am," she replied and took a sip of her drink, "but we can still have fun."

———

AFTER MY LAST class of the day, I drove home to eat dinner and get a head start on homework. Mom was out at a gallery show for a friend of hers, but the crisper was full of vegetables. As I waited for my pasta to boil, I texted Dylan.

We're still on for lab work tonight?

His answer came back right away.

ONE & ONLY   133

Yes. I'd love your notes from this morning if you have them. Took H to doctor's office.

Yeah, Dylan, I'd figured.

I also figured that I wouldn't return home between lab and the party, so I might as well get dressed now. After dinner I took a quick shower, then blow-dried my hair with a round brush so it fell in full, bouncy brown waves around my shoulders. My memories of Canton parties were that they were slightly more fashionable occasions than the occasional kegger I'd attended at State, so I chose a pair of skinny jeans and a gray knit top shot through with threads of silver that sparkled when they caught the light. I snatched a pair of high-heeled boots from my mom's closet that I figured I'd probably regret by the end of my lab session, but they gave me an extra two inches and looked really nice with my pants. As I was doing my makeup, the phone buzzed on the counter. I checked the screen: Cristina. A pang of guilt coursed through me—I hadn't kept my friend abreast of anything that had happened since I'd transferred.

I turned on the speakerphone so I could finish my eyeliner. "Hey, stranger!"

"Hi!" came the voice of my old friend. "I realized I haven't called you to ask how Canton is going, so I'm doing that now."

"It's crazy busy here, too," I replied. "I'm working insane hours just to make ends meet, but I'm also entering this symposium next month with a five-thousand-dollar prize, so...wish me luck."

"Awesome! What's your project?"

I told her, taking care to leave out the part where I was doing the project with Dylan.

"That sounds a bit like that thing you did with Dylan up here a few years ago."

"Mmm." I lined my lips a rosy red.

"Did you tell him?"

"I didn't have to," I replied sheepishly. "He's my partner."

Silence reigned on the other end of the phone. After a second, Cristina's screams bounced off the walls of my bathroom. "What the hell, McMann?" she asked. "How could you not tell me you two had hooked up again?"

"Because we hadn't?" I said. "We were just partners."

"*Were* just partners?" She pounced. "Spill. What's going on? What happened? What does he look like these days? Are his pants still too short?"

I hesitated, my lip pencil dangling in the air above my mouth. "He looks really good," I said at last. That was neutral, right? "And his pants are perfect."

But Cristina wasn't about to let me get away with it. "Are you *in* his pants?"

I sighed, then admitted, "Not all the way in."

She squealed again. "Oh my God, I knew it. The second you told me you were going to Canton, I was like, Dylan and Tess, sitting in a tree, k-i-s-s—"

"He...has a girlfriend," I said, interrupting her annoying little song.

"You man-stealing slut," she joked. "That is awesome."

I bit my freshly painted lip and looked in the mirror. "Please don't call me that."

"Oh, Tess—you know I don't mean 'slut' in a bad way," she said, sounding contrite. "I totally think women should own their personal sexuality and have as much sex as they want to..."

I let Cristina go on her Women's Studies-induced rant about taking back ownership of the word *slut* without saying anything else. Because, honestly, it hadn't even registered. The part that bothered me had been *man-stealing*. I didn't want to be a man-stealing anything—not slut, not bitch, and certainly not sister. Dylan swore to me that it wasn't about me, that it was about *him*, and I wanted to believe him.

But it would all be so much easier if he hadn't been dating her when we'd met again, if he hadn't been dating her when he'd lifted me up on his countertop and stuck his tongue down my throat.

"Tess?" Cristina's voice crackled out of my speakerphone, bouncing tinnily around the bathroom. "You're not mad, are you?"

"No," I said, and finished applying my lipstick. Not at Cristina, anyway.

Just myself.

DYLAN WAS ALREADY in the lab when I arrived, going over our notes and setting up our workspace. He seemed tired, with noticeable lines under his blue eyes and hair that looked like he'd run his fingers through it a few too many times. He wasn't wearing his glasses. His Tess glasses. I swallowed. Maybe this was all a mistake.

Ugh, that's idiotic, Tess. Don't read too much into a pair of freaking glasses.

"I've got great news," I said as brightly as I could. "I talked to Elaine this afternoon, and she said we can split the lab times Monday through Wednesday."

"You're kidding! How'd you work that miracle?"

I started unbuttoning my coat. "I did nothing. Apparently she had some kind of…stressed-out nervous episode the other week, and she deeply regrets her behavior and said we can have our lab slots back if we want."

"That's…great. So you actually had a civil conversation with her? That's possible?"

I chuckled. "You two should learn to bury the hatchet. She's not so bad. I even went to lunch with her and her roommate."

There was a pregnant pause. "Melanie?"

"Yeah." So at least he remembered her name. "And I have to say, Dylan, I was super surprised when I saw her. She doesn't strike me as your type." I slipped my coat from my shoulders and went to hang it up on the rack by the door. When I turned back, it was to see Dylan staring at me, open-mouthed.

"What?" I asked nervously, smoothing my hands down over my shimmery top.

"I...um...that outfit's really nice."

"Thanks."

He turned away. "Make sure to put on your lab coat so you don't get anything on it."

I rolled my eyes at him, then went to get one of the white jackets lining the wall. We started in on the evening's work, but a few minutes into it, as I was studying some cells in the microscope, Dylan spoke again.

"You're talking about the hair and the piercings and stuff, right? On Melanie?"

"Mmm?" I adjusted the magnification.

"She didn't look like that when I knew her," he went on quietly. "She was a little more conservative freshman year. Still figuring her style and stuff out, I guess. No piercings, no tattoos. Her hair was long...and...brown. Like yours."

I looked up at him. "Oh."

He gave me a gentle smile. "A lot like yours."

"Oh."

Dylan fell silent, and I wondered how many of the people he had dated resembled me. And then I thought of Hannah, and her eyes, and the genetics we shared, and the air in the room felt hot and impossible to breathe.

"Did you like her?" he asked now. "Melanie?"

"Yeah," I said, relieved to be back on safer ground. "She's nice. And Elaine spent the whole lunch apologizing, so maybe I'm going to give her another chance, too."

Dylan made a sound like a snort. "Then you're a better person than she is. She won't let go of something that happened freshman year, and I didn't even do anything to her deliberately."

"Well," I said, "they invited me to lunch, and to this party tonight, and it's not like I've made very many friends since coming here, so I'm willing to give it a chance."

"I'm sorry about that." When I looked at him this time, guilt had twisted his features into a frown. "I should be introducing you to more people. I did want you to come to the football game with me that time."

"And when I didn't, you brought your tailgate to my place of employment," I said wryly. "I remember. But my loner status isn't your fault, believe me. I've never had a lot of friends."

"I don't remember that about you from Cornell. You and Cristina were always really tight."

I smiled. "I talked to her tonight, actually. She says hi."

His eyes widened. "Did you tell her about…things?"

I put my hand on my hip and my tone became mock-scolding. "I thought you were all about telling people the truth."

"I am." He grinned. "I just want to know if anything incriminating is about to pop up on my Facebook page."

"Don't worry," I said. "Cristina is the soul of discretion." That was also the truth. I didn't have to worry about her posting something squealy on his wall while he was still "in a relationship."

Especially since right now we were the very definition of "it's complicated."

"So…," he said after we worked for a few minutes more. "Party?"

"Yeah. My first official Canton party." Should I invite him? Would that be weird, what with Melanie and Elaine and all the backstory with them? Not to mention how he and I should probably spend as little social time with each other as possible.

"Where's it at?"

"Beta house?"

He laughed.

"What?"

"Nothing," he said, a huge grin splitting his face. "That's just the frat your friend Todd is in."

Oh crap. Well, it was a party. The chances I'd run into Todd were slim, right? "What are you doing tonight?"

"Homework," he replied. "I've fallen a bit behind the last few days."

I nodded and looked down at my notes. "How was the appointment this morning?"

He shrugged. "Fine, I guess. The actual biopsy was fine. We're just waiting for results now. Hannah and her mom have gone up to Manhattan for the weekend. She wants to take her mind off it or something, I guess. Shows, shopping, whatever they do."

I knew what they did. And I knew that when they did it, my dad usually spirited my mom away for a weekend somewhere, too.

"So you're alone," I blurted without thinking. I raised my eyes. He was looking at me, too, and there might as well have been a big red warning sign flashing across his forehead. "I mean —it's nice Hannah is out of town."

"I know what you mean."

"No—I really am glad that she's getting her mind off things. Not just because—" My cheeks heated. Not just because I'd prefer she get her comfort from someone other than her boyfriend. I'd never been to Manhattan or seen a Broadway show, though once when I was young, Mom took Dad to see *The Lion King* on Broadway and they brought me back a beautiful mask from the theater gift shop. If you were trying to get your mind off things, that had to be a good way to do it, right?

"You know," he said now, "it's funny we're talking about your social life. Hannah asked me about it when she came by the apartment the other day."

The day I'd hidden in his bathroom.

"She mentioned seeing you at the coffee shop and said we should hang out sometime. She wanted to know if you had a boyfriend, if there was anyone she could set you up with."

I raised my eyebrows at Dylan. Didn't he know what that meant in girlspeak? She was fishing for information. I remember what her friend at the coffee shop had said. *Oh, honey, watch out.* Hannah was trying to figure out if Dylan was safe around me.

And he so wasn't. Hannah Swift didn't know the first thing about me, literally. And though he claimed to love me, Dylan didn't either. *How could he love me?* I thought suddenly. How could he love me when he didn't even know me?

FIFTEEN

AT NINE THIRTY, I left the lab. Dylan stayed behind, telling me he'd clean up and transcribe the rest of the notes. I have to admit, I was relieved—there'd be no awkward goodbyes or long, silent elevator rides down to the exit. Elevators were particularly dangerous for us.

I headed over to Beta house, texting Elaine on the way to see if we could meet outside. Though I'd crashed a few Canton parties with Sylvia back in high school, I'd always been the awkward, nerdy, probably obviously-far-too-young-to-be-there girl in the corner. This time, I belonged, but that didn't mean I wasn't nervous.

Melanie and Elaine were waiting when I arrived on the block where the Beta house party was, and they waved me over. Despite the chilly weather, the party had spilled out onto the lawn, where students were drinking and dancing under strings of lights. There was a beer pong game going on in one corner of the yard, and the porch was covered with other kids, sitting and standing, all holding plastic cups.

"Hey there," said Melanie. She was wearing a translucent red top and a short skirt over patterned tights. Elaine, whom I'd only ever seen with a messy bun, had let her hair down, where it shone like black silk in the lights from the party. She was in a soft white sweater and had lined her eyes with thick kohl.

"Ready to get your party on?" my old Bio-E nemesis asked.

I raised my hands and shimmied them in front of me like I was dancing. "Lead the way."

The Beta house was one of the nicer fraternities on campus and had the reputation of being the realm of the legacy boys. The furnishings showed it—leather couches and wood-paneled walls where pictures of Beta boys from years past in suits and tuxes smiled All-American smiles, and trophies from members' various sporting and academic accomplishments filled the bookshelves. The decor was at distinct odds with the house music, which filled the space with a persistent, pulsing beat so loud I was surprised the pictures didn't rattle right out of their frames.

"First stop: keg," Melanie announced, and we got in line near the kitchen. "Wonder if Jon's here tonight."

"Oh my God," Elaine said, rolling her eyes and pulling out her phone, "I can't believe you're still into him. You know he only trots you around to make his parents nervous."

Melanie tugged on her eyebrow piercing. "Yeah, but I don't care. I like making parents nervous. I give mine heart attacks."

Elaine laughed and nudged her friend. "Mine, too."

"Me, E? If they knew the truth about you, they'd fall over dead." Melanie turned to me. "What about you? Have your eye on anyone in particular?"

"Not really," I said. "Frat boys aren't usually my type."

"Don't knock it 'til you've tried it," said Melanie.

Elaine made a face. "Next time, I pick the activity, guys, and I promise you frat boys will not be a part of it."

"Let me translate that for you," Melanie shouted over the music. "She means we'll be watching ladies' field hockey."

"It's the skirts," Elaine said, looking wistful.

"I have to agree," said the guy standing behind me. "The skirts are nice. Sorry, couldn't help but overhear. I'm Chris." He stuck his hand out.

"Tess," I replied and shook it. Chris was half a head taller than me, with close-cropped sandy brown hair and broad shoulders. "Give us a break. The music's so loud, you had to do some serious eavesdropping to follow that conversation."

"Are you kidding me?" Chris asked. "Gorgeous lesbians? How could I live up to the stereotype of a frat boy if I didn't listen in?"

"Only one lesbian, thank you very much," said Melanie with a coy smile. "Jury's still out on me."

"Intriguing," said Chris. "And you, Tess?"

"Boringly straight."

"Me too," he said. "So dull, right?"

I rewarded Chris with a chuckle, and he grinned at me.

By this time, we'd reached the front of the line, and Melanie took charge of passing out the SOLO cups.

"So what are you doing at this party if you don't like frat guys?" he asked as Melanie held out her cup to the brother manning the keg.

"I'm here for the beer pong," Elaine said. "I'll kick your ass at it."

"She's telling the truth," Melanie added. "She had to get good because she can't hold her liquor at all."

"You don't drink, you don't like guys—I'm not sure we've done the right advertising for this party," Chris said to Elaine.

"But I did bring hot, straight friends," Elaine said to reassure him. "And they're both single, too."

"Fair enough," Chris replied. "You've earned your keep."

I stuck my cup out next but as soon as the brother turned on the tap, foam spluttered onto my hand.

"Sorry," he said. "Kicked." A moan went up from the line behind me.

Chris nudged me. "Let's not wait. Come on, I have a secret supply."

I followed him down the hall to a door marked Brothers Only. He knocked in some weird pattern on the door, which opened a crack. He held up two fingers and was rewarded with two cans of beer. "Cheers," he said, handing me one.

I popped the top. "Membership has its privileges."

We made our way back to where we'd left Melanie and Elaine, but by the time we'd arrived, they'd vanished.

"I'm guessing the beer pong table?" I suggested.

"Probably." He didn't seem in any hurry though. "So, what year are you?"

"Junior," I said automatically. "Wait, no. Sophomore."

"Um…?" He gave me a side-eye.

I was instantly transported back to high school, when we were the townie teens crashing frat parties. "I just transferred in, and I lost some credits, so technically I guess I've still got four semesters to go after this."

"I see." He looked relieved. "Where'd you come from?"

"State. But the Bio-E program here is way better."

"Bio-E?" He whistled through his teeth. "I had no idea I was in the presence of a genius."

I rolled my eyes and took a drink of the beer. "What are you studying?"

"Art history," he said with a shrug. "But the pertinent point, if you ask my parents, is that I'm pre-law. Going to Columbia next year."

"Nice."

"Thanks. Just heard last week."

"Cheers." I clinked my beer can against his and we both drank, but when I lowered the can this time, I caught sight of Dylan.

He was here. He was staring at me. I almost choked on my beer. Holy heaven, he was something. We were at a frat party and there were plenty of hot guys around, but Dylan… *Dylan*. There was something about him. Always had been. Every mitochondrion in every cell in my body seemed to get up and can-can whenever he was near.

"Hey, Chris!" Another brother swooped in. "Can I get you to give me a hand for a minute?"

"Sure." He turned to me. "You going over to beer pong? I'll catch up with you there."

I dragged my eyes away from Dylan. "Yep."

"Okay. I'll meet you there. Don't leave until you see me." He left with his friend, and Dylan and I...*floated* together. I don't even remember walking. We were just suddenly standing across from each other, so close I could smell him, touch him, kiss him if I wanted.

"Hey," Dylan called over the music. How was it I could spend all evening with him in a lab and when he showed up at a party, in that same sweater and jeans, it was like I hadn't seen him in months? I soaked up every detail, the errant curl flopping down over his temple, the blue eyes, bright as beacons, the dark crew-neck sweater soft enough to dive into...

"What are you doing here?" I asked, trying to ignore the heartbeat-skipping going on in my chest. "I thought you had to study."

"Too distracted."

"By Hannah?"

"By you," he admitted. "By the fact that you went to a frat party. By what you wore tonight."

Beer or no beer, my mouth went dry. We were in public. I lowered my voice until it was barely audible over the music. "You know, Dylan, you don't always have to tell the truth."

"I've spent almost every day since you got here pretending I don't want you back," he replied in that same soft tone. The heavy beat of the music rushed over and through me, as warm as the words falling from his lips. "I've spent years telling myself that. I'm done lying, to you, to myself, to everyone."

"Dylan!" I whispered harshly. "Stop. Anyone could hear you."

"I don't care."

I knew that wasn't true. He didn't want to hurt Hannah, and if this got back to her, with what she was going through... "Come here." I tugged the sleeve of his sweater, then turned and walked off.

I wasn't sure where we were going. I left my mostly untouched can of beer on a random table. I passed hallways, sitting rooms, a library, a bathroom—to judge by the line of people waiting outside—alcoves with couples entwined around each other, locked doors and open doorways filled with people...

"Here," I said, opening one narrow door and slipping inside. Dylan trailed in after me and I slammed the door shut, plunging us both into darkness.

Inside the closet, the music was muffled, little more than a background beat. I could hear him breathe, hear the blood rushing in my head. The space was slightly musty with the scent of winter coats. I could feel the edge of a pair of skis near my elbow, the curve of a lacrosse stick behind my hip.

"A closet?" Dylan's voice came from near my ear. Heat poured off him from inches away. I could smell him—soap and wool and something woodsy and wild. "This is less like a frat party and more like a middle-school sleepover."

"Dylan, we have to be careful." My voice came out like I was pleading with him.

He was silent. "Why is it you seem to care more about protecting Hannah than even I do? Am I that callous?"

No, he just wasn't practiced in deceit. "I don't know how you can say that when you spent all morning taking her to her biopsy," I blurted. "There are boyfriends who *don't* want to break up with their girlfriends that wouldn't bother doing that."

"I find that difficult to believe."

Did he really? I thought about my dad not coming to see me that time I was in the hospital. It was too dangerous for his reputation. And though appendectomies were rarely lethal, I was still an eight-year-old girl who could have used her daddy.

Dylan didn't strike me as the kind of guy who cared about appearances. It was people who mattered. And I loved him for it.

I loved him. It rose in my throat, almost escaped my lips, a safe soft sound in the closet, but he spoke again.

"I wish her friends were as sweet to her as you're being. I wish you two could *be* friends."

The bubble popped. "Not going to happen."

"I know." He sighed. Maybe so, but he had no idea why such a thing was so impossible. "I'm sorry I came here tonight."

I wasn't. He was *right here*. I imagined electrons leaping across from him to me, arcing tiny, microscopic connections between our bodies, invisible to the naked eye but stronger and brighter than steel. We could touch. Atomically, we already were. I could pull him to me right now. I balled my hands against my thighs.

"I could have lived without seeing you flirt with that guy."

What guy? I couldn't remember ever having talked to someone else. I didn't think I had ever set foot out of this closet. Dylan was a black hole, and I was falling in.

"I know I don't have the right to be jealous. I know. I know, but..." There was a soft thump on either side of my head and I jumped. His hands.

He laughed, low, little more than a breath. "You can't see me, can you?"

I shook my head ever so slightly.

"That's funny. I can see you." As if to prove it, he traced a finger down the side of my face.

I let out a shuddering breath.

"I can tell your eyes are wide, your pupils dilated."

"You imagine it, you mean." But I was pretty sure he could hear me panting. Was there a radiator or something in this closet? I was going to die from the heat.

"You're biting your lip."

I was. I stopped. "You're just listing stuff that happens when I get turned on." Shit. I just admitted I was turned on.

He chuckled. "Is it weird that I have worse eyesight than you, but better night vision?"

"More like I'm back here and you're getting some light shining on me from the crack in the door."

"Shhh." His thumb reached my chin and he tilted my head up. "Stop being rational."

He was going to kiss me. He was going to kiss me less than

two days after we'd agreed we couldn't be together right now. I turned my head to the side and his face hit my hair.

"Tess, Tess..." His words were hardly audible, but they hit my soul like a distress call. He leaned against me, pushing me back to the closet wall, chest to chest, hip to hip. I stumbled and clutched his shoulders for balance, taking a wider stance on my spiky-heeled boots. His sweater was soft but scratchy. This was right but so, so wrong. I felt his cheek stubble graze my jaw. His knee nudged between my parted thighs.

I moaned—just for an instant—then clamped my traitorous mouth shut. I was *not* that girl.

He brushed my hair off my neck, and I felt the soft whisper of his mouth on my skin, right where my throat met my collar.

For a second, neither of us moved, each waiting for the other to come to our senses and stop.

But there was no being sensible in the dark. We weren't in a real place, this wasn't a real time, and nothing counted. He pressed against me, his leg rubbing between mine, turning the crease of my jeans into the most delicious friction. I bit back another moan and my hands migrated to his hips, pulling myself closer until I was almost resting my full weight on his thigh. Oh, *yes*.

The music was far away, the party was in another galaxy, but I could hear the rhythm, pounding, pounding. My hips moved, ever so slightly, to the beat, a fraction of an inch—press, tilt—not enough, of course. Not even close, but it felt more necessary in that moment than breathing. He moved closer, too, pressing in opposition. Press, release, press, release, until I thought I'd explode.

The back of my head thunked against the wall near his hands. As I arched my back, I felt the tip of his nose trace the line of my throat, his lips a millimeter away from my skin, a path of wet heat from my pulse point to my chin. The ache between my legs deepened, throbbing to the beat of that far-away music. He leaned over me, his sweater brushing against my breasts, and I longed for his hands on them, but he wouldn't, he couldn't. That would make it too real, too concrete, too obvious that we were actually doing this.

The bargaining continued as he braced his hands on the wall above my head and breathed harshly against my ear, as lost as I was, as desperate to go on. *It's okay,* I wanted to tell him. *It doesn't count. We're not even kissing.*

Like whores do.

The thought fell like a sheet of ice between us. My hands dropped to my sides and I slid off his leg. "Stop. Stop, Dylan. Stop."

He backed off immediately.

"I'm not this girl," I mumbled. "Not this girl who fucks some guy with a girlfriend in a closet at a frat party. Oh, God, what are we doing?" I fumbled for the door.

"Tess, don't—" He reached for me. I needed air, I needed light, I needed out. *Reality.*

I practically fell out of the closet. Blinking in the light, I saw a handful of people staring at me.

"That's *so* not a bathroom," I trilled, pretending to be tipsy. "Oops." I hope I didn't look as mussed, as flushed and hot and turned-on and *guilty* as I felt.

Eyes downcast, I hurried down the hall and through the house out on to the yard. The lights on the lawn bathed everything in harsh, multi-colored reality. Spilled beer and crushed plastic cups. Trash and crowds and cold, grim air. Reality. Escape. My car—still parked outside the lab—

"There you are!" said Elaine. I practically ran right into her. "Where did you disappear to? That Chris guy is looking for you—"

Chris. Right. That guy in line for the beer. He'd been cute, he'd been funny...but he hadn't been Dylan. God, what was wrong with me? Why couldn't I like the nice, available frat boy?

"I have to go home," I said, and I completely failed at keeping my voice in acceptable levels of calm.

"Tess, what's wrong?" Her eyes narrowed and she reached for me. "Do you feel all right? What did you have to drink?"

"Tess!" It was Dylan. "Wait."

Elaine looked from me to Dylan. "What's going on?"

I squeezed my eyes shut. This was a nightmare.

"Tess is fine," Dylan said to Elaine. "I'm going to walk her back to her car..."

"No," I said. If he walked me back to my car, we'd end up doing it on the hood. "I'm fine. I just want to go home."

"Let me go with you," Elaine was saying now. "It's late, and I'm not sure you—"

"I've got this," Dylan said to her. "She's fine."

"Back off, Kingsley," Elaine snapped. "She was fine twenty minutes ago, and now she looks like she might cry."

I took a deep breath and gave them both a long, hard glare. "I'm fine. I don't need anyone to walk me anywhere. I just want to go home." I looked at Elaine. "Don't worry about me. I had two sips of a beer I opened myself. No one has slipped me a roofie." I turned to Dylan. "Don't. Just...don't."

He looked stricken but gave a tiny nod. I almost gave in right there. But I didn't. I turned on my stupid, sexy, too-high heels and walked away.

I was not that girl.

SIXTEEN

I WAS halfway home before my heart stopped pounding, and it wasn't until I was in the shower that the queasy feeling in my stomach subsided. I pressed my palms flat against the tiled walls of our shower stall and took several deep breaths.

It was close back there. And I had no idea how it had happened.

There were times in my childhood, especially once I was a teenager and understood the truth behind my existence, when I'd wondered what my mother had been thinking. At what point in her early interactions with my father she had thought to herself, "I don't give a shit that he's married and has made a commitment before God and man to some other women, I'm going to take all my clothes off and have sex with him anyway." I thought there had to have been a moment where she made that decision, where it lay before her, a giant YES/NO button for her to look at and then choose.

But that hadn't happened back in the closet. We were having a discussion and then we were doing...*things*, and I'm not sure where one ended and the other began.

I had made a decision, though, before things got too dire. I'd left. I'd *run*, to be perfectly honest. But I'd had to. If I didn't leave right then, right that very second, I would have capitulated. I'd have pressed the giant, blinking red YES button and become that girl. The one who slept with her sick sister's boyfriend.

I started feeling queasy again.

What was it about Dylan? Was it that he was taken? Was *that* the kind of person I was—the one who liked boys who weren't available? Would I want Dylan as much as I did if he were free? He had been free, back at Cornell, and I'd been able to walk away. What had changed? Why couldn't I walk away now?

I got out of the shower, toweled off, and brushed my teeth. Once my hair was dry enough to stop dripping, I changed into a pair of my mom's old silk pajamas. Over the years, Dad had bought her plenty of sexy negligees, but they seemed to gather dust in the bottom of her lingerie drawer. I'd never seen her wearing anything but these—loose, silky drawstring pants and matching tops. Sometimes they were fancy, kimono-style tops with embroidered dragons and palm fronds, but this was a simple blue button-down. The material shivered over my feverish skin, cool and soothing, a sensual delight that had nothing to do with sex.

Suddenly, it was very easy to understand what Mom liked about these PJs.

It was barely eleven thirty, but I climbed into bed anyway. Mom had already retired to her bedroom, but though I could see the light from her bedroom TV flickering under the door, I opted not to bother her. What would I say?

Mom, when you started having sex with Dad behind his wife's back, did you ever have a crisis of conscience, or did you just decide that he looked so handsome and smelled so good and felt so amazing that you really didn't care whose lives you'd be ruining?

Mom, I'm thinking of continuing the family tradition of having an affair with a guy who should be with a Swift woman. Thoughts?

Hey, Mom, just wondering how you feel about me sleeping with my sister's boyfriend. Think it violates Dad's rules? What if we just don't tell her? After all, it's worked for you all these years.

I threw my arm over my face to muffle my cry of frustration.

Mom, I'm screwing up. I don't know what to do. I don't want to be that girl. But I love him. What do you do if you love him?

I knew what she had done. She'd thrown caution to the wind and taken what she wanted, even though it belonged to someone else.

He was mine first.

Yes, there were differences. Dylan and I—we had history, long before Hannah. And nobody was married yet. And the big one: I *hadn't* slept with him when I'd had the chance.

And I wouldn't, either. Not until everything was resolved. I could offer my secret sister that, at least. Maybe I'd take her boyfriend, but I wouldn't betray her.

My phone buzzed on my nightstand. I didn't even have to see the screen to know it was Dylan. I let it ring, once, twice, three times, then lost my nerve and picked it up.

"Don't hang up," he said at once.

"I'm not going to. I wouldn't have answered if I didn't want to talk."

He sighed in relief. "Thank God. The only reason I'm not at your door right now is because I realized I don't know where you live." He stopped. "I don't even know where you live, Tess."

I imagined him running up the stairs to my apartment, banging on the door, waking up all the neighbors and my mom like he was the hero in some romantic movie. Jesus, Tess. What was next? Picturing him out in the parking lot, holding up a boom box as the sun rose?

Of course he didn't know where I lived. How could I invite him by when there was a good possibility my dad might show up at any time? To be perfectly honest, I wasn't used to having people over to my house. Friends would visit when I was younger for play dates and later, sleepovers, and now occasion-ally Sylvia stopped in, but nothing else. I didn't even know what Mom's policy was about guys coming over. It had never been an issue in high school, and I'd had my own apartment at State.

"What happened at the party," he was saying, "I thought—I don't know. I wasn't thinking."

I hadn't been either. That was the problem. One dark, empty closet and I was going to break the promises we'd made just a few days ago.

"Where are you right now?" he asked. "Home? Let me come over."

No freaking way. "No. I'm in bed."

There was a pause. "Oh, then definitely let me come over."

He said it like a joke, but I knew better. If he came over, that would be the end of all my good intentions.

"No."

"Tess—"

"I can't be around you," I whispered. "I can't stop myself." Maybe it was genetic. My parents couldn't stop themselves, either.

"I can't *not* be around you," he replied. "How's that for a conundrum?"

My insides thrilled at his words, even as my conscience pinged. "Dylan, please…"

"You know, I couldn't actually see you tonight," he went on. "Not really."

I had no idea what he was getting at.

"But I still knew exactly what you looked like." Another pause, and some rustling. Where was he? Back in his studio apartment in Swift? Sitting on his rumply futon bed? Lying on it? "Want to know why?"

Yes. "No."

Dylan went on like he hadn't even heard me. "That day at Cornell. You weren't only the first girl I'd ever slept with, Tess. You were also the first girl I'd ever made come."

I caught my breath.

"The first girl I'd ever *seen* come. Clearly I was watching all the wrong porn in high school."

I laughed nervously. "You've found better porn?"

"I don't need porn," he said softly. "I just remember you."

Oh my God.

"A lot."

Oh. My. God.

"Your eyes, wide, like you were surprised and happy—thrilled, maybe? Your face flushed. And your mouth open, your lips pink and wet and perfect." His voice was soft and languid and I knew he must be lying in his bed too. Maybe that was the rustling. Oh, I was in *so* much trouble.

"And the sounds you were making," came Dylan's voice in my ear, soft and close as if he were sharing my pillow.

I don't think what I was doing could properly be called breathing anymore. It was panting.

"Kind of like now." He chuckled, low and smooth, and I felt moisture pool between my legs. "Like you didn't want me to know how hot I was making you. But I knew, Tess. I knew, and I've never forgotten."

I shifted under the covers as if I could escape him, escape his voice, but he went on, slow and steady and insistent, and even the silk of my pajamas was an affront. My nipples were hard and tingly against the fabric, my skin felt too tight, too hot, too sensitive, and that throbbing I'd felt in the closet was back in full force.

"It's really clear to me, Tess, because I've thought about it quite a bit. For two years."

My hand drifted lazily over the waistband of my pants. *No. No, Tess.* I was not going there. Phone sex was off-limits as much as closet sex.

"Every time I touch myself." Was it my imagination, or was he breathing heavily too? I lay there, listening, my body sobbing for release, and I thought of Dylan, for two years, touching himself and remembering me, imagining me, wanting me…

"What do you think about?" he asked, and there was no mistaking it now. Breathless. "Tell me, Tess."

No. I would not respond. I couldn't control Dylan's imagination, but I wasn't going to cross the line.

"Tell me," he coaxed.

"You," I admitted miserably. I took a deep breath. "Of course it's you. It'll be you for years after tonight, you jerk."

He was quiet for a long, long moment. I thought I'd lost him.

"Dylan?"

"See?" he said, his tone all smug and satisfied. "You can avoid me if you want, but it doesn't change things. Believe me. I've wanted you for two years, and I didn't see you once."

"What the hell, Dylan!" I barely kept my tone low enough not to wake the whole building. "That was supposed to be a *lesson?*"

"No," he said. "Just the truth. I love you, Tess. Goodnight." The line went dead.

I wanted to throw my phone across the room. But instead I turned off the light, rolled over, and finished the job Dylan had started.

EARLY THE NEXT MORNING, I emailed Dylan.

I've canceled our lab reservation this evening, since Elaine has offered to share and I could use the shift at Verde. She told me we can use it Tuesday and Wednesday next week. Have a good weekend.
-Tess

There. That should do it. The hints were heavy enough. Three blissful days in which I wouldn't see him once. Three miserable, interminable days in which I would never even set eyes on Dylan Kingsley.

The only way to get through this was to work, and work hard. After my Friday classes, I headed straight to Verde and changed into my waitress uniform. Once the lemons were sliced to within an inch of their lives, the silverware and napkin rollups bundled so tightly they could have passed for tourniquets, the candleholders polished, and the liquor bottles on the rail refilled, I decided to wash down the prep fridge.

Sylvia found me elbow-deep in the ice machine. "You know

we have a duty roster, right? And you're only supposed to pick *one* task?"

I wiped my hands off on my apron. "Yeah. I just needed to work off some extra energy."

"I don't believe it," she replied, crouching beside me. "Canton Bio-E, working here four nights a week, and that whole symposium thing? No one with your schedule has extra energy."

Would she accept sexual frustration? My solo session the previous evening had barely even taken the edge off. Every time I closed my eyes, I remembered that dark closet. I couldn't look at my clothes hangers without blushing this morning. "You should talk. You've got voice lessons, band practice, and every night you aren't here you're either performing or babysitting Milo."

"Yeah, and I only do one task on the duty roster," Sylvia pointed out.

I tossed the rag into the laundry bin. "Fine. Someone else can finish the fridge."

"Besides," she went on, "Annabel keeps saying if I were really serious about my career I wouldn't stay in Canton."

Annabel was right, but that didn't make a difference. Sylvia would never leave her sister and her nephew. Not while they were all alone. The Warren girls were a team, always. No matter how much Sylvia wanted to be a professional singer, if it meant abandoning her sister, it wasn't going to happen. At least not until Milo was a little older and Annabel had her nursing degree and some extra income. There was no point in saying any of this to her, either. It was all known, open, easy. Sylvia lived by rules just as ironclad as my own, but where hers required her to stay near her sister, mine required me to stay away from mine.

"Any big shows coming up?"

"Big? No. And 'shows' might be pushing it, too. We're going to be making noise at a coffee shop down the street the week of Thanksgiving. You know, when all the students are home and we aren't in competition for the open mic night."

"Hey, congrats!" I said. "I'll come."

"Please don't." She rolled her eyes. "It's humiliating."

"Yeah," I replied, "but the singing will be good."

Sylvia rolled her eyes again, but this time, she was smiling. "And we should make a plan for the big two-one, right? Next week?"

I nodded. "Monday."

"What do you want to do?"

Get drunk and sleep with Dylan. "I don't know. Nothing fancy. Or gross. I hate those twenty-first birthday parties where they make the person do shots and stuff."

"Absolutely not," said Sylvia. "We should go to a fancy bar where they card and order gourmet cocktails."

I made a face. "Don't you think we spend enough time at a bar? Seriously, why does the theme of every twenty-first birthday have to be alcohol?"

"What theme would you prefer, birthday girl?"

Silk sheets and candlelight. "I don't know. Maybe I won't even drink on my birthday." The last two times I'd had so much as a sip of alcohol, I'd wound up making out with my secret sister's boyfriend.

But I couldn't tell Sylvia that. First of all, she didn't even know I had a sister. Second, she'd probably cheer me on. Hannah, to her, was a Lady Who Lunched.

Sylvia frowned. "I'm pretty sure that's against the rules."

"I'm sick of the rules," I said, probably more vehemently than I needed to. But I was. I was sick of rules that kept the most important things about my life from the people I cared about. I was sick of rules that meant I couldn't tell Dylan exactly why this whole situation freaked me out. I was sick of all of it.

She raised her hands in defeat. "Fine. Fine. We'll have balloons and a cake and those little pointy paper hats. Like you're six. Better?"

I gave her a weak smile. "You win. We'll go out. Maybe that new fancy Mexican place? Pitchers of margaritas and bottomless bowls of guac sound about right."

"Yay!" She squeezed my shoulder. "There's the spirit."

The rest of the day passed as Fridays do, with the genteel lunch crowd making way for the rowdy college kids at night. On Saturday, the cycle started all over again. I didn't hear from Dylan—not even his usual "Eureka" emails where he told me about every new thought or plan he had for our project. I was simultaneously relieved and terrified. This was what I wanted, wasn't it? For Dylan to leave me alone while he sorted everything out with Hannah? This was what I'd begged him for, right before he'd done exceptionally naughty things to me from half a town away...just to prove that he could.

He wasn't teaching me a lesson this time. He was just doing as I asked. I'd wanted him to leave me alone this weekend, and he was. But he was still right. I didn't need him around to think about him, to miss him, to long for him with an ache so strong I could barely sleep nights. Every time a dark-haired guy came through the front door at Verde, I looked to see if it was him. I thought I heard someone call his name a dozen times that weekend. It never was, and I hated myself for wanting it to be. I hated the times I picked up my phone, scrolled to his number, and almost pressed Call. I hated the times my mouse hovered over the Reply button of the last email he'd sent me. I hated the fact that if we did make contact again, if I did break down and call him, if I so much as glimpsed him on the street, I'd lose every shred of my self-control and leap into his arms.

Worst of all, I didn't actually hate any of those things. I just wished I did.

SEVENTEEN

ON MONDAY MORNING, I awoke to the smell of butter and cinnamon. Still wrapped in my robe, I padded out into the kitchen, where I found my mom hard at work at the counter.

"Sweetie!" she cried. "Happy Birthday!"

I gave her a kiss. "French breakfast puffs?"

"For my girl? You bet."

I had no idea why we called them French, but they were a house specialty. The "puffs" were essentially little muffins dipped in butter and then rolled in cinnamon sugar, and they were every bit as decadent as that sounds. Mom reserved the treat for holidays and birthdays, and I could eat two or three at a sitting. "Mmm. Is there coffee?"

"Yes, and I used some of that chicory your father brought back from New Orleans last month."

I poured two cups of the fragrant, rich coffee as my mom rolled the last of the puffs in the cinnamon-sugar mixture. The secret to French breakfast puffs was eating them warm.

"Besides," Mom said. "I figured it was important to get some nice, fatty food in you today before you go off and do tequila shots with your friends."

"Sylvia promised no one would make me do shots," I said,

snatching a puff off the plate. "But yes, we will be having a ton of tequila."

"Who is your designated driver?" When I rolled my eyes at her, she held up her hands. "Sorry, I'm your mom. Can't turn it off."

"Annabel. She has a big test tomorrow and wants to make sure she's rested. Thank you for volunteering to watch Milo, by the way."

"No problem. I remember those days," said Mom, taking a sip of coffee. "Desperate to find anyone to watch you while I went out with my friends once in a while. And I remember being the designated driver at all my friends' twenty-first birthday parties. It's easy when you're pregnant."

I nodded, realizing I was now the same age Mom had been when she'd had me. There'd been no tequila on her twenty-first birthday and no fancy dinner out with her boyfriend, the father of her child. I couldn't imagine what I'd do if I were facing the same choices my mom had been at this age. Pregnant? Babies? Dropping out of school? No way.

"Don't go getting pregnant," she added, winking when she saw what was probably a look of horror on my face. "You need to get that PhD first."

"You bet."

"Are any friends from school going out with you tonight?" she asked.

Fishing, Mom? "I invited these two girls I went to the party with last week."

"Any boys? What about that mysterious lab partner of yours? Dylan?" It had been a few weeks before I'd even been willing to tell my mom his name, I was so nervous she might mention it in front of my father. There were probably several Dylans at Canton, but the Bio-E connection might raise his suspicions that my Dylan was the same as Hannah's boyfriend Dylan, and if I was lab partners with him, I must be hanging out with his girlfriend, despite our rules. Eventually, however, I decided that not saying his name was even more suspicious than just mentioning it offhand. But Mom seemed to think there was nothing more to our relationship than that.

It may have helped that I'd made a face when she'd asked if Dylan was cute.

I shook my head. "I think this'll be a girls' night out."

"That sounds fun, too."

Mom and I finished our breakfasts and made plans to meet after lunch for birthday pedicures, and then I got ready for school. My organic chemistry class started at nine.

I arrived at campus at ten 'til, parked, and walked over to the chemistry department, feeling good and filled with French breakfast puffs. It was my birthday, so I'd had four.

As I went to my usual seat in the classroom, I noticed something on top of my desk: a small red leather jewelry box with a silk ribbon tied around it, and an envelope sitting underneath.

"Where did this come from?" I asked Liz, the pre-med who sat across from me. Near the front of the class the TA, Jess, caught sight of me and came over.

"Your boyfriend brought it," she said, bouncing a little bit, a big grin plastered on her face. She was the only chem student I'd met who ever bounced. "He asked me where you sat. Happy birthday, by the way."

"I don't have a boyfriend." I slid the card out from under the box.

"Black hair, blue eyes, super cute?"

And as if that wasn't enough, I recognized the handwriting on the envelope immediately. "Oh. He's just my Bio-E lab partner."

"Come on," said Jess the TA. "Open it. We've all been dying for you to get here."

I looked around. There were at least half a dozen pairs of eyes on me.

"It looks like a ring box, is the thing," Liz said. "*Just your lab partners* don't give rings for birthdays."

I shook my head to dismiss that thought from anyone in class who might be getting the wrong idea and opened the card.

Dear Tess,

    There's a good chance I won't see you today, and I didn't want to miss the opportunity to tell you Happy Birthday.

    I hope it's everything you want.

    Dylan

"What does it say?" Jess asked dreamily.

"Happy Birthday." I turned to the box and untied the bow, worrying my bottom lip with my teeth. It did look remarkably like a ring box. What was Dylan thinking? I opened it.

Inside, nestled against the crush of white satin, was a small silver charm, about an inch and a half long, of a capital letter T. The vertical line was in the shape of a double helix, and the bases —the "rungs" of the twisted ladder — sparkled as I held it in the light. The charm was attached to a silver chain, and I lifted it out, to the oohs and ahhs of my observers.

"Ohhhh, that's so sweet," cooed Jess. "And so perfect for you."

It was. I traced my finger along the edge, staring at it in wonder, and then quickly caught myself. "It's really nice," I managed to say without the words catching in my throat. I found the clasp and fastened it around my neck. I swept my hair out of the way and let the T slide down over my collarbone to nestle just above the curve of my breasts.

"It *is* really nice," Liz agreed. "I think *just your lab partner* doesn't want to be *just* anything."

I waved her off.

"I have to go start class," said Jess, "but I'm with Liz. That boy wants you bad."

I wished they'd stop. There was a chance Hannah had a friend in this class. As the hour progressed, I caught myself fingering the charm around my throat—the smooth horizontal top, the jagged, sparkly edges of the helix. I had no idea where Dylan had found this crazily perfect piece of jewelry for me, but I loved it more than anything I'd ever worn.

After class, I met my mother for my birthday pedicure at her favorite nail salon. Like the breakfast puffs, it had become somewhat of a tradition. We picked our colors—shell pink for me, a fiery coral red for her—and climbed into the big leather massage chairs. As our footbaths filled, Mom told me all about the new commission she was hoping to get, and I stared off into the distance, touching the silver charm and wondering if it would really be that bad if I invited Dylan to dinner with us tonight. Just as friends, of course. There'd be plenty of people there. It was a chance for him to maybe mend fences with Elaine.

And he could see me wearing the charm and know how much his gift meant…

Yeah. No. Bad idea. Terrible. I dropped the charm back on my chest like it had burned me.

"Oh, that's pretty!" my mom said. "How cute. DNA, right? Or…RNA?" She looked at me helplessly.

"DNA," I assured her.

"Who is it from?"

I shrugged. "Secret admirer. I hope if I wear it, he'll show himself to me." Funny how easy lying came if you did it your whole life.

My mom laughed. "Oh, honey, let me tell you about secret admirers. Trust me, if they're secret, it's almost always because you don't *want* to know who they really are. It's probably some total geek who's been making eyes at you all semester across the beakers."

Right on both counts. Dylan had been making eyes at me all semester—eyes and much more. And he was definitely still a geek, even if you couldn't tell to look at him. I mean, who got a girl a DNA necklace?

And what kind of geek was I for loving it so much?

"Well, it's nice to imagine he's some hot stranger," I said again. "In my head, he looks like Henry Cavill." Actually, that wasn't too far from reality, though he had nowhere near the Man of Steel's build. Where Superman looked like, well, an alien superhero, Dylan was a bit leaner, like a runner. Still, the eyes were right.

I shook myself free of the fantasy, realizing I hadn't listened to whatever my mom had been saying.

"Actually, speaking of birthday presents, I have your father's." She reached into her bag and pulled out a long, narrow jewelry box.

I looked at her suspiciously and opened the box. Inside lay a big, beautiful string of vintage pearls. I swallowed. "They're really nice."

She looked relieved. "It was his aunt's. He's been feeling bad that you don't have any of his family's jewelry, but his mom's stuff all went to Marie or…"

"Hannah," I finished. I guess no one would notice one of his aunt's necklaces missing, and a set of pearls weren't distinctive enough to recognize if anyone ever saw it on my neck.

"Try it on," she said. "I want to see how it looks!"

I hesitated. The pearls were pretty enough, but I didn't want to take off Dylan's charm.

"Come on, Tess."

The manicurist started clipping my toenail cuticles, and I stiffened, my muscles tensing in spite of myself. I fastened the pearls around my neck. They were bulky, heavy. Clunking against my collarbone in a way I wasn't entirely sure I liked.

"Oh, they look so beautiful!" My mom exclaimed as a woman went after her heel with what looked like a cheese grater.

"Yeah," I said awkwardly. "I'll have to find someplace nice to wear them." I unfastened them and set the choker gently back in the box. I didn't think I was the kind of girl who wore pearls.

After our pedicures, Mom and I went our separate ways, and I tried to get homework done while counting the hours until I met my friends for my first legal drink.

I'm proud to say I never once called Dylan.

———

TUESDAY MORNING, slightly hung over, I popped two Advil,

drank a large glass of Gatorade, and went to Biotransport class in a blouse cut low enough that the double-helix T was on full display. As I slid into my seat, I caught sight of a bleary-eyed Elaine across the room. She gave me a halfhearted wave. Even though she doesn't usually drink, she joined in on the margaritas last night. Guess she was still paying for it.

"Hi," Dylan said as he sat down beside me. If he saw what I was wearing, I didn't notice.

"Hi," I said. "Thank you." It hardly seemed enough.

"Looks good on you."

"I love it."

He faced me then, his blue eyes hard and piercing.

I love you. I love you, Dylan. It's the most wonderful thing anyone has ever given me and I love you. I tried to communicate it with my eyes, but telepathy, unfortunately, was not a real thing.

"I'm glad." He turned to his notes.

I dropped my hands to my lap, rebuffed. Was he still mad about Thursday night? I'd thought, since the present he'd given me... I stole a glance out of the corner of my eye but he looked like the epitome of studiousness. My left hand migrated under the table to rest on his thigh. He put his hand under the table, too, and covered mine. Our fingers entwined. I squeezed.

He squeezed back.

We stayed like that for the rest of class, me taking notes one-handed on paper while he occasionally pecked something out on his laptop. It was worth it. From time to time, he'd brush his thumb in circles over the back of my hand, kneading that spot between my index finger and my thumb. I could hardly concentrate on what our professor was saying, but it was the best Transport class of all time. When the lecture ended, I reluctantly let go of his hand to pack up.

In silence, side by side, we put away our books and papers, not daring to look at one another. When all my stuff was put in order, I glanced up. "So, tonight? Lab?"

He nodded, his attention focused on his bag. "See you there."

I saw his forehead crease and then he looked up, and the force of his gaze almost blew me backward. "Tess?"

"Yeah?"

He opened his mouth, but nothing came out. After a minute, he shook his head. "Have fun last night?"

"Yeah. Went out for Mexican."

"Nice. How are you feeling this morning?"

Desperate. Impatient. Sexually frustrated. Crazy for you. "A little woozy, but otherwise good."

There was a ghost of a smile on his face. "Yeah, that happens. Try to eat something greasy to soak it up. Do you want to go...?" He stopped himself. "I'll see you tonight."

And then he left. I stood there at the table, wanting very much to kick myself. All those stupid, high-and-mighty ideals of mine. I couldn't see him, or I wouldn't be able to control myself. Well, he was giving me what I wanted. Not even a hangover breakfast at a greasy spoon.

And he'd been right, last Thursday on the phone. It didn't matter if I spent time with him or not. Especially not now, with the soft, T-shaped reminder resting over my heart. Maybe I hadn't been giving my parents enough credit all these years. Lust you could ignore. Lust you could forget. But this was way worse. I was in love with him, and he was never, ever off my mind.

EIGHTEEN

AT FOUR FORTY-FIVE THAT EVENING, a text appeared on my phone from Dylan.

Can't make it tonight.

I wrote him back asking why, but there was no response, so I went to the lab and worked alone for a couple of hours. We were nearing the end of our project, and things were coming together nicely. With no decisions left to be made, the rest was just a matter of data compilation, analysis, and, of course, writing up our final report and presentation. I figured we'd be done in plenty of time for the December symposium—as long as my overenthusiastic partner didn't decide we just *had* to include all kinds of extras.

I smiled, imagining it. That was the Dylan I'd always known, the Dylan of the 3:00 a.m. emails and the Eureka moments and the insistence on bumping whatever it was we were doing up to the "next level" by exploring a new avenue of research or upgrading our charts or including a whole bunch of unexpected extras. It was why I'd decided to work with him back at Cornell, when he was just a cute teenager in too-short pants. It was why

I'd decided to work with him again here at Canton. He was a good partner, and it had nothing to do with how much I wanted him.

When I got home that evening, I sent him a short email, updating him on the progress I'd made at the lab. It was simple and professional, but I'd be lying if I said I didn't keep waiting for the ping of his response for the next few hours. It never came, and the next morning, when I woke up, there was still no new mail from Dylan.

I tamped down my confusion as best I could and headed to school, but no matter how loudly I played the radio in my car, worries crept in. This wasn't like him, to not respond to a progress report. This wasn't like him, to not respond at all.

The day passed. I took notes in Org 3, aced a pop quiz in Stats, and met with my advisor to review my plan for next semester. By noon, I was worried that Dylan might not make it today, either. Actually, I was worried, full stop. He'd never *not* replied to me. Never. Was he sick? Dead in a ditch? Lost his phone in a freak water buffalo stampede? I decided to text him, just to make sure.

We still on for lab tonight?

Fifteen minutes later, there was no response. Another half-hour had passed by the time I finished lunch. Before I left for my 1:00 p.m. class, I tried again.

If you can't come, let me know so I can tell Elaine we don't need the lab slot after all.

A minute later, my phone buzzed.

I'll be there.

So here's the thing. I used to pride myself on not being one of those girls who read into every single word a guy ever said or wrote. But I looked at those three words over and over, trying to figure out why he was being so terse and distant. Yes, we'd had an argument last Thursday, after the…closet. Yes, we hadn't seen each other all weekend. But he'd come in with that necklace on Monday. If he'd been mad at me, he wouldn't have gone out of his way to surprise me in Organic Chemistry.

He wouldn't have held my hand like that all through Transport on Tuesday morning.

Right?

So it was with trepidation that I approached the Bio-E building that evening after dinner, prepared to start our lab session.

Dylan was waiting when I got up to our assigned room. Well, waiting wasn't quite the right word for it. He was working, already set up with print-outs of results spread out on the tables, reviewing the slides on the big overhead projector hooked up to his laptop.

"Hey," I said, setting down my bag.

"Hi." He didn't look up from the computer. "Did you get the readouts from strain seven last night?" He pointed to one of the green test tubes in the long row. "I don't see anything here on that."

"Let me look in my files," I replied. Okay. No chit-chat. "I think it's on the fifth page—"

"Found it," he broke in, his tone terse. "We should really cross-reference that with specimen twelve, because they both showed a significant die-off after we introduced the 'night frost' variable…"

I nodded as he shifted slides on our presentation, talking about green levels and efficiency and all the other things that I could usually discuss with him for hours. But not tonight.

"Dylan—" I could barely get the words out, "—is there something wrong?"

His shoulders lifted in a shrug.

A horrible thought occurred to me. It had been a week since those tests. "Is it Hannah? Is she okay?"

His head still bowed over our work, he replied, "No, she's really not."

My heart stopped. *Hannah.* "What—what is it?"

He looked up at me, and his eyes were tired, wrung out. "I broke up with her."

I leaned against a stool for support. "You—"

He let out a long breath. "I broke up with her last night, Tess. It was really unpleasant and I'm not…I'm not happy with myself right now. It's not your fault. It just is."

I didn't understand. He'd sworn he wouldn't break up with her until she was out of the woods. "But Hannah—her tests—"

He threw his pen down on the table. "She's fine. Her results came back yesterday and she's fine. The nodule on her thyroid is benign. They're going to try her on a medication at first and if it continues to bother her, she's going to have surgery to remove it…but the bottom line is, she's going to be fine."

I slumped against the table. "Thank God." Hannah would be okay, my dad would be relieved, and Dylan and I—well, we were free.

And that hope, that anticipation, must have shown on my face, for he shook his head, disgust painted all over his features. "I…wish I wasn't here, that I wasn't seeing you. I know this is what we wanted, but right now, I feel like a real asshole."

The excitement and relief curdled inside me and I forced myself to nod impassively. "I understand." And I did. Mostly. "Do you want to tell me what happened?"

He looked away. "I haven't…been with Hannah in quite a while. I couldn't. Not when all I wanted was to be with you. And last night, after she got her results back, she wanted to celebrate."

I take it back. I didn't want to hear this. Hannah was healthy. They were broken up. That was all I needed to know.

But Dylan was always one to tell the truth. "And, of course, I didn't want to. It was a betrayal of you, and then I realized that whatever else I'd been trying to be for the last week, I was betraying her, too. I couldn't." He shrugged, helplessly. "So I broke up with her. I told her that I cared about her very much, that I was glad she was going to be okay, and that I thought it best if we went our separate ways."

My heart broke for Hannah right then, for my sister who was getting dumped. "What did she say?"

"What do you think she said!" he snapped. "She cried. I made a really sweet girl cry on the day she found out she didn't have cancer. I'm a big jerk."

For me. He'd done it for me.

"So if I'm a little grumpy today, you know why." He bent back over his work.

I came around the table now and laid my hand on his arm. "Dylan—"

"Don't." He shook me off. "I just…I can't right now, Tess." He looked at me, the expression in his blue eyes stark and crossed with pain. "And I'm not here to collect my reward for hurting her, to just jump from her bed into yours like her feelings don't matter."

"I don't want you to!" I cried. Her feelings did matter. That was what this past week had been about.

His eyes searched mine, looking for some kind of comfort. "I kissed her last night."

I blinked as my stomach dropped to the vicinity of my knees. I knew he must have—on some level, I knew. But knowing it and hearing it was still different.

"I kissed her when she told me, because…I don't know. Because of habit? Because she expected me to?"

I stepped back, and he flinched.

"Yeah, I thought so," he said miserably. "I thought you'd react like that. I betrayed her with you, and now I've betrayed you with her, because she told me she didn't have cancer and I was so happy for her I kissed her. Shit." He stood there for a second, shaking his head, his face downturned. "And then I broke up with her because I realized what an awful thing I was doing. I understand now why you said you didn't want to see me. And back at the party, why you didn't want to kiss me. You were right, even though I wasn't listening to you. It was wrong because it was a lie."

My eyes began to burn. Dylan Kingsley had no idea what it was to lie. Not really. "I would have kissed her, too," I said, honestly. "And I don't even know her."

He laughed mirthlessly.

"Do you think I'm *mad* at you?" I asked, incredulous. "Because you kissed your girlfriend when you were planning to break up with her?" Oh, boy. He had no idea who he was speaking to, did he? My dad had spent twenty years sleeping with my mother and his wife, and never once had he felt guilty enough about it to stop being with either one of them.

"No, Tess." He turned to me again. "*I'm* mad at me."

My heart pumped ice through my arteries. Something was wrong. Something was very, very wrong here. This whole time, I'd trusted Dylan to tell me that this would be okay. That he would break up with Hannah and get together with me and it was all possible. That this was something normal, healthy people with positive relationship examples did. How was I supposed to know—me, the dirty little secret who had no basis to judge— what was right and what was wrong?

He'd sounded so reasonable when we'd made our plan. *I don't want to be with Hannah. I want to be with you. I don't want to hurt anyone, but I can't lie to Hannah.* The path seemed simple: break up with Hannah, in the kindest way possible, and then we'd be able to be together.

Were we kidding ourselves? Were we poisoned now because of the way we'd begun?

"But it's over now," I said, nearly desperate. "It's over."

"Yeah," he replied flatly. "But it's not that easy."

None of this was easy. It hadn't ever been with Dylan. It never would be with Hannah. I'd known it wasn't going to be easy. But I thought it would be enough. Hard, yes, and maybe unpleasant for a little while, but worth it in the end because we loved each other. We wouldn't have bothered with all of this unless we truly loved each other.

"Tell me what you want," I said to him. "Do you want me to go away? Do you want us...to...wait? Do you—" A lump formed in my throat and I found I couldn't speak anymore. *Do you not want to be with me now?*

I felt like I could handle any option but that last one. The silver T around my neck seemed heavy enough to leave a mark. What had all this been for? How could I face the rest of the semester, the rest of this project, without Dylan?

"I don't know." His jaw was clenched. His hands gripped the table. "I shouldn't have come here tonight. I'm not ready. I need to work some things out."

"*Work some things out*"? I repeated. The room closed around me. I couldn't breathe. I was standing here, wearing his necklace like a talisman, waiting for him like it would be okay, like it would happen, like I deserved to be happy after I'd stolen my sister's boyfriend...and of course I didn't. Of *course* I didn't. I wasn't that kind of girl. I was the kind you sneaked around with, the kind who was only exciting if it *meant* sneaking around.

I whirled on my heel and headed back to my bag. It was self-preservation, really. If I didn't leave, I was going to fall to my knees and beg. "Fine, you work some things out. I'm going home."

"No, wait. It's not like that. I just—it's just really complicated, and I—"

Oh, did I ever understand how complicated it was. I had a lifetime worth of experience with complications. He had no idea how complicated it all was. And he never would. I made a beeline for the door, not even daring to look back. It was against the rules. All of this was against the rules, and I'd been a fool to think I could break them.

ON THURSDAY, I was the one to skip Biotransport. I didn't want to see Dylan. Clearly, I needed space just as much as he did.

I logged on to Facebook. I'd been so good all this time. But I had to know. Hannah's profile had, in fact, been updated. It listed her status as "Single" and her wall was filled with "you go, girl" and "he doesn't deserve you" posts from those pretty blonde friends of hers. I thought of what Dylan had said about the lack of support she'd been getting from her female friends over the past week. I didn't know her relationship with the redhead in the coffee shop, but Hannah had kept quiet about her medical news to her. Was Hannah as self-contained in her way as I was in mine? I wondered how many of these posts were from people who really knew Hannah, who knew what she'd been dealing with, who knew how she felt about Dylan, what she wanted from him.

If she loved him.

There was no message from her, no comment about why they'd broken up. Nothing at all, really, in her updates except pictures of her and her mother on their recent trip to Manhattan. Marie Swift was very pretty. A good decade, at least, older than my mom, and blonde, like Hannah and Dad were, her hair a sleek cap that shimmered on her shoulders.

But there was little hint as to Hannah's state of mind. Was she happy about her medical news? Devastated by Dylan dumping her? Had she been talking to friends about it? Had she gone out drinking with a bunch of Ladies Who Lunch to drown her sorrows in martinis and girl-power anthems? If so, it hadn't been at Verde. Sylvia would have told me.

I did finally drag myself away from my laptop and go to Verde for my shift, but around three thirty, I asked Sylvia if I could go home. I claimed a headache, but the pain was much farther down. Close to my heart.

Mom was out when I got home, off helping an artist friend with a studio crisis, so I curled up on the couch and watched mindless TV for hours. At some point I realized I hadn't eaten, so I grabbed some junk from the kitchen and snacked, flipping channels. How long had it been since I'd just vegged out? Forgot about work, about classes, about the lab—just let everything go?

No wonder I hadn't been thinking straight. I hadn't even given myself *time* to think.

Not that I was deep in contemplation now. I wouldn't let myself be. If I found my mind wandering to anything other than the show I was watching, I flipped channels. Thrillers, sitcoms, reality shows—it didn't matter. Anything to distract me from obsessing over whatever had gotten Dylan and me so messed up. Anything to keep from wondering if all along, our case had been hopeless.

After a while, though, the thoughts crowded in, too adamant to ignore.

Fact: He'd been mine first.

Fact: He'd told me he didn't love Hannah and wanted to be with me.

Fact: No one was married. No one was even engaged. We were just in college. It was normal to date lots of people, to break up with lots of people. What, he should marry Hannah just because he'd dated her?

Fact: I'd been fair to Hannah. I'd refused to sleep with her boyfriend while she was still with him.

All of this was fine. But I didn't think I'd spent enough time thinking through the rest of it.

Fact: Even if Dylan didn't love Hannah, he broke up with her for me. For me.

Fact: Dylan wasn't used to deception, and he'd deceived her twice. First when he'd kept dating her after we'd made out. Second, when he didn't tell her he was dumping her for me.

Fact: I was deceiving Dylan, too. If he knew Hannah was my sister, he'd never be with me.

Fact: Never.

Because of me, Dylan had become a liar. Maybe this was my

fate. I was the child of lies. Everything I did was touched by that poison. I'd been so stupid to think there was a happy ending here. Every time Dylan looked at me, he'd remember the look on Hannah's face when he broke her heart. And really, if I stepped back from it all, what did I envision? Keeping my connection to Hannah a secret from him forever? What did my parents envision? What became of our rules when I got old enough to actually bring a guy home, to start my own family? Who was my "father" on the day I got married? Had my parents thought about it at all? Did Dad expect me to wear his aunt's heirloom pearls on my wedding day? Would he even come to my wedding?

Ugh, I was really going down the rabbit hole now. I wasn't getting married, to Dylan or anyone else. I was barely twenty-one. Like Mom had said, I had a whole PhD to wrangle before I started making those kinds of life decisions.

I picked up the remote and switched channels again, finding some sort of home improvement show marathon. Good. No familial dramas there.

I awoke a few hours later to the jingle of Mom's keys in the door. Outside the apartment, the windows were dark, which meant it could be any time from six to eleven.

"Hey, sweetie. I didn't expect to see you home. No work tonight?"

"I was feeling a little under the weather," I lied. Again. All I did was lie.

She switched on the light and looked at me as I blinked. "I'm worried you're pushing yourself too hard. Is it a cold? Did you take anything for it?"

There was nothing to take. And as I sat there under her examination, it all bubbled up inside me, hot and slimy and impossible to ignore. My throat closed up, my eyes burned, and before I knew it, I was overflowing, tears rolling from my eyes and choking sobs emanating from my throat.

"Oh, honey! Honey, what's wrong?" She sat down beside me and slid an arm around my back. "What's going on? Is it your classes?"

I shook my head miserably.

"Is it the money? Because if I get this new commission, I'll be able to help you some with those costs. I knew it was going to be more expensive than you'd figured—"

Another shake of my head. I buried my face in her shoulder. I'd heard the "new commission" talk before, and it never amounted to anything.

"Sweetie, talk to me."

No way. What was I going to say? *Mom, I'm a real chip off the old block. I make men into cheaters, too. Sure, I did insist the guy break up with his girlfriend if he wanted me, but it turns out that doesn't make it any better.*

"I messed up with a boy," I sniffled at last.

She squeezed me tight. "A boy? For real? Oh, Tess..." She chuckled a bit. "You know, most moms I know would figure that was it first off. It says a lot about you that I didn't even think of it." Taking me by the shoulders, she looked into my face. "What happened?"

"I...thought we were going to be together, and we're not."

She gave a knowing nod. "Well, that one, sadly, I have some experience with. Is it Mr. Necklace?" She gestured to the silver T.

I bit my lip, tears flowing anew.

"That's secret admirers for you," she said. "Like I said, there's a reason they're secret. Either you don't want to be with them or they can't be with you. What's up? He have a girlfriend?"

"No." Not anymore.

"Religious differences?"

"No." I didn't even know if Dylan had religion.

She eyed me warily. "He didn't—did he just want to get you into bed?"

I groaned. "I didn't sleep with him, Mom." Not this time, anyway.

Back at Cornell, what Dylan and I had was pure and perfect. We'd met, we'd fallen in love, we'd had sex. There were no rules, no restrictions. No Swifts or secrets hanging over me. We'd both been free and clear and we'd chosen each other. Now, I feared that was all tainted. Tainted by our deception, by my lies, by the rules I lived by and the ones we'd made in the past week. No wonder once he looked at the whole picture, he didn't want me anymore. Maybe I *was* that girl—the one who only worked if it was all a lie.

"Well, that's good!" Her expression had lost none of its concern. "Oh, honey, I don't know what to say. If he doesn't realize what an amazing person you are, then he doesn't deserve you."

It was the right thing to say. It was the patented mother script. It made perfect sense. But Mom hadn't followed it herself. Dad didn't love her enough to leave his wife, and she let him have her anyway.

"Mom," I asked now, in a voice so soft I wasn't even sure it was audible. "If it hadn't been for me, do you think you and Dad would still be together?"

Her eyes widened. "Don't even think about getting pregnant to tie a guy down, Tess. I'll wring your neck."

That wasn't what I'd meant, but it was all the answer I needed. Even now, she was defining it as losing Dad, rather than choosing Dad.

"And don't measure yourself by the choices Dad and I have made."

How could I avoid it, when history kept repeating itself?

NINETEEN

"AND THEN WHAT HAPPENED?" Annabel asked. It was late Friday morning, and we were seated at a big-top table at Verde, rolling silverware in cloth napkins. The powers that be at the restaurant had decided to change from green napkins to black for a "sleeker" look, but that meant doing a buttload of rollups before our shift today.

I was giving the Warren girls the rundown on the latest Dylan developments. Annabel was staring with her mouth open as if I was relating the end of an action movie. Sylvia had stayed very, very silent.

"Then...nothing," I said. "I haven't heard from him since. I even skipped class on Thursday so I didn't need to see him."

"You?" Sylvia gasped. "Skipped class?" She pressed a hand to her heart in mock shock. "Jesus. Annabel, check to see if the Four Horsemen of the Apocalypse are on the reservation list for tonight."

"Ha ha," I said and grabbed a few more forks.

"But seriously," said Annabel. "What's the next step?"

I shrugged as that squeezing feeling started in my chest again. "I don't know. I think...I think maybe we're doomed." My fingers went to the T hanging around my neck. I don't know why I'd put it on again today. Funny how in four short days it had become such a part of me.

Sylvia snorted. "Doomed? Come on, Tess, I'm supposed to be the dramatic one around here. You're the practical, scientific member of the group."

"Fine," I replied. "The hypothesis doesn't fit the data set and is therefore invalidated. Satisfied?" I rolled up a napkin full of silverware and slammed it a little too hard onto my finished pile.

"The data set being what, exactly?" Annabel said. "That he didn't want to jump into bed with you the second he dumped his girlfriend?"

"No…"

"Can you blame Tess for being suspicious?" Sylvia cut in. "He didn't seem to have a problem jumping into bed with her when he *had* one."

Annabel pursed her lips. "What kind of man do you want him to be, Tess? The kind who cheats on his girlfriend with you or the kind who actually cares about a person he dates enough to not want to go running into some other woman's arms before his ex has even had time to process the situation?"

"Haven't you been listening?" Sylvia said. "Dylan's both."

"Dylan's neither," I said. "He didn't cheat—"

"That's debatable," Sylvia mumbled.

"—and not wanting to be with me the other night…that had nothing to do with Hannah. She never would have known what Dylan was up to."

"She didn't have to know what he was up to if he just sneaked around with you, either," Annabel pointed out. "Lots of people cheat on their significant others without their significant others knowing anything about it."

She was telling *me* this? Honestly, sometimes hearing the comments people made about Cheaters and Other Women and Sugar Daddies and Mistresses and whatever else made me want to, first, laugh out loud and, second, give everyone a lesson in reality. We weren't exactly living in a penthouse suite, and my mom's boobs were one hundred percent real.

"But you're not wrong," she continued. "I think the other night had nothing to do with Hannah. It had to do with Dylan. Him wanting some time to himself was just as much about *his* own sense of morality as you not wanting to be with him until he'd broken up with Hannah was about *yours.*"

I blinked at her.

"It doesn't matter what she knows and does not know," Annabel explained. "You didn't want to be the other woman, right?"

"Right."

"And he didn't want to be the guy who bed-hopped." Annabel looked at me triumphantly. "See?"

I remembered what Dylan had said to me, back at the lab. *I'm mad at me.* "But if that were the case, wouldn't he say, 'Okay, let's wait a week and then we can be together'? After all, I gave him rules." Rules like no sex, no kissing, no *phone sex* until he'd broken up with Hannah.

"*Rules?*" Sylvia repeated, incredulous. "What rules?"

I lost my voice. Fortunately, Annabel filled in for me.

"She said she wouldn't be with him until he was single. Which I think was the right move. You respected yourself, you respected Hannah, and now he's trying to show the same respect." She shrugged. "He just…maybe wasn't quite as explicit about what he needed as you were when you asked him?"

"Yeah," said Sylvia, grinning. "Tell me more about these *rules* of yours, Tess. Because in my head, they look that that contract Christian gave Anastasia in *Fifty Shades of Grey.*"

I blushed furiously and stared down at my silverware. Fucking rules. Chalk that up as another thing normal people don't have in relationships.

"I like the idea of rules," Annabel said. "Written down or not. Spells out your relationship. No one is left confused, or hurt, or…" She lifted her shoulders and went back to rolling.

Or alone and pregnant without a clue of what she might expect from the father of her child, as Annabel had been. Yeah, rules could come in handy. At least by following the rules, my mother knew she could count on her lover to take care of her and their baby.

The trouble was, I was already in the middle of a game with Dylan, and I had no idea what we were playing.

———

SOMETIME DURING MY shift that evening, I felt a text buzz through to my phone. I pulled it out of my pocket to look at the display.

Can I see you tonight?

I showed Sylvia, who was passing with a tray. She shook her head, skepticism painted all over her features. "Last-minute enough for you? Might as well say, 'Can I see you tonight for a booty call?'"

No. At work, I typed back.

I checked on a few tables, then looked at my phone again.

After work is fine. I can come to Verde.

Sylvia snatched the phone from my hand. When she handed it back, I saw she'd typed:

After work is time for my beauty rest. You think this happens all by itself?

I shrugged and pressed send.

"Good girl," said Sylvia. "Make him sweat."

Except I was the one sweating. If he wanted to see me tonight, did that mean he was ready to be together, or did it mean he wanted to tell me it would never happen?

Either way, Sylvia probably had it right. I should play it cool. Don't let him know how much I needed him. My fingers went to my throat again, where I'd put on Dylan's silver T, though I'd hidden the necklace beneath the neckline of my shirt. Only I knew it was there. Only I knew how much this would break me.

A few minutes later, another buzz in my pocket.

Then tell me when.

Oh, now it's my turn to say when? I typed back furiously. I went to press Send, then thought better of it. Instead, I deleted the message. I put the phone away. Make him sweat, Sylvia had said. Fine. It was his turn, anyway.

But my fingers itched to pull my phone out of my pocket, to tell him to come now now now. I'd had enough of lying, enough of playing games. All I wanted was Dylan. If he was ready for me, I was here.

I forced myself through the next fifteen minutes without pulling my phone out of my pocket. Finally, in a lull at work, I gave in to temptation.

No new messages.

Shit. Shit shit shit. I really hated Sylvia. And Dylan. And me, for ever trying to play some stupid game instead of just telling him the truth. Because hadn't that always been Dylan's M.O.? Telling me exactly how he felt? No games, no pretenses, no lies unless it was absolutely necessary to help Hannah for one of the most miserable weeks of her life?

And worst of all was that sad, sick voice in the back of my head, that drumbeat of *see? You are that girl. He wants you now, there's nothing keeping you apart, and you can resist him. You are that girl who only wants the boys you shouldn't have.*

I felt a hand on my shoulder and looked up into Sylvia's concerned face.

"Girlfriend, you look like crap. Finish your tables and go home."

Just what I needed. More time alone with my thoughts. I shook my head resolutely.

"I'm not suggesting. I'm telling." She slipped my phone out

of my pocket. "You can have this back tomorrow. Go home. Get some sleep."

I stared at the phone. "You realize this doesn't stop me from just going over to his place."

"I give you more credit than that. Go home, Tess."

I went home. I found half a bottle of white wine in the fridge, poured myself a glass, drew a bath, and had a nice, long soak while I sipped wine and read a magazine.

That lasted for about fifteen minutes. Then I got too tired to hold the pages of the magazine high and dry above the bubbles and pitched it over the side to land on the bathmat. I sank further into the suds, bringing the stem of the wine glass with me. I tilted the wine into my mouth so the bowl and my chin all got bearded in white foam as I drank, the sweet wine mixing with the scent of lavender and rosewater from the bath. I remembered the way Dylan had tasted when we'd kissed, like the retsina we'd been drinking. Wine and wood and warm.

I lifted my hips in the tub, bubbles popping against my more sensitive parts as they crested, then sank, then crested again. And it was nice, really, this tease, relaxing and comforting, like the way the water sloshed and echoed around the outdated, dark tiles of our tub. But not enough.

My chest was half-covered with bubbles, the silver of Dylan's chain tracing a sudsy V from my neck to the hollow between my breasts, the double-helix T like an exclamation point at the bottom. Bubbles clung to the metal, melting and sliding in a trail down from my breasts to my navel.

I closed my eyes, lay my head back against the rim of the tub, and let my hand follow the trail, longing for release, longing for *relief*, really. I'd been on edge for a week now, ever since the party, the closet, the *phone*…

The silver cooled against my skin, and I shifted in the bubbles, trying to find the purchase and pressure to get me where I needed, to no avail. I could always handle things myself, but that did nothing to slake the need Dylan had planted in me.

The problem, of course, was that it wasn't sexual. Not wholly, anyway. Yes, I wanted to tear Dylan's clothes off, but more than that, I wanted him with me, the way he'd been all semester, talking to me about algae and laughing with me about typos in his notes and lighting up when I served him meals at Verde. I missed that, too. Maybe, in time, I could have been happy with that. Just that.

No. Abruptly, I stood and pulled the plug. As the suds drained down, I turned on the shower and stood beneath the spray until the bubbles were gone and sanity had returned. We couldn't go back. The next time Dylan called, I'd answer.

But it wasn't until I was washed, dried and in bed, safely covered up in a nice pair of silk pajamas that I remembered Sylvia had swiped my phone.

———

THE NEXT MORNING, I woke up, exorcised. I made tea, I made toast, I read the paper. It was easily 9:00 a.m. by the time I sat down in front of my computer to check my email.

Among the new messages was one from Sylvia.

Subject: *Returning Your Phone*
> *Okay, in retrospect, it was a bad idea to take it last night. I totally can't remember your mom's home number. We'll be lucky if I remembered the address right. I hope you get this in time.*
>
> *And forgive me.*
>
> *-S*

I furrowed my brows at the screen. Sylvia talking in code again? I wasn't angry at her for taking the phone. She'd been right—I'd have driven myself crazy with it last night. And what was that crap about my address? She'd known where I lived for years. I sincerely hoped she hadn't mailed the phone when we'd be seeing each other at work in two hours.

Our doorbell rang.

"This is early," Mom called from the kitchen. And unexpected. Maybe a neighbor looking to borrow a scoop of coffee? I pushed away from the desk, but by the time I'd left my room, she was already at the door.

"Hi," said a voice I recognized. "You must be Mrs. McMann. I brought donuts."

And now I could see him standing on the threshold, in jeans, a hooded Canton sweatshirt, and those damn, damning glasses. His hair was almost as floppy as when I'd first met him, but the scruff on his jaw told an entirely different story. It was years since high school; it was days since we'd last spoken.

He saw me, too, and blindly handed off the pastries to my mom. "Tess." Two steps, and he was in the room, and his hands were sliding up to cup my jaw, his fingers weaving into my sleep-mussed waves. "I can't wait anymore," he whispered, and then our lips touched, a soft, sweet press of mouth on mouth. A greeting. A promise.

"Well," said my mom. "I'd ask who you are, but I think I can guess. Necklace Guy."

He turned to her and stuck out his hand. "Sorry, where are my manners? I'm Dylan Kingsley."

"The lab partner?" My mom narrowed her eyes. "My daughter's been holding out on me."

"That's fair," Dylan replied. "Turns out, I've been holding out on her."

———

"DON'T SAY things like that to my mom," I said. We were out on the street, breathing in cool, crisp November air, the box of donuts forgotten on my kitchen counter as we walked and talked and figured ourselves out.

"Things like what?"

"That you've been holding out on me."

"But it's true," Dylan replied. "And it was also funny."

I gave a little shake of my head and looked away. "Your two favorite things."

"You're my favorite thing."

I bit my lip. When he said things like this, I wanted to believe they were true. But Wednesday night...

"Don't worry about your mom," he said now. "I'm really good with parents."

I could believe that. I'm sure he'd charmed the pants off Dad, right before breaking his other daughter's heart.

"So Sylvia gave you my address?"

"And your phone." He pulled it out and handed it over. Our fingers brushed, and I nearly fumbled.

"You think you're good with parents?" I asked to cover my nerves. "Sylvia's the toughest nut to crack of all. I can't believe she told you where I lived."

"I swore I'd cause a scene if she didn't. Since you seemed determined to avoid me at school and at home." He shrugged. "And even on text."

"Sylvia took my phone," I pointed out.

"I meant your replies."

I walked on, quickly, so he had to jog to catch up. "So now what?" I asked. "You're ready to come scoop me up? I'm not a library book you put on hold."

"No. Tess..." He scrubbed a hand through his hair. "If I hadn't seen you on Wednesday—if I'd called in sick to the lab that night and taken a day or two, all by myself, and then come to you and told you it was over with Hannah, would we be standing here right now?"

If, if, if. If I had never left him after Cornell, if Hannah hadn't been sick last week, if Marie Swift hadn't gotten pregnant with Hannah at the beginning of my parents' affair ... What was the point in thinking about ifs? We were here now.

"Probably not," I admitted. "Maybe it's not always a good idea to tell the truth."

"I will never believe that. But yeah, timing might be an important factor." Dylan reached for me, and I let him curl his fingers around mine.

We walked that way for a while, hand in hand, not saying anything.

"I want to be with you, Tess," he said softly, squeezing my hand. "Tell me how to make that happen."

"It's happening. It's already happened."

He stopped, so abruptly I swung around on the sidewalk until I faced him. His expression was filled with wonder, his blue eyes with wild relief. "Why didn't you tell me?"

My free hand flew to my throat, to the silver T hanging there. "What do I need to tell you, Dylan? I'm here, you're here. There's nothing to keep us apart anymore. Am I happy about what happened at the lab last week? No. Were you happy when I stopped calling you two years ago? Of course not. But that didn't stop you when I came back, and I'm not going to let one stupid night stop us now."

He tugged me into his arms and lay his head down against the crook of my neck. "Jesus, Tess," he whispered. "I thought I'd messed everything up. When you walked out, when you didn't show up to class…"

"It is messed up," I agreed. "Everything has always been messed up. It's been messed up for us for two years. But we finally have the chance to make things right." I couldn't let all the bad choices we'd made—all the bad choices of two generations—ruin what I had with Dylan. I wouldn't.

We'd done the best we could with what we had. And now we could start anew.

TWENTY

IT WAS the Friday before the Thanksgiving holiday, and Dylan was taking me out on our first real date. We'd had a hectic week, working long hours on our project and even longer on the last big round of tests, quizzes, and problem sets for our respective classes. After the Thanksgiving break, we'd have one more week of classes, then a week of studying, then final exams...and the symposium on which I was resting all my financial hopes. I'd begged off work at Verde, which was probably going to be pretty dead anyway, as students left Canton for their hometowns. Even some of us who called Canton our hometown, like Hannah, had vamoosed for points unknown this weekend—at least, according to my mom's report that Dad was out of town with his family.

And I had to admit, there was still some small part of me that wondered if that was why Dylan had waited until now to take me out on the town. Our relationship up until now had been stolen kisses at the end of lab times, a few lunches here and there. Technically not so very different than what we'd been doing before we were officially together. We might be boyfriend and girlfriend for real now, but no matter how many times I told myself that, I didn't really believe it. My slim experience with boyfriends in the past wasn't sufficient to teach me how one behaved with this boyfriend. This man I loved. This man I was in a week-long relationship with that felt like it should be so much more.

Dylan planned to head home Saturday afternoon, but he'd promised me he'd be back right after Thanksgiving so we could put the finishing touches on our project before the department review period and, he added, spend some quality time together before exams made everything crazy. That meant that if we didn't go out tonight, it wasn't going to happen until sometime after break or—knowing the way Dylan attacked his lab work—maybe even after exams. After Christmas Break? By then we'd have been together a month, but would it still feel like no time at all, and also like entirely too long.

These were the thoughts running on a loop while I showered, dressed, and did my makeup. I kept it subtle tonight—none of Cristina's peacock-inspired eyes. A simple swipe of mascara, a touch of gloss on my lips. I wore a black wrap dress of my own instead of something from my mom's extensive wardrobe. It had a wide, swirly skirt and a plunging v-neckline that displayed the silver T to perfection. I blow-dried my hair so it had a nice wave but left it down so it floated over my shoulders. And when I was ready I took a long, appraising look at myself in the mirror.

I was not my mother, not my father. I had his eyes, her face and figure, but I hadn't followed their path. The boy I loved loved me enough to choose me. Loved me enough to make me his for real. It was everything I wanted, everything I'd asked him for, everything I'd thought wasn't possible for a girl like me.

So why wasn't I happier?

My doubts plagued me until I heard Dylan's knock at the door. I answered and the second I saw him, it all fell away. He wore a pair of dark pants and a charcoal-gray sweater that made his eyes practically glow with blue fire. Or maybe it was his expression that glowed.

"Tess," he said, his voice nearly a whisper. "You look beautiful."

I fingered the skirt. "Yeah, once I'm out of the lab coat, I clean up nice."

"No," he replied. "You look beautiful in the lab coat, too."

He made small talk with my mom, took me by the hand, and led me to his car.

"Where are we going?" I asked once we were seatbelted in.

"Verde."

I turned to him, eyebrows raised.

"What, don't you like that place? You spend enough time there. I thought it was your favorite." He winked at me and pulled out of the parking lot. "Nah, don't worry, algae girl. I didn't get to take you out for a birthday drink, and I know a place I think you'll love. They're a little swanky and they definitely don't serve the underage collegiate crowd, so this will be your first opportunity to try it out."

And so he hadn't taken Hannah, either, if you couldn't go until you were twenty-one. Was he purposefully taking me to someplace off the campus radar so we didn't run into anyone who knew him with Hannah?

Stop thinking like that, Tess. Just stop.

After about fifteen minutes of driving, he pulled up in front of an unassuming brick storefront. A black awning out front had a name painted in gold block letters that I couldn't quite read from this angle. We approached the front door.

"Alchemy," I said when the name finally became visible.

"After you, lab partner." Dylan opened the door for me.

The inside looked like something out of a Sherlock Holmes movie, all exposed brick walls and copper pipes leading every which way. Giant glass vats suspended over the bar were lit from within so their mysterious contents glowed green and gold and blue. The walls were lined with dark glass bottles featuring hand-stenciled labels. We weren't in a bar—we were in some sort of Victorian apothecary.

Dylan and I found seats at a small, high table, and I perched on the leather-covered barstool, the full skirt of my dress sliding to the side. We opened the leather-bound menus and I perused the offerings, divided into "subjects" like Brews, Elixers, and Potions. We certainly weren't in Verde anymore. There wasn't an Amaretto sour to be seen, and despite my own bartending experience, I didn't recognize half the liqueurs they listed.

"Adorable," I stated, eyeing him over the rim of the menu.

"Yeah," he replied. "So...do you have any idea what elder-flower tastes like?"

Our waitress arrived, dressed in a high-necked shirt with puffed sleeves and a bustle skirt. After she went through the usual patter, she informed us of a special promotion available that evening. Apparently they'd hired a palm reader to help guests concoct the perfect drink, based on the fortune the reader gave us.

"Interested?" the waitress asked. "I didn't get a drink because my shift started, but I have to say, I liked my fortune."

"I'm pretty skeptical about stuff like that," I said.

"It's just a drink," Dylan pointed out. "Not a prescription for life."

"Oh, honey," the waitress said to him as she took our menus. "You clearly haven't had one of our cocktails before."

In the end, we decided to let the fortune-teller choose for us, just for the story.

She came over, a middle-aged woman in flowing dresses and more than her fair share of bangles. "I'm Madame Misty," she intoned. "Give me your palm."

I shied away, chuckling nervously. "You first, Dylan," I said. "This bar was your idea."

He shrugged, then gamely held out his hand. "To be fair, I was going for the chemistry angle, not the mysticism."

I expected her to read the lines on his palm, but she did nothing of the sort. Instead, she looked deep into his eyes for a second, slapped his hand up and down a few times, turned it over once, then took a deep breath.

"You're on the right track," she said.

"That's good to know," Dylan said with a smile. "What should I drink?"

"Whatever you want," she replied, her tone just as matter of fact. "Your decision will not be wrong. You are intelligent and ambitious, but you never let that lead you astray. You live by your heart, and your heart is pure. The work you do arises from true passion. The love you know is the same. You do not doubt, and your aim is true. What do you *want* to drink right now?"

"I think we need our money back," I said. I looked at the lady. "I thought you were supposed to pick for us."

She rolled her eyes at me. "Fine. I will write down what I think, and then we'll ask your boyfriend."

"How do you know I'm her boyfriend?" Dylan asked.

Madame Misty turned back to him. "The same way I know she won't like what I choose for her." She pulled out a pen and scribbled a note on a cocktail napkin, then slid it to me. "You hold it." She looked at him. "Now tell me what you want."

"Whiskey," he said. "Something with a little spice, but not too sweet so it overwhelms the flavor."

I unfolded the napkin. "It says, 'The Golden Heart.'"

Dylan consulted the menu. "It's on here. Rye, cognac, Peychaud's, absinthe—what's that?"

"Sounds kind of like a Sazerac cocktail," I said. Whiskey, spicy, a tiny bit sweet. "It's just what you asked for."

"A believer now?" Madame Misty asked me, her eyebrow raised.

I sighed and held out my hand.

She thwapped it up and down a few times, and a frown crossed her features. "Oh."

"Oh?" Dylan echoed with a sly grin.

"You will never be free until you let go."

Well, there's a tautology, I thought.

"Maybe she has us mixed up?" Dylan asked. "I was the one who needed to get free," he explained to the fortune-teller.

No, she had Dylan exactly right. He always followed his heart, he was always true to himself, and he only wanted to do the right thing.

"There is a fire within you, but you'll smother it in darkness if you aren't careful."

"Ouch," I said lightly. "You're right about one thing. I don't think I'm going to like what you choose for me."

"But you should let me choose anyway," Madame Misty replied. "For no choice you make can be true while your heart holds lies."

I snatched my hand back as if she burned it with her touch. How dare she say that aloud—I mean, how did she know?

"What should I drink then?" I stated as flatly as I could manage. I would not let her or Dylan know she'd rattled me.

"Love Lies Bleeding," she replied, then wandered off.

"Ugh, what a fraud," I said as soon as she was out of earshot. Seriously, what the hell was that? Was she trying to wreck our date? Trying to wreck my life? I mean, that was the only option, right? It wasn't like she was *actually* psychic.

But he seemed unconcerned by the fortune. "Love Lies Bleeding," Dylan read from the menu. "Blood orange, campari, gin... That sounds tasty."

"That sounds bitter," I said, realizing only after the words left my mouth that bitter was what I sounded.

"It's just a game," he said, his tone consoling. "You can order a martini if you want. It's not binding arbitration."

And when the waitress came around again, I ordered what the menu called Elderflower Tonic, while Dylan went ahead and got the suggested Golden Heart. We also ordered food. Now that the fortune-teller was safely handling customers on the other side of the restaurant, I started to relax. Dylan obviously hadn't ascribed any great meaning to her palm reading, and I shouldn't either. It was just a lucky guess. Or maybe she sucked up to guys while cutting down the women, on the expectation that it was men who'd give her her tips. I knew some waitresses at Verde like that.

The Elderflower Tonic was a strongly herbal concoction served in a tall, slim glass with a sprig of rosemary. The Golden Heart came in a brandy snifter. Both were delicious and as we sipped our beverages and chatted, the date quickly got back on track.

"Do you have plans for the summer yet?" he asked me as we ate.

"I'm not sure if I can plan past next semester," I replied. "If we don't win this symposium, I may not be able to afford to finish at Canton. I might have to take a semester or two off to make some money."

His eyes widened. "Tess—it can't be that bad, can it?"

I shrugged. It might not be. My mom might be able to talk Dad into at least loaning me the money. Now that he was over his anger at me transferring to Canton behind his back, surely he wouldn't begrudge me a few thousand dollars a semester. Not after all the money he was saving on my apartment out at State. "Well, I was getting money from my father when I was at State, but he's not giving it to me anymore."

The problem was, I didn't want his money anymore.

"That sucks." He eyed me, frowning with concern. "You never talk about your father."

"We aren't very close."

"Does he live here in Canton?"

Alarm bells started ringing in my head. "Yeah." I took a drink.

Dylan didn't pursue the topic. "I guess we'll just have to win the symposium then."

"I'll drink to that!" We clinked glasses and Dylan's blue eyes met mine as we sipped.

"But seriously…plans for this summer?"

"Why?"

He put down his drink. "Because I got a paid internship with Solarix, and when I was speaking to my contact this morning she mentioned they may have another opening."

My fork dropped to my plate. "In Colorado?" The bioengineering firm was responsible for the largest-scale protype algae farms in the country.

"They pay for housing, too." He looked hesitant for a

moment. "Is it too early to ask you to spend the summer with me?"

Yes. No. We were barely together, in fact, but it felt like we got some credit for the two years that came between.

I decided on the safe option. "Probably too early to ask for certain, at least," I said with a laugh. "Unless you've also been empowered to offer me a job."

"But Tess, you're perfect."

"How much does it pay?" I asked. Even with housing covered in Colorado, if I stayed here and worked at a lab at, say, Canton Chem, I could still pick up shifts at Verde to help make some extra cash.

But then, I wouldn't have Dylan. Solarix meant we could be together, far from Canton, far from Hannah and Dad and all our secrets, like the old days when we were at Cornell and I didn't feel like I was lying to him with every breath.

Ugh, that stupid fortune-teller. Was she going to ruin my whole night?

Instead, I let Dylan tell me about the job. I let him weave a beautiful fantasy of the two of us, the scientific power couple, living together in an apartment in Colorado, working together day after day in a lab.

"And summers in Colorado, they're so gorgeous. I don't even know—do you like hiking or fishing or any of that stuff?"

"I definitely like walking," I said. "And eating fish. I've never caught one, but I'm willing to let you teach me." I'd like to do all those things with him. And more.

By the time they cleared our plates, the specter of the palm reader's warning had all but vanished. The waitress handed us dessert menus, but Dylan put his hand over mine.

"I've got something waiting at home," he said, his face full of promise.

A shiver rippled over my skin. "Something sweet?"

"I hope so."

I couldn't wait.

TWENTY-ONE

WE COULDN'T PAY the bill fast enough. We walked back to the car, hand-in-hand, and Dylan was frustratingly vague about what exactly his plans were for dessert.

"Is it animal, vegetable, or mineral?" I asked. "Tell me that at least."

He grinned as we drove back to campus. "As soon as you tell me what mineral it is that you eat."

"Salt?" I suggested after a moment.

"Touche. Then there's definitely some mineral in it. And animal. And vegetable, for that matter."

"You're impossible."

But Dylan just grinned wider.

As we walked up the path to the Swift building, my skirt twirling about my thighs, Dylan slipped his arm around my waist. When we reached his floor, I saw two guys exiting the room across the hall. They stopped and waved. He told me their names—John and Gary— then introduced me. "This is my girl-friend, Tess."

I had only a moment to revel in the title. I don't think he'd ever used it aloud before. But then I saw the boys' reaction. John's eyes widened. Gary said, "Oh—well, nice to meet you."

I felt the words he didn't say. The ones that included *What happened to Hannah?* Awkward.

Still, why did I care what someone else thought? It was Dylan who mattered, Dylan who called me his girlfriend to anyone who cared to listen. It was a fact that he'd recently broken up with Hannah. Oh, well. The salient point was that they were broken up.

All thoughts of Hannah fled as Dylan pushed the door open and pulled me inside. He shut the door with his foot and pulled me against him.

"You didn't really make dessert," I murmured against his mouth.

"You underestimate me." Hand in hand, he guided me down the hall to the main room of the studio. What I'd taken for lamplight from the hallway coalesced into something soft and flickering. Mason jar candles winked at me from the bookshelves and the bar countertop of the kitchenette. The effect was magical, sweet, unprecedented. I spun around to look at him. Already setting out plates in the kitchenette.

"You shouldn't leave candles burning when you aren't around," I admonished teasingly.

"You don't know I didn't ask a friend to light these right before we came back." He put down two forks.

"You didn't..." I trailed off. He didn't what? Ask a friend? Fill a room with candles for me? Choose me over Hannah? Love me? He'd done everything else. My mouth went dry as I watched him arrange napkins and silverware, as he whipped the foil cover off a dish of pastry with a flourish. Dylan was a constant mystery. He'd picked me, loved me, and now had made some kind of truly complicated dessert in order to...impress me? Get me into bed?

Come on, Kingsley, I thought. *Last time I slept with you, you hadn't even bought me dinner first. Don't you know I'm easier than this?*

Yet just because I was, didn't mean he didn't want to impress me anyway.

I realized he was waiting for some kind of response.

"It's baklava," he said at last. "I made it myself."

I swallowed, then came up to the counter to meet him. "Thank you."

"You haven't even tasted it yet," he said. "There's nuts and honey and filo dough—and really, it's the most complicated dessert I've ever made—"

"And you made it for me."

"Well yeah, but hopefully, you'll share..."

"For me."

He regarded me carefully, then reached over and dipped his finger in the honey dripping off each triangular piece. "For you," he repeated and brushed his honey-laden thumb across my lips.

I captured the tip of his finger in my mouth and sucked all the sweetness off.

His breath hissed through clenched teeth. "Careful, Tess," he warned. "Do that again and we won't have the chance to eat the baklava, and I've been dreaming about it all day."

"I've been dreaming about something else for much longer." I hooked my arms about his neck.

Dylan tasted of whiskey and honey. I caught his bottom lip between my own and sucked on it, echoing what I'd done to his finger moments before. He moaned, and his hands slid around my waist, half pulling, half lifting until our bodies pressed together. Our tongues touched, parted, and slid together again.

"What about the baklava?" I mumbled as he started walking me backward, away from the counter and toward the futon.

"Never heard of it," he breathed against my neck.

We fell back on the futon, a tangle of arms and legs, sliding against each other, rubbing and twisting as if we could, if we tried hard enough, entwine ourselves tightly enough to become a single person. It was with effort that I worked my hands between us to fumble with his belt buckle. He yanked his sweater over his head; I kicked off my shoes.

And then we were kissing again, breathing the same breaths, matching each touch of lips with weeks of built-up longing. And that was when I realized it: Dylan was mine. *Mine.* I could do whatever I wanted with him and not feel guilty. I had fought, I had waited, and this—this was my reward.

I laid a hand on his chest and pushed him back against the futon. He froze, staring up at me, his blue eyes curious.

I stood and grabbed the ties holding my dress together. I tugged them free, then shrugged out of the sleeves. The material pooled around my feet, leaving me in a pair of black lacy hipsters and a matching demi-bra.

There was no denying the naked lust in Dylan's eyes as he looked me up and down. He was propped up on his elbows on the futon, staring at my body.

"Is it like you remembered?" I asked, twisting a bit in the flickering candlelight.

"No," he replied. "You didn't have underwear half so inter-esting when you were eighteen."

I dipped my fingers below the lace trim lining my bra cups and ran them along the edge, catching one and then the other on my nipples, which had hardened into nubs under Dylan's watchful gaze. "That all?" I leaned forward as the peaks of my breasts popped up above the lace.

I heard a gasp from the bed. "My memory isn't all it's cracked up to be, Tess."

"That's categorically untrue, Phone Boy."

A laugh sputtered from his lips. "Phone Boy?" And then he grinned. "Ah, that. Well. Those memories certainly can't match reality."

"We'll have to refresh them for you, then," I replied and sank to my knees on the mattress, straddling him as he lay back down. His hands went to my hips, then slid up to cup my breasts as I leaned over him, grinding my hips against his. The silver T dangled between us, flashing like fire in the candlelight. "Memory jogged?" I teased.

"*Something* is jogged." His thumbs brushed across my nipples, easing my breasts further out of the bra. "God, you're beautiful, Tess."

"You keep saying that."

"I always mean it." He rose upon his elbows and took one of my nipples in his mouth, doing things with his tongue the eighteen-year-old Dylan had probably never even dreamed of. The hollow, throbbing ache between my legs intensified, and I moved my hips against him, feeling his erection through the layers of clothes he still wore.

"You know what I never got to do two years ago?" I asked him, and then, without waiting for a response, I wriggled down, taking his pants and boxers as I went. When he was laid bare, I took his penis in my hands, wrapping my fingers around the base and tugging slightly, sliding my hands up and down in a tease. Then I leaned over and took him in my mouth.

"Tess...," he hissed, his hands going to my hair, weaving into the strands without holding on tight or applying pressure.

I loved the feel of him, thick and heavy, the slightly salty tang, but I'd barely even gotten started when he dragged me up against him and kissed me hard, full-mouthed and hungry. His hands slid around my back to pop the clasps on my bra, then went to my waist and shoved my panties down, too. Dylan rolled so I was beneath him, whisking away the last of my clothing until I was as naked as he was. Then he stopped, staring down at me in the flickering light. The candles were doing strange things to his features, casting the planes of his face in hard shadows, in golden glow. His eyes seemed to shine in the light, and his gaze took on greater reverence, like he was looking at some great work of art in a cathedral.

"Last time I saw you like this," he whispered and traced four of his fingers across my torso, "You were striped from the sun in my window. This time you look like a painting..." He lifted his face to mine and our eyes locked.

"I'm not a painting," I said, reaching out my hand to cup his cheek. "I'm not a memory."

"I want you in every light—sunlight, candlelight, twilight—"

"I'm going to have to veto fluorescent light," I joked.

He kissed me softly, then, when I didn't dissolve into nothingness, with more energy. His hand went between my legs, teasing, circling, stroking, as I arched in his arms, bucking my hips when the pressure, the need, threatened to overwhelm me.

He went to the bathroom for a condom and returned to find me kneeling on the futon, waiting for him.

"Tess—"

I stopped him with a finger to his lips. "Do not say I'm beautiful again."

"I was going to say you're brilliant."

"That's better." We kneeled, chest to chest, our hands entwined before us.

"I was going to say I'm sorry it took us so long to get back here."

"Mmm." I leaned in to taste his collarbone, his throat.

"I was going to say that if I don't get inside you in the next five seconds, I might explode."

I pushed him down. "We can't have an explosion," I said. "It'll wreck your baklava."

Seconds later I was sinking down upon him, catching my breath as he filled me, stopping for a moment to look down at him. He pulled himself up again, cupping my breasts in each hand, depositing a simple kiss on one, then the other, and then, at last, lifting his mouth to mine.

We kissed and started to move, coming apart and crashing together, closer and closer each time, the years of separation disintegrating with every thrust. I could see the tension in his face, in his arms as he held himself in check for me, and it drove me wild. I wanted to make him lose control. I pushed his hands down over his head and swiveled my hips against him, moving until the silver chain around my throat slammed rhythmically against my chest, until my name on Dylan's lips became a chant, a plea, a primal cry, until the ache wound tight within me spun free and I pulsed around him, my orgasm spurring his.

He pushed inside me one last time so deep, so hard it almost hurt, and I collapsed over his chest, our hearts beating frantically against each other's chests, our breath coming in pants.

At last, I drew my fingers across his damp brow. "So…"

"So?" He smiled at me.

"About that baklava?"

———

WE ATE IT IN BED, by candlelight, still naked, which made it all the easier to lick dripping bits of honey off our skin when we were done. And then, since he'd already started the licking, he decided to do the rest of my body.

After I'd come back to myself, he gathered me close in his arms.

"Well, that hasn't changed," I said sleepily.

"Sorry to hear that. I would have thought I'd gotten better in two years."

I felt my muscles tense at the reminder and prayed he didn't notice. I didn't want to think of him doing this with other women. With Hannah. "Well, it's tough to improve upon perfection," I said to cover.

"Flattery, Tess," he said as he rolled on top of me and slid inside, "will get you everywhere."

After that, we drifted off into a sated sleep, still tangled in each other and the futon sheets. At some point in the night, I felt him leave me to blow out the candles and bring us a heavier comforter. Then he took me in his arms again and I fell into a sleep so deep I didn't even dream.

When my eyes fluttered open the next morning, the gray November light was already sifting through the blinds on the windows. I rolled over to meet Dylan's sleepy smile.

"Hi," I said, snuggling against him.

His arms went around me. "I really wish I wasn't going home today."

"Me too."

He raised himself on his elbow and looked down at me. "What are the chances I can get you to stay right here, naked, the whole time I'm gone?"

"Slim to none?" I replied, stretching luxuriously. His pupils dilated and I smiled in triumph. "I have stuff to do, Mr. Kingsley. Reports to write. Jobs to apply for, apparently."

"Right. I'll make sure to forward you all the information. God, spending the summer with you again..."

I chuckled and shook my head. Summer, winter, it didn't matter anymore. I'd be with him.

He reached out to trace the T resting above my sternum. "I'm glad you like this."

"I love it." I ran my fingers up and down his arms as he weighed the jewelry in his hand. "Where ever did you find me something so perfect?"

He was quiet for a second, and when he spoke, his tone was soft, almost confessional. "I had it made, actually."

"In a week?" I asked impressed. "You just found out when my birthday was."

His smile faded. "No. I had it made two years ago, after I got home from Cornell." He let the charm fall back on to my skin. "A cousin of mine does silverwork. I—wanted to give you something. But I never saw you again."

I met his eyes. "I'm sorry, Dylan."

"Don't be," he replied, smiling. "The wait was worth it. It was always worth it for you, Tess."

I closed my eyes and cuddled close against his shoulder. This was real. This was really real. "And you kept it all this time?"

"I guess there was a part of me that never gave up. That never would. I don't care how long we had to wait, I don't care what we had to go through to get here. I love you, Tess. All my life, I've loved only you."

I breathed in, deeply, as if I could draw his words into my lungs, my soul. "I love you, too," I whispered back.

We showered and dressed, then I waited while Dylan packed up his stuff for the trip home to Pennsylvania. We ate the rest of the baklava for breakfast, and Dylan dropped me off at home on his way out of town. We talked about what we'd each need to do to finish our project before the due date, and what steps I'd need to take to apply for the internship in Colorado. We talked big game about our future.

I really believed we'd have one.

TWENTY-TWO

THE NEXT FEW weeks passed in a blur of classes, studying, and final preparations for the symposium. My days were spent working and reading by Dylan's side, most of my nights in his arms. My mom didn't even bother giving me a look on the few times she and I ended up at our apartment at the same time. She knew my bed was empty most nights, but she hardly had the moral high ground to tell me off. Unlike her, I was sleeping with a monogamous boyfriend. Unlike her, I was being very safe.

Because I spent so little time at home, I hardly saw my dad at all, which was fine by me. Every time we met, I thought of Hannah. I wanted to ask him how she was doing. How was her thyroid? How was her heart? Did her breakup with Dylan still sting? But of course, I didn't.

"Your mother tells me you have a boyfriend," he said to me once as I was folding laundry on the couch. It was a rare moment for the two of us to be alone. Dad rarely dropped by unless it was to hang out with my mother. "How's that going?"

"Fine." I hoped Mom hadn't told him that the boyfriend's name was Dylan. "He's a junior at Canton, like me."

"That's nice." He hesitated. "Your mom says he's very polite. I hope he's treating you right."

This was a point where a normal father would tell his daughter that he wanted to meet this man who was coming after his girl. But of course, that was off the table for us.

"He is treating me right," I replied coldly. "I'm in a committed, monogamous relationship with a man who isn't lying to me or anyone else. It's everything I could ask for."

Dad didn't bother responding to my comment, and I didn't see him again for more than a week.

I knew it couldn't last forever. Eventually I'd have to tell Dad what Dylan's name was. Maybe if and when I got the job in Colorado for the summer and had to inform my parents I'd be living with my boyfriend. Maybe if, next fall, we decided to continue the arrangement in an off-campus apartment here in Canton. Maybe a few years down the road, if things got really serious. If we got married.

I probably shouldn't get ahead of myself there.

But someday, Dad would have to meet the man in my life, wouldn't he? Had my parents ever bothered making up rules for that?

Still, I rarely let thoughts of my father or Hannah intrude upon the new bliss I'd found in Dylan's company. Everything seemed brighter now: my shifts at Verde less arduous, my crush of schoolwork simpler to handle, my dwindling bank account easier to bear. There were even nights when we went out with friends—Sylvia had decided she loved him, and even Elaine had grown friendlier. Elaine had gotten the hang of her classes, and her competitive streak had died down somewhat. I finally felt like I had a group of friends in the Bio-E department, a social circle at Canton.

Dylan, of course, was endlessly optimistic. In his mind, we'd win the symposium, get me my money, get matching jobs at Solarix and matching 4.0 GPAs. Every night he told me he loved me and every night I repeated the words back to him, like it was some sort of talisman against an unknown future. I tried not to think of what would happen if it didn't turn out that way. If I didn't get the job, if we didn't win the symposium, if my mom mentioned the name Dylan to my father and he put two and two together...

But that wasn't how it happened at all.

Even after we'd finished our project and turned it in for departmental review, the work didn't let up. Final exams were upon us, and Dylan and I spent every spare second studying. My mom was out late at a monthly arts salon meeting, and Dylan had come by the apartment with takeout Chinese and textbooks. And that was where we were—me curled up on the couch, Dylan in the kitchen fetching drinks—when I heard a key in the door. I barely had a chance to look up, when the door opened and there was my father on the threshold.

"Oh, hey, Tess," he said. "Is your mom—"

There must have been something awful, something unspeakable and terrified on my face, because his voice stopped liked I'd changed the channel on him. And then Dylan was there, holding two glasses of water, and he was staring at my father.

"Mr. Swift?" It was a simple question. Just like that.

"I'm sorry," Dad said abruptly. "I must have the wrong house." And then he was gone, the door clicking into place behind him, nothing disturbed and everything smashed to pieces.

My knuckles were white as I held my pen, and my tongue seemed frozen to the roof of my mouth. My brain spun like wheels on an icy road, fifty thousand RPMs and not a single useful thought.

Dylan turned to me, his face twisted with confusion. "Do you know that man?"

"No," said a voice that sounded like mine. I was very far away, tumbling down a black hole of imploded rules.

"He came into your house."

"Apartment." I looked down at the textbook in my lap. "Just had the wrong door number. Happens a lot. All those doors look the same from the outside."

When I dared to look up again, he was blinking at me, even more mystified. Had he heard Dad call me by name? Ask for my mom? His scientist brain was reviewing the data, trying to fit it to my hypothesis. I knew it never would. "But how did he get in?"

"Huh?" Perhaps play dumb. "I must have forgotten to lock the door after you came in." I prayed he didn't hear Dad's key jingling in the lock.

"It locks automatically."

Damn. Trust a genius like Dylan to notice a detail like that. I shrugged. No. Not right. I was acting too calm for a girl who'd just had a strange man walk into her house. I stood up and crossed toward the door, wheels spinning, wheels spinning. I turned the deadbolt, threw the chain. "Oh, I guess the lock didn't catch. It sticks sometimes. Piece of junk."

When I turned around, Dylan had put the glasses down on the coffee table and crossed to me. I backed against the door, wishing I were on the other side of it, scared he'd see the rules broken all over my face. He certainly wasn't buying anything I'd said so far.

"Tess." There was something flat in his tone. "You don't know who that is?"

I swallowed. Shook my head. "Nope." *Wait, maybe I should say yes. He's a client of my mom's. I think I saw him once on TV. An alumni function...* "I'm a little scared, that's all. Some guy just broke into my house."

"Burglars don't wear three-piece suits."

"I didn't really take stock of what he was wearing."

Dylan was shaking his head at me, very slowly, as something —*God, please don't let it be the truth*—worked itself out in his head. "That's my girlfriend's dad."

My breath caught in my throat. "*I'm your girlfriend.*"

He stared at me, still, silent, and after what seemed like forever, he swept his hair off his brow. "Sorry. Yeah, I meant ex." But he'd been right the first time, too, even if he hadn't known it. That *was* his girlfriend's father. "That was really weird for me."

"Yeah," I replied. "Me, too. It was my house some strange dude just came in."

And it remained weird for the next hour. Even though we were discussing the geometries of unsteady state transport, I could see unrelated questions in my boyfriend's eyes. He was asking himself why Steven Swift was at my apartment building, why he'd just walked in the door.

All the Chinese food was gone when Dylan's phone rang. He glanced down at the display.

"It's Hannah," he said flatly.

My heart stopped pumping blood through my body. It was the only explanation for how cold I suddenly felt.

"Hello?"

As close as we sat on the couch, I could hear every word she was saying to Dylan. She was crying. "I'm really sorry—I wouldn't do this if I had any other option—"

"Hannah," he said, "calm down."

"...can't get the car to start. I think the battery's dead. My mom is out of town—"

"What's happening?"

"My dad," she sobbed. "They just called me. My dad was in a car accident."

Oh my God. Dad. *Daddy.*

"Okay." Dylan's voice sounded very far away, but his tone was warm, like a blanket. "It's going to be okay. I'm on my way over. I'll take you to the hospital."

Without realizing it, I was nodding my head. *It would be okay. He would take me to the hospital.*

He hung up the phone and looked at me. "This just keeps getting weirder. Hannah's dad was in a car accident. It must have been after he left here."

I swallowed. Like maybe he was so distraught at seeing Dylan in the apartment that he'd had an accident? If so, then it was my fault. My fault that I hadn't warned him in advance that my new boyfriend was his real daughter's ex. My fault for breaking the rules so completely that they'd fallen on his head.

"Take me with you," I blurted.

"What?" He shook his head, distracted. "No, Tess. I'm just taking Hannah to the hospital so she can be with her father."

There went my head again, nodding like it all made perfect sense. "Yes. Take me with you." And I needed to text Mom. She could meet us there.

"No," he repeated. "That's ridiculous."

Reality crashed in on me. Of course. Of course that was ridiculous. My mother and I couldn't visit Dad in the hospital, no more than we could visit him at work or at his home. We weren't family who could stand by his bedside. I lowered my head, my face burning with shame. Right, right. My boyfriend could go be with my father right now, but not me. Never me.

Dylan was scowling at me, completely misinterpreting the look of anguish that no doubt graced my face. "Don't be difficult about this, Tess. I'm giving her a ride to the hospital. Hannah and I are over. Come on—you're not the jealous type."

"Oh?" I scoffed, because otherwise I would cry. "I've never been more jealous of Hannah in my life."

His eyebrows furrowed, but then, for the second time today, he sighed at me and shook his head. "I don't have time to talk about this right now. You're being really petty. I have to go take Hannah to the hospital." He grabbed his things and left.

I plopped down on the couch. I wasn't being petty. Petty would be resenting Hannah for everything she'd been given all her life. Petty would be resenting her right now for having Dylan by her side while she went to see our father.

I couldn't get past the idea that I'd had something to do with the accident. I was to blame. If I'd warned Dad in advance that I was dating Dylan, if I'd made sure to bolt the door so he didn't walk in on us.... We'd been so careful all these years that no one, not even childhood friends like Sylvia and Annabel, knew that the famous Steven Swift was my father. There was a reason I so rarely had people over to my house. And there'd been no reason for Dad to suspect I'd bring Dylan by today, either. By mutually unspoken agreement, we'd been avoiding each other ever since our last pointed exchange.

Oh, God. I hoped it wasn't our last. Hannah had been crying, but she'd given no indication of how serious Dad's injuries were.

I jumped to my feet and started pacing the floor. I called Mom, but there was no answer. Either she'd forgotten her phone in her car or she was ignoring it during the salon. Both, for Mom, were par for the course. I texted her.

Dad's in the hospital. Car accident. Waiting for more info.

We might wait forever. There was no plan in place to deal with situations like this. The best source of info I had was Dylan, and he thought I was acting like a brat. Maybe if I'd gotten hold of my mother, she would have talked me back from the ledge. Maybe she would have explained to me that she and Dad had prepared for what would happen if he was hurt. Maybe my mother was somewhere on the phone tree in his office, listed under something innocuous and discreet.

But all I could think about were the last words I'd hurled at my father. All I could think of was the shock, the utter horror on his face when he'd seen Dylan standing inside our apartment. All I could think of was that no matter what kind of screwed-up half-relationship we were forced to have, he was still my dad.

Dylan had gone to pick up Hannah. If I left now, I might be able to beat them to the hospital.

I didn't give myself time to think, just rushed to the car and drove.

I didn't see Dylan's car in the parking lot, nor a silver BMW that meant Hannah had managed to get hers started. I practically sprinted into the emergency room, then up to reception.

"Steven Swift?" I panted at them.

The nurse at the desk nodded at her computer screen. "Are you family?" she asked mildly, not even looking up.

"Yes." Somehow, I expected the word to choke in my throat. This was the biggest rule of all, and I'd just broken it. But the nurse didn't ask for proof, for ID. She didn't demand to know our relationship. She didn't even seem to care. I scribbled my name on a sheet and followed her directions down the hall.

Dad was asleep on the bed. His face was badly bruised, and remnants of blood had caked in his hair and along the curves of his ear. One of his arms was wrapped in bandages, and the other was strapped to his chest.

I should probably go. He wasn't going to die on us tonight. He looked hurt but okay. He wasn't even plugged into a heart rate monitor or anything. No machines beeped near his bed. No IVs stuck out of his arm. I should probably go. We could see him later. I could apologize some other time.

Instead, I approached cautiously, like trying to sneak up on a wild animal. "Dad?" I whispered.

His eyelids fluttered open. "Tess," he croaked at me. His eyes seemed unfocused, probably from pain medication. That was why they wanted Hannah here. Not as a bedside vigil. Just to pick her father up. It was silly to have come. Silly and dangerous. Hannah and Dylan could show up at any minute.

"I'm so sorry, Dad. I should have warned you about—"

"What are you doing here?" His voice slurred, but his tone was one I'd heard before. This was against the rules. This was all, all against the rules.

"I came to see you!" Tears blurred my eyes. "I was worried you were really hurt. When Dylan heard you'd been in an accident—"

"You have to leave, Tess," he said. "You can't be here. You're not family."

I *am*, I wanted to shout, as petulant as a child. I wiped ineffectually at my eyes, hoping he was so out of it that he wouldn't be able to see.

"I appreciate it," he went on. "More than you know. But you can't be here. Go home, Tess. I'll call when I can."

Was that what he said to my mother? *I'll call when I can? I'll let you be a part of my life when I can?*

I didn't want to be his daughter *sometimes*. I didn't want to sit at home, twiddling my thumbs, while his real daughter went to his hospital bed. Maybe that was enough for my mother, but it would never be enough for me.

"Daddy," I whispered, and my voice broke on the last syllable. "Please."

He turned to me, and I saw from the pain that creased his features how much it cost him to do it. "Go home now, Tess," he said firmly. "I mean it."

I turned and ran from the room.

I could hardly see where I was going, but I had almost reached the exit when the automatic doors parted and Dylan and Hannah walked in. Her silky blonde hair was straight and shiny. She had a colorful scarf wrapped around her neck, and the flaps of her expensive white wool coat streamed out like the wings of an angel. They weren't holding hands or cuddling, but all of Dylan's attention was on her. I stopped short.

So did Hannah. "What is *she* doing here?" she spat at me. They were the same words our father had used. They were right. What *was* I doing here? Why had I come?

Dylan turned to Hannah. "Go check on your dad. I'll be right there."

She swept by me, regal and infuriated, and up to the front desk.

Dylan's hand was on my elbow. "Come with me." He led me through the big doors and out to the front receiving area of the hospital, where there was a wide, awning-covered space lined with potted plants and park benches. There he dropped my arm and took two steps back.

I wrapped my arms around myself for warmth, for comfort, for protection, but nothing could guard me from the expression on his face. He was bewildered, angry, lost.

"What the hell, Tess? Have you gone crazy?"

I said nothing.

"I told you to stay home. I was taking a friend to the hospital. That's all. We weren't running off together. We weren't having some hot hookup." I'd never heard him mad at me. Even in that last email he'd sent, when I'd abandoned him after Cornell. Even when he told me how I'd broken his heart. Even when I'd run from him at the frat party.

"Well?" he prompted.

I made no statement of defense.

"You'd better tell me what you're thinking right now. You're really scaring me."

There was nothing I could say. The lie he believed—that I'd come because I thought he'd reunite with Hannah if I wasn't there to stop it—was awful. The truth was impossible. There was nothing in between. I hadn't had a sudden hankering to become a candy striper. I didn't have a neighbor who'd slipped in the bath and needed transport to the ER.

He was shaking his head in disbelief. "What's going on, Tess?"

I found my tongue at last. "Did you tell Hannah we saw her father tonight?"

He blinked at me. "No—it didn't seem…" He trailed off, his expression growing even more confused.

I turned and walked away from the doors, away from the light of the loading dock. Down the path everything was dark and quiet. Safe. There was another bench there, far from the entrance. A stone urn filled with cigarette butts sat at the base. This must be where employees went to smoke.

Dylan caught up with me. I felt his hand on my arm. I looked up into blue eyes burning with questions. He was wearing his glasses. He was mine.

I didn't take time to think. I didn't take time to breathe. I spoke before I could stop myself. "Steven Swift is my father."

I had never spoken those words aloud before. I expected a crack of thunder, a whiff of brimstone, but the Earth remained steady beneath my feet. My heart didn't stop beating. Then I caught sight of Dylan's face. He looked so surprised I was afraid his glasses might fall right off his nose.

"He's my father," I repeated. "Hannah is my sister. She doesn't know it, but she is."

A strangled sound came from Dylan then. I plowed forward anyway.

"That's why he was at our apartment tonight. To see my mom."

"Your mom…and Mr. Swift—"

But I wasn't holding a press conference. I wasn't here to answer questions. "No one knows about me. No one *can* know."

Except I'd just told Dylan. I'd just broken every rule there was.

He stared at me for a minute, silent with shock. "You…you knew I was dating your sister?"

I jerked my head up and down in some semblance of a nod.

"Is that—that's not why you—"

"No!" I cried. "Of course not." I wanted to say the mantra I'd repeated to myself during that awful week of waiting. *We were together first. We were together first.* But it suddenly sounded hollow in my ears. I stepped forward and placed a hand on his jacketed chest. "Dylan, I love you."

He reared back as if struck. "You *lied* to me."

My hand dropped uselessly to my side.

"You've been lying this whole time. Every time I talked about Hannah, every time I talked about her family…" A shudder seemed to pass through him. "You lied to me like it was nothing."

I was cold and hot all at once. A giant lump of hot lead seemed to have taken up residence in my lungs, scalding my breath, scorching my throat, bleeding from my eyes. "I *had* to."

"I have never lied to you," he replied. "Never."

"You don't understand—"

"You never gave me the chance to!" His eyes were like ice, so frigid and distant I could have been looking at a glacier. "You just let me believe… Fuck, Tess. You're *sisters*. That's—"

"What?" I croaked. "*Against the rules?*"

"Yeah, usually," he replied, as if that should be obvious. "I have no idea what to think. No one has ever lied to me like this. I don't know what to believe."

"I just told you everything."

"Have you? You've just been lying about who you are—"

"No!" I said, my heart shattering. "You have always known who I am." His lab partner, his first lover, the girl he thought of for two years... I wasn't just Steven Swift's dirty little secret. I wasn't just the product of my parents' long lies.

But all of that was gone now. I could see it on his face.

He cast a long glance back at the hospital doors. "I think you should go home now. Mr.—" He stumbled for a second, as if deciding whether or not to call him my father. "Mr. Swift's injuries aren't that bad. Hannah says they told her on the phone that they'll release him in a few hours."

"Dylan—"

"You should let your mother know, too, I guess," he went on. "I can't believe I'm saying that. I—I should probably get back to Hannah."

"Please," I said. "You can't tell her. You can't tell anyone."

He glared at me, so long and so hard I thought I'd melt under the intensity of his gaze. The glasses were there, but he was no longer mine. "Yes, Tess," he said at last. "You've made a liar out of me, too."

And that, I realized, was the worst thing of all.

TWENTY-THREE

MY FATHER DID COME home from the hospital that night, but due to his broken arm, it would be a while before he'd be able to drive himself to our apartment. My mother managed to meet him two days after the accident, but I didn't see him at all, a fact that I think we were all okay with.

"Is he very mad?" I asked her.

She shrugged.

"Does that mean yes?"

Again, she shrugged. "Your father and I disagree on this matter. He was in the hospital. Of course you wanted to see him."

Except he hadn't visited me when I was eight and had my appendix out. To Dad, trips to the hospital were no excuse to break the rules. I didn't point this out to Mom, though. I was just glad she'd taken my side for once. I'd actually never seen her disagree with him before.

Which made me wonder how angry he'd be about Dylan, once the drugs wore off.

I didn't see Dylan, either. Classes were over for the semester —we were well into reading period, where we spent our days studying for the upcoming exams. When Sylvia texted, asking if

I had shifts this week, I told her to redistribute my hours to some of the other servers. She seemed excited about the idea, and I needed to study. I knew Dylan was deep in his books, too, but still… He didn't call; he didn't email.

Though to be fair, I didn't either. I wasn't sure what I could say. The few times I'd opened the Compose box on my email, the only thing I could think to type was something I was far too terrified to put into words.

Are we broken up?

I wondered if this was how Dylan had felt, after Cornell, when he'd sent me text after text, email after email, and I'd never responded. Maybe Dylan figured turnabout was fair play. No contact meant it was over. And I was totally capable of getting the message more quickly than he had back then.

Except…that was never the way Dylan had been. I was the one who lied, the one who thought silence was better than speech.

The symposium was held three days after the hospital. When I woke up in the morning, there was a message from Dylan waiting.

Tess,

Sorry I didn't get back to you yesterday. I'd had a long night. I've been over all our notes for the public presentation. I hope you've done the same. Unfortunately, my morning's pretty booked up with study groups, but if you want to rehearse before tonight, I can meet you in Lab C at 2.

Dylan

The lump of lead where my heart once lived clanged, reading his note. I fingered the T around my neck. *Did* I want to meet him? Would we really be rehearsing? Would he be breaking up with me? Could I bear to go into the symposium with this question hanging over my head? Could I even do a presentation at his side if he told me we were through?

Dylan,
 I'd like to meet beforehand, but not to rehearse.
Tess

Yeah, no way I could send that. What if he thought I was propositioning him? I pressed Delete and started typing again.

No, I think I'm ready for whatever comes my way tonight.

There. I hit Send. Now, if only it were true.

———

I ARRIVED at the symposium that evening with my mother. I was dressed in a smart gray suit for the presentation, and I'd pulled my hair back into a French twist that I thought made me look older and intellectual and my mom said made me look like I was going for "sexy librarian." But when I went to pull the pins out, she stopped me.

"Sexy librarian might help with the judges," she pointed out.

That was my mom. Never let months of hard work and scientific rigor get in the way of good old-fashioned sex appeal.

Dylan was already waiting in the auditorium, in a suit that fit him so well I knew Hannah must have originally picked it out and a tie that brought out the scary gorgeous levels of blue in his eyes. My heart dropped to my stomach as I approached, afraid of what I might see in his expression, but he met me with a smooth, confident smile, then greeted my mother.

"Mrs. McMann," he said and shook her hand. "I'm so glad you could come out tonight to be with us. My parents would have come if they lived closer."

"Of course," she said. "Though I'll warn you in advance, I can't promise I'll comprehend anything you say."

He laughed. "Just clap when we say, 'Thank you.'"

She found her seat, and Dylan went back to staring resolutely out at the crowd. There had to be over a hundred people here tonight, plus all the students waiting to give their podium presentations.

I straightened my notecards and cleared my throat. "All ready?"

"I see your father didn't bother showing up to see you win tonight."

I whirled to face him, but he still wasn't looking at me. "Is that supposed to be some kind of joke?"

He turned to me and beneath the polished exterior, I noticed nervousness behind his eyes. "No, Tess, I promise you I'd never joke about something like that."

Before I could think of an adequate response, the presentations began. I watched each with careful eyes, comparing their science to the work Dylan and I had done. The style of the presentations ran the gamut from high-school level science fair, complete with amateurish posters, to hipster cutesy cat-gif brigades. Dylan and I had chosen a straightforward, professional-style PowerPoint presentation, and when it was our turn we took to the auditorium stage, notes and pointers in hand.

I began by introducing us and stating the subject and background of our experiment. To go along with this portion of our presentation, we'd compiled an array of short videos and photos about similar algae-related experiments and the potential for implementation in the renewable energy field. Our particular experiment examined the potential for small-scale changes to microstructure fluid flow and its applications for increasing efficiency in algae production for biofuel.

Dylan took over the talk portion and began discussing the parameters of our project, and I stole a glance at the screen behind us. My jaw dropped.

Where we'd arranged for simple, clean-lined graphs to chart our subjects' progress throughout the experiments, there were now detailed 3-D images like wavy lines of seaweed that snaked their way up and down the number lines in time with Dylan's words. I turned to him, gobsmacked.

He flashed me a glance and kept talking. Our upgraded presentation continued as he spoke about breakthroughs and setbacks throughout our weeks of work and how we'd built upon the study we'd performed back at Cornell.

Once again it was my turn and, swallowing my surprise, I began to tell the assembly about the places where our findings matched and diverged from the expected results. A quick check on the screen showed animated images that matched my explanations. The crowd was riveted—not so much by the super-exciting world of algae growth, but by the TED-level graphics we'd brought along for the ride.

"And that concludes the presentation," Dylan said at last. "Thank you very much."

Out in the audience somewhere, my mother heard her cue to clap. But everyone else was clapping, too, and I couldn't help but smile, if only in relief that it was over.

As we came down the steps from the stage, I shook my head at him. "What the hell was that?"

But he just shrugged and ignored all my nudges to go out in the hall and talk while the rest of the presentations went on.

I thought we might have a chance to speak after the formal portion of the symposium ended, but we were soon accosted by professors and other onlookers filled with questions. We spent a good half an hour clarifying and defending our work, especially to members of the jury panel from Canton Chem, who expressed great surprise that we'd picked a subject outside of the field of biomed.

"Risky," said one, skeptical.

"Ballsy," corrected another.

We didn't get a moment's privacy until the jury retired to discuss their rankings and the cocktail hour commenced. I bypassed the trays of canapés and plastic glasses of wine and tracked down my partner. He was deep in conversation with Kathleen Hamilton, the Canton Chem VP he'd brought to Verde that time. We made chitchat for a good fifteen minutes before I wrested Dylan away.

"I think this is the time we should be schmoozing," he pointed out as I pulled him into a quiet corner.

"Where did those new graphics come from?" I pressed. "You think you have free rein to keep secrets now? You almost screwed me up out there!"

"The graphics come from me now owing an enormous favor to my sister," he said with a sigh. "She's got a master's in animation and she pretty much lived with me on Skype for the past day and a half in order to get them done on time."

"Why?" I asked. "The charts we had were fine."

"*Fine* doesn't win you five thousand dollars, Tess." He looked at me. "The last time you didn't have the money you needed to go to Canton, I lost you for two years. I can't risk that again."

It was like a thunderclap to my heart. I'd thought he hated me for lying. I'd thought he was avoiding me because he felt betrayed. But really he was spending every spare second making sure we didn't lose. I didn't know what to say. I simply reached out and laid my hand over his. "You wouldn't," I said. "Not now."

But Dylan went on like he hadn't heard me. "And we especially can't let your father win."

"What?"

"All this time I thought you had a deadbeat dad, and that's why you were on scholarship. Turns out it's true, only he's a bigger deadbeat than I could have ever imagined."

I stared at him in awe. "I thought you were mad."

"Are you kidding? I'm *furious*." Beneath my palm, his hand had closed into a fist. "If my father wouldn't have had to take several days off work to travel here, he'd be sitting in this audience right now."

"That's not what I meant."

"I know what you meant. And now I know why you keep doubting our future every time we have some dumb fight. You can't even count on your own father."

"That's not—"

"Your dad's here in town, it's a huge crowd, he's a Canton alum and booster, no one would even blink if he showed up tonight, and yet you and I both know he would never come."

"He was in an accident…" I trailed off. The words sounded hollow in my mouth. Why did I keep making excuses for him?

"Were you expecting him to come before?"

"No," I admitted.

"He's got all the money in the world and he won't give you any for your education. You're working every night you can and trying to earn extra scholarships on the side and you're living with your mother and *none* of this is necessary. I've been to your father's house. He could find five thousand dollars in the couch cushions."

"Yeah," I said, "but Dad's money comes with Dad's rules. That's how I ended up at State for two years."

"So that's it," he hissed. "I thought maybe it was. Why didn't he want you to go to Canton?"

"Too expensive."

"Lies."

I nodded. Yes, yes it was. I'd known that, even at eighteen. "You know why."

Dylan said nothing for a while. Then, "You know, you were still following his rules, even after you came back here."

I felt as if my breath had been knocked out of me. *No,* I wanted to shout at him. *It was breaking the rules to be with you, to steal Hannah's boyfriend. It was breaking the rules to go to the hospital the other night.* "That's different. Canton is about me, about what I want from my life. Exposing him—that's about *his* life."

"Bullshit," Dylan scoffed. "He's made you lie your entire life to protect his money, and he won't even share it with you. He takes advantage of you and your mother, of Hannah and her mother…" He clenched his jaw. "He's a liar, Tess. And he's made us both into liars—for *him*. It's about our lives, too."

The panel judges got back up on the stage, and the lights flickered, indicating they were ready to announce the winners.

"Tell me," Dylan whispered in my ear as the noise of the crowd settled. "What bad thing would happen to you if people knew your secret?"

"I'd lose him." It was the truth. The only truth to live behind a lifetime of lies. "I know you don't think he's much of a father, but he's the only one I've got." I caught sight of my mother approaching. She beamed at me. My mother, so proud of me. My mother, so weak. "And she'd lose him, too."

Dylan followed the path of my gaze. "Fair enough," he said. "You can only make decisions for yourself, not your mom. But maybe it's time for your mom to pick a side, too."

There was a rash of feedback as Dr. Cavel fiddled with the mic, and everyone fell silent. "I want to thank you all for your participation this evening."

My mom had arrived by my side. She leaned in. "Is that one of your professors? She's very pretty."

"Yeah, Mom," I replied, rolling my eyes. "Plus, she's got a PhD and a Sloan Fellowship."

Out of the corner of my eye, I caught Dylan stiffen. I could practically hear the pieces clicking into place in his brain. At last he understood why I felt it was nice he thought I was beautiful, but not as important as everything else.

I thought of what Mom would do without the crutch of my father to lean on. If she'd have to get serious about her art or the jobs she took on. I thought of the time she'd agreed with my father about sending me to State instead of Canton. And I thought about what she'd said the other morning, after my dad had gotten out of the hospital, still angry I'd dare to visit him there. *Your father and I disagree on this matter.* Maybe things *could* change.

"As you know," Dr. Cavel went on, "the First Semester Design Symposium is one of the most prestigious competitions for bioengineering students here at Canton, and I'm so pleased that this year's crop of projects has been the most competitive and impressive yet. Every student who has presented tonight should be extremely proud of the work they've accomplished this semester and of their contributions to this growing field. I look forward to see what you bring us in the new year."

There was a smattering of applause.

"And now, the moment you've all been waiting for. The winner of the symposium, and the recipient of the five-thousand-dollar grand prize is..." She paused. I breathed. Dylan grabbed my hand. "Elaine Sun, for her work in Targeting Drug-Loaded Nanoparticles to Prostate Cancer Cells Using the PD36 Minibody."

All the bones in my body turned to swizzle sticks. I slumped. My hand went wet fish in Dylan's. We'd lost. We'd lost?

"Clap," he whispered. "She's your friend."

So I clapped. Tears burned my eyes as I clapped for Elaine. She stepped up on the stage, her smile bigger than I'd ever seen, to accept her plaque and the envelope with her check. She and Dr. Cavel smiled for the pictures.

I was happy for her. I was. I certainly wasn't going to be as sore a loser as she'd been back when Dylan had beaten her freshman year. Elaine had also been working her ass off, and she deserved recognition for that. She'd played fair, too, giving us all the lab time we'd needed, in the end. It wasn't her fault we'd lost.

Dr. Yue came up behind us. "Better luck next time, you two. It was a great podium presentation, but biofuel is a tough nut to crack at Canton. Half the jurors are from Chem and they don't give a crap about anything they can't package in a pill."

I nodded, trying to look staid. To most entrants, this was just a minor disappointment—oh well, one little bullet point that didn't make it on their resume. Back to studying for finals.

Of course, it was so much harder to study for finals if you still weren't sure how to pay for the books in your hands.

I was going to have to take a semester off. That was the only option. I could work a few jobs, build up some reserves in my bank account—maybe they would hold my scholarship. Maybe I could take out a few more loans. A few more.

The clapping went on and on, rising like a storm, matching the rush of blood in my ears.

"You want to get out of here?" Dylan was saying to me, but I could barely make out the words.

I shook my head miserably. I didn't have time to hang out with my boyfriend, to have long talks about where this was all going. It was going nowhere. *I* was going nowhere.

I pulled away from him, mumbled to my mother that I'd see her back at home, and left the hall. It was raining now, freezing cold drops spitting down from the sky. I got in my car, tore off my suit jacket, and yanked every last goddamn pin out of my hair. Nice clothes hadn't done the trick, and neither had sexy librarian or fancy animated graphics or impeccable science. If they only wanted to give their prize to biomed, they should have expressed that in the rules.

Stupid Canton and their stupid expensive, best-in-the-country program. I hated it. It had ruined me. All of Dylan's fantasies of the scientific power couple were revealed for what they were: dreams. I couldn't afford Canton, even with the academic scholarship. And Colorado? Ha. It would take me *two* jobs this summer to work my way out of the hole I'd dug in a single semester. And I still had the spring semester looming ahead, with new books, new fees, new bills.

"Three jobs," I murmured to no one in particular as I drove off the campus. I'd always had to fight, hadn't I? If it took losing a semester of credits, if it took moving in with my mother—I'd done everything else to have Canton. I could do three jobs, too.

And there was no time like the present, was there? I'd been lax in my shifts at Verde recently, prioritizing study time over my job. Oh, who was I kidding? It was only when it was study time with Dylan that I'd blown off work. I'd rationalized that if Dylan and I worked hard enough, we'd win the symposium, and I'd make up all those lost tips in one fell swoop.

Well, it was time to face facts. Girls like me didn't get breaks like that. No, we were Sylvia, waiting tables and performing at campus coffee shops and never leaving this town for New York or Nashville or LA or wherever it was singers actually got jobs singing. We were my mother, who swore she loved art but would settle for beauty. I could have Canton, but not unless I let it wear me down.

Why waste time? I had so much money to make and so little time to do it. Maybe they needed an extra hand at Verde tonight. I made a U-turn and started heading to the restaurant. Screw the fact that I'd left my uniform at home. Who cared that I was wearing pumps instead of standard-issue waitress sneakers? I'd been an idiot to expect my life at Canton would be one of fancy, science-symposium afterparties. I had tables to bus and drinks to pour.

I walked into Verde, and Sylvia sprinted to my side.

"What are you doing here!" she said under her breath. "I told you not to come in."

I made a face. "No, you said you didn't need me this week." Verde was decorated for the holidays, with sparkly lights dripping down from all the trees in the atrium.

"That was a heavy hint," she replied. "Now, out of here, quick, before she sees you."

"Who?" I asked, but then I saw her, her back ramrod straight in the booth, her hair falling like liquid gold down her back.

Hannah.

TWENTY-FOUR

"SHE'S BEEN COMING HERE and asking for you." Sylvia wrung her hands. "Since yesterday. I can't get rid of her. She's polite and she orders and Bill says unless she causes a scene we can't refuse service."

I looked over the tops of the booths at our customer. Verde was quiet tonight. Most people were probably studying.

"Well," I said. "She *is* a regular."

Hannah saw me. She didn't wave. She didn't smile. She just sat there, like a princess waiting to receive her audience. And God help me, I started walking over. I held onto the silver T like a talisman, like it could ward off the worst of her wrath. I'd never meant to hurt her.

"Tess, don't," said Sylvia. "I'm serious. What if she does have a vial of acid in her purse—"

I waved her off, uninterested in Sylvia's theories. I arrived at the booth. "Hi."

"Hi," she replied. "Have a seat?"

I slid onto the bench seat across from her. It was odd, being so close. Hannah was shorter than me and thinner, too. Her skin was a gorgeous peaches and cream, her hair was straight as rainfall, and her eyes were like looking in a mirror.

"So…," I said. "My friend thinks you're here to attack me for stealing your boyfriend."

There was the tiniest twitch on her polished, aristocratic expression, but it was gone in an instant. "What do you think?"

"I don't know. I didn't even know you knew I worked here." And I wasn't sure how it made me feel, either. I'd spent most of my life believing it absolutely vital that Hannah Swift never thought about me at all.

"Dylan told me. He talked about you a lot." She gave a small, self-mocking laugh. "Should have known, right?" She waved down a server. "Would you like something to drink? I have to order something every hour or they kick me out."

"What do you want from me, Hannah?"

But Hannah just smiled at our server, a guy named Phil I didn't know very well, and ordered two iced teas. Once he was gone, she spent a great deal of time rearranging the cocktail napkins on the table.

"You've apparently been hanging out here looking for me," I continued.

"I don't know what I want," she said abruptly, still looking down. "I want to hate you, I guess."

"That seems fair."

"Doesn't it?" She looked up, a rueful smile on her face, but as soon as our eyes met, it vanished. "It's been a bad few months for me, you know? I didn't get into any of the classes I wanted, I totally flunked my Stats midterm, I had a big medical scare, and then some bitch stole my boyfriend."

"I'm sorry," I said.

"About what part?" She raised her eyebrows.

"All of it." I wanted to add something about how I wish I'd known she was having difficulty in Stats, because I totally could have helped her, but of course, I couldn't have. I wouldn't have. The rules.

I *should* have.

Phil came back with our iced teas and a small plate of lemons, which both Hannah and I reached for at once. Our knuckles brushed and I snatched my hand back. She took two slices, then pushed the plate over to me. I nabbed the rest as my pulse sped.

Hannah liked lemon in her iced tea, too.

"So, yeah," she went on, squeezing the lemon into her drink and watching me as I did the same. "But what that whole health thing did was make me think about how, as much as life sucks sometimes, I should really appreciate the things that I have. I shouldn't go out of my way to make enemies." She paused. "And even if I want to hate her, I should probably at least *try* to get to know my sister."

I choked on my tea. "You—how did you—"

"Dylan told me. The night after the hospital. Don't get mad."

"He promised—"

"I basically made him," she said calmly. "Well, I basically guessed, and he's not much of a liar."

He was the best liar. "You...guessed?"

She was silent for a long while, staring down into her tea. "I knew my dad cheated on my mom before I was born. My mom told me about it once, a long time ago. They almost broke up, but then she got pregnant."

Stop, I thought at Hannah. *Just go back to hating me.*

"I thought that's all there was to it. But you were there at the hospital that night. When I went in to see my dad, he was so out of it on drugs, he thought I was still you. He kept telling me to go away but calling me Tess, he kept mentioning someone I assume is your mother. So I Googled."

"You Googled?"

"I *can* Google things, you know. I'm just not good at math." She frowned. "I knew your name. I found out hers. I saw pictures of her art and recognized a few paintings. My father has some just like them hanging in his office."

"He does?" That didn't sound like him. That didn't sound like the rules.

"So I went there. Do you know what else he has in his office? I do, because I went through everything. I told his secretary I needed some records for his doctor. Anyway, I found a picture of you. You're young in it—maybe middle school? But I recognized you."

That definitely didn't sound like following the rules! "Is it the one with the off-center ponytail?"

"And the zit on your nose," she finished a little too gleefully. "And your eyes. Your Swift eyes."

I closed those eyes, unable to bear the accusation on her face.

"So what would *you* do, Tess?"

I opened my eyes, those eyes that were so much like hers, and met her gaze.

"I want to hate you, because you stole Dylan from me. I want to hate Dylan, because he left me. But you guys slid right off the top of the list. Right now, I want to hate my father even more."

Sorry didn't seem strong enough for what I needed to say to her. "I'm not supposed to talk to you," I said lamely. "Ever."

"That's ludicrous," she said. "You have no idea how insane that sounds to me."

Spoken aloud, the rules did sound crazy. I remembered Sylvia making fun of me, here in this very restaurant, when I dared mention rules.

I stirred my straw around in my drink as silence descended between us once more. The rules were smashed to smithereens, but it didn't feel at all like I thought it would. Where was the part where Hannah and I hugged and braided each other's hair and gossiped about boys...boys we *hadn't* both slept with, that was?

"I wasn't in love with him, you know," she said at last. "Dylan, I mean. I thought I was, but I know now I couldn't be, because he didn't love me back. I guess he was always in love with you."

She waited, as if expecting me to respond. But I couldn't. What was I supposed to do, thrill to the confession? I already knew it, since honest Dylan had told me. And I wasn't here to gloat.

"That's what he said to me, you know. As soon as I figured

out he didn't just dump me, he dumped me for his *lab partner*. He apologized, and he told me he'd always been in love with you." She looked me over, appraising every inch. "I wonder if that's why he dated me...because in some way, I reminded him of you. I don't think we have many similarities, though."

This glittering, blond Lady Who Lunches and her science nerd bastard sister? Not really. "I recognized you by your eyes when we met," I said at last.

"You already knew what you were looking for," she snapped and sipped her tea. "But you never answered my question."

"What question?"

"What would you do if you were me?"

I twirled the straw in my iced tea, batting at the slices of lemon until they drowned. "I don't know, Hannah. I have no idea what it's like to be you. I have no idea what it's like to have a father who lies to you every day. Dad—" She flinched, and I fumbled. Yeah, we were so not ready to put it like that. "Your dad...he cast me in the role of accomplice."

"And I'm the victim in your scenario?"

"Not what I meant—"

"No, it's fair," she conceded, then frowned as if her tea was too sour. "I know what I'm doing first."

I waited.

"I'm getting out of town. I'm not coming back to Canton next semester. I'm halfway through my junior year and I still can't land on a major. I need to go away for a while, figure some shit out. School. Boys. Family..."

I nodded in understanding. "That sounds...nice."

"Yeah," she said. "I thought maybe Europe."

"How are you going to afford it?" I could have cut my tongue out the second the words slipped from my lips.

She stared at me, alternately amused and pitying. The gulf between us was massive. Hannah had never worried how she'd pay for something in her life. "So that's what I'm doing here," she said instead. "Partly."

"Partly?" I wasn't sure how there could be anything left after this, the most bizarre conversation of my life.

"I'm going away. I probably won't see you again for a while. Four months? Six? And I hate you a lot right now. But maybe once I get back"—she gave a little, self-mocking giggle—"once I've slept my way through my fair share of Spanish pool boys and Swiss ski instructors and forgotten all about that jerk Dylan you're dating…"

I almost snorted iced tea up my nose. She was funny, this sister of mine.

She looked away now, off into the distance, and her voice dropped a few levels. "Maybe I'll be ready for us to get to know each other." She shrugged. "If you want."

I thought of the horror movies on her Facebook page. Of the friends Dylan said didn't understand her. Of the way I'd wished to sneak her my bone marrow if she were really sick. "I would," I said softly as my nose burned and my eyes watered. "I really, really would."

"Okay then." She folded her cocktail napkin, then unfolded it again. "That's all I came for…except also, Dylan told me you're here on scholarship, but it's not covering everything."

"Yeah. Well."

Her pretty pink lips formed a thin line. "Dad's going to pay for your school from now on."

"I don't want to live by his rules anymore," I replied. It was easier than I'd ever thought it would be. Dylan would probably say that was because it was the truth. Dad's money came with Dad's rules, and I was done. I was here with my sister, and she wanted us to try. What was fear of my father to that?

Hannah rolled her eyes. "These aren't his rules," she said. "They're mine. I went to Dad and told him I knew. I told him that unless he supports you in school like he's supported me, I'm telling my mother he had a child with his mistress." She stopped. "I mean…your mom."

My eyes widened and my heart pounded at the very idea. It wasn't the words that had bothered me—my mother *was* his mistress. Hadn't I said it to myself a thousand times? But if Hannah's mother knew, if it was public... My mom might be his mistress, but she also loved him. The rules weren't just for me. "Please don't do that."

"What would you do, Tess," she repeated, "if you were me?" I knew what I'd do. I knew because I'd done it. I'd followed the rules. I'd stayed silent. I hadn't argued with my parents when they'd arrayed themselves against me. I'd acted just like my mother, letting Dad's desire for secrecy keep me from Canton for two years. I'd nearly let it keep me from Dylan forever.

And I was done. I was not that kind of girl anymore. I was the girl who'd risked my father's wrath to pursue my dream school. I was the girl who refused to follow in my parents' path of betrayal and lies when it came to Dylan.

I was done playing by the old rules. I was determined to make my own.

"Besides," she added, "you and I both know Canton costs a lot less than he'd lose if Mom created a scandal or sued his ass for divorce."

"What do you mean?" I asked. "Wouldn't she just make him break up with my mom?"

"Yeah, because that worked out so well last time," Hannah scoffed. "You haven't seen my parents in action. Trust me. I know exactly how all this would go down."

My sister was kind of ruthless. I kind of loved it.

"But what if he takes it out on you?" I asked, worried. "Withdraws his money for your school or...Europe?" I gestured vaguely to reference imaginary chalets and ski instructors.

She laughed at me, shaking her head. "I was left a million-dollar trust fund from my grandparents, Tess. Your grandparents, too, I suppose. So there's even *more* money my father screwed you out of. The least he can do is pay for your college."

I was speechless. A million dollars? I was ready to drop out of school over a couple of thousand. "This feels a little like blackmail."

"It is blackmail. But so was what Dad was doing to you."

This time it was Hannah and I calling the shots. Making the rules. Hannah and I. The very idea seemed impossible.

"He owes you this, Tess. He owes you a lot more, but this is a start. Please take it."

I regarded her carefully. "You know, you aren't acting like you hate me a lot."

"Let me try again," she said. "Please take it…bitch?"

I laughed and for a moment, I thought she would, too, but instead all the humor slipped off her face, leaving only raw pain as she looked at a place behind me.

I turned too, but what I saw only filled my heart up. It was Dylan, standing at the door of Verde and watching us.

"I think I should go," Hannah said, and motioned for the check.

I stopped her. "On the house."

She nodded and rose from her seat. I thought perhaps we'd hug or shake hands or something, but none of that happened. It was too soon.

And yet, it was real. I'd just sat there and talked to Hannah Swift for a good half-hour. And though it was horribly painful and terrifically awkward and very, very odd, the world hadn't ended. It had only grown, ballooning up so large I was afraid it might snap its strings and blow away.

I watched her walk toward the exit. Dylan met her halfway. They hugged, briefly, and she said something to him that I couldn't quite make out. And then she was gone. I ached for her. She might not have been in love with Dylan, but it still hurt. And there was nothing I could do. Not yet.

I threw some bills on the table for a tip—I was still a waitress, even if I could comp a couple of iced teas—and met Dylan in the aisle between the trees. Fairy lights twinkled down on us, white and golden as starlight. I'd forgotten how pretty Verde could be.

"I've been looking everywhere for you," he said. His black hair was mussed, wet with mist. His coat was wet near the shoulders, as if he'd walked through the rain. His hands in mine were cold to the touch. But I didn't care. "I went to the labs, your apartment. Your mom is back there, by the way. We should probably give her a call and let her know you're okay."

"I am okay." And I was. This time, I really was. "I'm sorry I ran off."

"So am I," he said. "But I guess you had somewhere to be?"

"I didn't know it," I replied. "Sylvia didn't tell me that she's been hanging out here looking for me."

"I'm sorry about that. I had planned to tell you about Hannah. After the presentation."

"Don't be sorry," I said firmly. "This...she and I needed this." I hadn't realized how much we'd each needed it.

Dylan took a deep breath. "Okay. By the way, Elaine was looking for you at the reception. She was worried you were snubbing her, and though I think she probably deserves it after what how she treated me freshman year, I have to say, you kind of looked like a sore loser."

Funny, I didn't feel like a loser at all. I didn't win the symposium tonight, but I still ended up with the best prize. A new sister. A life without secrets. And then there was Dylan. Dylan, who'd made me feel like I wasn't a dirty secret or a second choice. That being with me was worth waiting for, worth fighting for, worth shining a light on the lies that had ruled my life for so long.

"Thank you again, for everything you did," I said.

He shrugged. "The graphics? Whatever. My grand romantic gesture didn't mean too much in the end, did it?"

"That's not what I meant."

Dylan looked down at me, and the corner of his mouth quirked up in a little smile. "I know what you meant."

Then he bent his head to mine and kissed me, and my new life began.

EPILOGUE

Six months later

DYLAN REARRANGED the last box in the back of the car and slammed the door shut. "I think that's all we're going to be able to fit."

I shrugged. The May sun bounced off the cars in the parking lot. It was a beautiful day in late spring, and classes had just finished. "It wasn't my idea to bring an entire box of kitchen utensils."

"You want to go a whole summer without my baklava?" He winked at me from behind his glasses.

I slid my arms around his waist. "Okay, chef. You win." I kissed him on the nose.

We turned and, hand in hand, walked over to my apartment building. Sylvia and Annabel had come with Milo to see us off and were waiting on the curb. I'd had a goodbye drink with Elaine last night. She was spending the summer working for Canton Chem and was subletting Dylan's campus apartment while we were away. In her opinion, the chance that he was going to move back in come fall was slim to none.

"You two will want a bigger place than a studio," she'd said.

"We aren't necessarily going to keep living together next year," I'd pointed out.

"Yeah, right."

As we joined my friends, Sylvia asked, "How far are you going to get today?"

"Kentucky," I said. We were budgeting three days to drive to Colorado, planning to take it easy and enjoy the countryside. We weren't even due to start work at Solarix until next week, so we had plenty of time to get there and settle in. "Dylan has mapped out a course based on all the local specialties he wants to try."

Annabel laughed. "Just don't eat one of those butter sculpture things, okay?"

"Don't be ridiculous," said Dylan. "Those aren't for eating. They're *art*."

My mom joined us on the walk. "You're sure you haven't forgotten anything?" she asked. She was dressed for class, with her bookbag over her arm.

"It's Colorado, Mom, not the far edge of the world. I'm sure they've got stores there if I need shampoo."

"Well, I still worry." She gave me a hug. "Call me from the road, okay?"

"You got it."

She pressed a wad of twenty-dollar bills in my hand. "For gas."

"Mom—" She needed this money for tuition. I knew very well how expensive school could be. She still had twenty credits to go to complete her master's degree in art education.

"Please," she said. "Let me contribute, too."

I took the cash. It meant so much to her that she was paying for things herself these days, even if it meant spa pedicures and designer clothes were things of the past.

"Are you going to be okay all alone here?" I asked her.

"Are you kidding?" she replied. "I'm so busy I don't think we'd even see each other."

That was true. It was amazing how much bigger your world got once you stopped letting it revolve around a man who wanted to keep you a secret. Between our respective friends, classes, and jobs, it had been quite a while since we'd managed even a simple dinner together.

Of course, it didn't help that I spent most nights at Dylan's place. Maybe Elaine was right.

It had all gone down back in December. My father hadn't taken too well to Hannah's ultimatum, but my sister had refused to budge. He'd railed at me, railed at Mom, and my guess was he'd railed at Hannah, too, but whatever happened, it had no effect. For the first time in his life, none of us were letting him have his way. In the end, he wrote me a single check large enough to cover the final four semesters of school, telling me gravely that if I squandered it, I was not to expect any more.

"I guess he doesn't know you very well, after all," my mom had said. "I've never seen you squander anything in your life."

I'd immediately opened up a high-yield savings account to handle the money until I needed it.

Soon after Hannah had left for Europe in January, Dad had stopped coming around. Mom never explained what exactly happened between them, but I got the distinct impression that she was done with his rules, too. She'd taken a full-time job at a gallery in town and enrolled in night classes to finish her degree. I was so proud of her I could burst.

Dylan had been right. The truth did set us free.

"I guess it's time to hit the road," I said now.

Another hug for Mom and she headed off to work. Sylvia and Annabel next, and a special cuddle for Milo, who was growing so fast I wondered if I'd still recognize him come fall.

We climbed in the car—Dylan had offered to take the first shift driving—and waved at everyone. As we drove off, I touched the silver T around my neck.

Dylan reached across the console and squeezed my hand. "Are you excited?"

"Yes."

And so was he. He'd been bouncing like a kid all morning, his eyes sparkling, his teasing grin a permanent fixture on his face. His enthusiasm was infectious. Then again, it always had been. I leaned over and kissed him on the cheek.

"Careful, Tess," he teased. "We've got six hours of driving before we hit the hotel tonight."

"Drive fast," I whispered in his ear.

I was twenty-one years old when I found my true family, when I realized that no one, not even my father, could tell me who my sister was or what my life would look like or who would fight for me. This was the year I stepped out from the tangle of lies that had made up my childhood. Thanks to Dylan. To him, I was a girl worth bringing into the light, his first love, his one and only. And because of Dylan, I realized it was all true.

———

The Canton Series continues with Hannah's book,
Sweet & Wild.

ACKNOWLEDGMENTS

Even though it's called indie publishing, I did not pull this book together on my own. I am in debt to all those who gave me advice during this process, including (but by no means limited to): Julie Leto, Mari Mancusi, Carrie Ryan, Amanda Brice, Lavinia Kent, Rhonda Helms, Erica Ridley, Courtney Milan, Dahlia Adler, Cora Carmack, Jennifer Armentrout, Gennifer Albin, Simone Elkeles, Holly Black, Sarah Brand, Julie Kenner, my awesomely understanding and forward-thinking agent Michael Bourret, everyone on the NAAU! Facebook group, Marie Force and the members of her self-publishing email loop, the fabulous writers and conference organizers at NINC, and all the readers, bloggers, and fans of college love stories who have been cheering me on.

Special thanks to editors Rhonda Helms, Dahlia Adler, and Dan; and to cover designer extraordinaire Sarah Hansen of Okay. Creations.

As always, love to my family, who were very supportive during the feverish writing of this project.

And thank you, thank you to the loyal readers of the Secret Society Girl series. I hope you've found another couple to root for.

ABOUT THE AUTHOR

Viv Daniels is a pen name for critically acclaimed author Diana Peterfreund, who has written a dozen books for adults and teens that span the gamut from post-apocalyptic science fiction to contemporary fantasy about killer unicorns.

Yes, really.

As Viv, she writes love stories. She hopes you love them.

Viv lives in Washington, D.C., with her husband (whom she met in college) and their daughters. You can learn more at vivdaniels.com

————

The Canton Series

- Book 1: *One & Only* (Tess's Story)
- Book 2: *Sweet & Wild* (Hannah's story)
- Book 3: *Tried & True* (Sylvia's Story)

www.ingramcontent.com/pod-product-compliance
Lightning Source LLC
Chambersburg PA
CBHW020321200626
46814CB00006BB/2350